# SACRED LEGACY

## Branded Trilogy, Book 3

# KAT FLANNERY

SACRED LEGACY: BRANDED TRILOGY #3

www.katflannerybooks.com

SECOND EDITION Paperback
June 8, 2018

ISBN: 978-1-989189-03-0

Cover designed by Carpe Librum Book Design

# Praise for
# Sacred Legacy

"A Cherokee man, a Gypsy woman, a magic ruby, a wonderful, captive love story. One of the few stories that captured me from beginning to end."
> —*USA Today* Bestselling author, Rosanne Bittner

"Sacred Legacy will immerse you in a harrowing journey of anger and bitterness that only love and forgiveness can heal. You won't soon forget Tsura and Red Wolf's journey."
> —Kristy McCaffrey, Award-winning author of the
> WINGS OF THE WEST series

"If you loved the first two books in this series, you will absolutely love this one!"
> —PARANORMAL ROMANCE GUILD

"Two wounded souls, two hardened hearts, and a tradition of magick that must be protected at all costs. With a deft touch and an elegant understanding of the fine line between good and evil, happiness and despair, Kat Flannery gives her best to *Sacred Legacy*. Red Wolf and Tsura prove it is possible to find what has been lost—not only within the real and magical worlds, but also within the human heart. Flannery has created characters worth rooting for, a legacy worth dying for, and a love worth living."
> —Kathleen Rice Adams, award winning author
> of the PRODIGAL GUN

# ACKNOWLEDGEMENTS

This book took a lot to write. Not only was this the last of the trilogy, and of characters I grew to love, it came at a time when I'd lost someone so very close to me, my brother Joe. After he passed I could not pick up a pen, much less type any words. My mind simply was not there. However, I had made a promise not just to my readers, but also to Joe while he was in the hospital, and I could not go back on my word. I promised to write him a happy ending…to give him the love of a woman he never received while living on this earth. I had strict instructions too. She had to be good looking, which of course Tsura is, and love would conquer all, which of course you'll have to read to find out.

I'd like to thank my brother, Joe for always being there, for making me laugh, for being an awesome big brother. I love you and I miss you.

Thank you to my readers who patiently waited for me to write this book. I hope you enjoy this last installment of the Branded Trilogy, and experience all the emotions I did while writing it.

I love you all!
Kat

# NOVELS BY KAT FLANNERY

*For my brother, Joe*

*Strength, Courage, Love and Faith…you showed them all.*

# PROLOGUE

*Willow Creek, Colorado, 1890*

Nora stared at the dilapidated trunk next to the fireplace. She hadn't looked at it after pa died last year. The old wood turned up at the edges, warped from the many times they'd traveled across the country. Pa was resigned to saving Nora from herself, which hadn't done either of them any good. As a gifted child she'd not been able to turn away from someone in need no matter the idle threats her father issued.

She closed her eyes, seeing him now. The too-short brown slacks he wore, his weathered shirt, stained and in need of repair. No smile lifted his lips, or creased the skin around the eyes. His face stiff as stone, rigid, and unmoving. Within the blue depths surrounded by black lashes lay disappointment.

Nora shuddered. Even now, months later, she could not see him without the cloud of disdain he'd placed around himself. The anger he'd cast upon her so many times. He'd been wrong. He'd seen her only as the rest of the world had…a threat.

The house was quiet. Morning Star napped in the small bed in the corner of the room, and Hawk was outside doing chores. She inhaled and stepped toward the trunk. Pa used the heavy crate for his clothes and whatever else had needed storing. She never really cared what was inside and had forgotten all about it until Hawk brought it in from the barn last week. He thought she might want it in the house. She wasn't so sure. The trunk held distant and unsettling memories of the life she led with her father, of resentment and hate…of a little girl who longed to be loved.

Her stomach turned. She needed to face the past sooner or later, and what could be inside but a few of Pa's things? She stared at the trunk once more as she feasted on her bottom lip. Pa wasn't a saint. He sure as hell didn't leave her fond memories of him. In fact almost all of her memories were tainted with the sloshes of whiskey, dreadful words thrown her way, and him passed out across the sofa. She had to search the recesses of her mind to draw any hint of the father who raised her. And even then, her mind foggy, she wasn't sure if it was a dream she'd had or the real thing.

She took another step. Her toes touched the side of the trunk. She glanced behind her to where Morning Star slept.

"To hell with it."

She bent, flung open the lid, and knocked it against the stone wall that made up the fireplace. She winced and waited. No cry. No small feet running across the floor toward her.

She sighed and stared down at a pair of folded denims and a woolen blanket. She pulled out the blanket, not the least bit surprised to see two bottles of whiskey hidden beneath. She rescued them from the musty confines of the trunk and set them on the floor beside her. Next she pulled out Pa's denims and stared at the bottom of the trunk. There was nothing else left and yet the trunk seemed so much larger on the outside than what it appeared to be inside.

She peeked at the contents beside her and then inside the trunk again. Standing, she placed her left leg up against the trunk and took a mental note that it came to just below her knee. She lifted her skirt to place her foot inside the empty trunk. In doing so, she lost her balance and fell into the wooden box. The timber snapped, breaking beneath her, and dropped her foot another three inches.

She stared at the bits of broken wood. Another compartment was concealed beneath. She slowly pulled her leg out and knelt. She pushed her insecurities aside and reached her hand past the broken wood to explore the space. She felt some sort of fabric.

She withdrew her hand and stared at the small hole. What was underneath? Without further hesitation, she pulled the wooden board up and snapped it from the edges of the trunk. Placing the broken board to the side, she peered into the trunk once more. Nestled on the bottom was a blue blanket wrapped around something hard. She pulled it out and carefully unraveled the cloth to reveal a rectangular jewelry box. Nora had never seen anything as beautiful as this handmade piece. The side bore intricately carved flowers and on top a sparrow etched into the wood. She lifted the lid and found a book, a ledger of sorts, which fit perfectly inside. She plucked it from the confines of the box. The cover was fashioned out of deer hide. She inspected the binding which was held together with leather strips. She ran her fingertips along the worn book, and thumbed through the yellow pages with what appeared to be feminine handwriting. She turned to the beginning of the book and gasped. It was a diary...

# CHAPTER ONE

Tsura Harris lifted the hem of her green skirt and stepped up onto the wooden plank. She clutched her reticule in her right hand and reached for the rope with her left. The planked bridge swayed as the boat rocked against the seas. She stared at the water below. White-capped waves crashed along the ship's hull, rocking the boat. She inhaled, forced her chin up, and took another step. She walked the short distance to the boardwalk, releasing the breath she'd held when her boot touched land. She planted both feet upon the wooden dock and set her shoulders, but the reminder of why she was here intensified the weight upon her chest. Despair was her shadow, and it was with her today.

"Sister!"

Her brother's deep, masculine shout came from above.

She shaded her eyes from the hot afternoon sun and peered up at him. His stature always shocked her. Micah Walker was six foot with broad shoulders and strong arms, a spitting image of their father, Kade. His white shirt gaped open to show the tanned skin beneath, a sign of too many days out on the water. Long blond hair waved in the breeze. Her handsome brother had his pick of the ladies, but still hadn't settled down. It was a shame. She knew he wanted children and a wife of his own, but his heart belonged to the sea and time would lend him those favors only when he was ready.

"You must wait," he called and raced past his men carrying crates of goods onto the wharf.

She placed her bag onto the wooden walk and clasped her gloved hands together.

He reached her, his cheeks glowing and dark eyes lit with mischief. Before she could discourage him, he picked her up and swung her around.

Her boots kicked the bag, knocking it over, as his strong arms held her tight.

Micah had always been affectionate. He never shied away from holding her hand, kissing her cheek, or teasing her like a brother would. He'd come to her side when she needed him the most. When her life had fallen apart, and she couldn't see past her own misery to pick herself up. He had carried her, and she loved him for it.

"You cannot go off without wishing me well." He smiled down at her.

"If you would simply release me, I'd be able to make it so," she retorted. He was the only one, aside from her mother and father, who she allowed to touch her.

"Very well, nit." He set her in front of him. The nickname he used for her was one of endearment and came from her pestering him as a child.

"Thank you." She smoothed her skirt before bringing her eyes to meet his.

"You do not need to do this."

She glanced away unable to stare at him any longer.

"Come sail with me."

She shook her head. The urge to leave caused her legs to shake. She couldn't be around him any longer. His cheerful disposition haunted her and made her think of things she'd rather forget.

"I know you don't want to speak of this, but—"

"No, Micah."

"Tsura, you need to forgive—"

"Forgiveness is not within my heart."

"It surely is."

She shook her head, careful not to release the many pins holding her thick corkscrew curls in a loose chignon.

"It is in all of us."

She glared at her brother.

"Do not speak to me of forgiveness, brother. My heart is cold to it."

His dark eyes watered, and she knew her words had hurt him, but she didn't care. It was better this way—it was easier.

"Will you not reconsider?"

"No."

"Please stay. I will protect you."

Protection was not what she needed. She could care less if she died. It'd be a relief from the constant pain she felt each day.

"I should've taken you to mother and father."

"Do not speak to them of my presence here."

"They will understand."

"Not one word."

Micah sighed. "As you wish."

"I must go." Anger pressed on her spine, and she straightened.

His shoulders dropped.

"Be safe. Trust no one."

She nodded.

"I port back in Jamestown one month to this day. You will be here."

It was not a question, and she didn't know if a month would be enough. Would the time between then and now ever fade from her soul? Would she be ready to return? She didn't know if she could go back and so she didn't answer.

"Hiram knows of you coming?"

"He does."

"Very well." He straightened and smiled. "Know that I love you."

She fought the tears. If Micah saw one ounce of sadness within her, he'd throw her back aboard the *Jade* and take her with him.

"As I you." She refused to say the words.

He picked up her bag and handed it to her.

"Thank you. Now go. You have work to do and whores to see." She smirked.

"Ah, that I do." He pulled her into a final embrace. "You will find your way. I am sure of it." He held her away from him, and his eyes searched hers. "Remember who you are."

She pressed on his chest and stepped out of his embrace. She couldn't help the furrowing of her brow or the set of her chin. The reminders of the life she led were never to be forgotten, and because of that she'd be forever lost.

Micah sensed the change in her and left it alone. He bowed, and with a final kiss to her forehead he walked away.

She turned, unable to watch him go, raised to believe it was a sign of weakness, of regret to watch one leave your life. This was meant to be. The world around her had tilted, and even though she wanted nothing more than to go back in time to the lavish house on the hill where she'd felt content, where laughter was but an expression upon her lips, she could not. What had been was no more, and she'd do right to remember it. One year had passed, but the ache inside her soul still remained.

Her eyes watered, and she pulled out the ripped piece of cloth her mother had given to her. She placed it to her lips and nose, inhaling the scent of lavender and honey. The need to turn around and yell for Micah washed over her, and she spun on her heel. Hope took root within her heart as she searched the wharf for one last glimpse of him. Her eyes roamed past the men and women fumbling their way through the crowds.

Micah was gone.

She reprimanded herself for being foolish—for thinking she was strong enough to watch him leave. She picked up her reticule, tucked her mother's cloth back into her pocket, and carried on.

"Tsura?"

She halted, the voice unfamiliar to her. She pulled her shoulders up and searched the faces in front of her. A blond man with fair skin and blue eyes came toward her. He was not Hiram, but instead a younger version of him.

"Tsura Harris?"

She nodded.

"James Monroe, your half-brother. It has been a long while since we've seen one another." He stuck out his hand.

She gripped her bag and leaned away from him.

His blue eyes searched hers, and he smiled. She sensed the kindness within him and shuddered. It'd be simpler if he were crass or rude. She despised those who were jovial.

"Please, refrain from any sleight of hand," she said.

He raised a brow.

"Do not *touch* me," she said with a little too much force in her voice.

He shrugged and reached for her bag.

She stepped back.

"I…I will carry my things."

He retreated, and she knew he'd not missed her hesitance when he came near, nor did he misunderstand her unwillingness to be touched in any way.

"Right this way. I have a carriage waiting for us."

She followed at a short distance, leaving two feet between them.

The carriage was beautiful. Dark mahogany wood framed the vehicle, and velvet curtains hung in the windows offering privacy from the world outside. She expected nothing less from the wealthy plantation owner. Hiram Monroe was one of the richest men in the colonies. He was the sole owner of the biggest tobacco plantation in Virginia, and their exports were sold all over the world. Her father had transported them for years, and now Micah did.

"After you." James held the carriage door open.

Tsura eyed him. She trusted no one, and propriety or not, she'd let him climb into the carriage first.

"Go on," she said.

"A lady must go first."

"Do not flatter me, Mr. Monroe. I am quite capable of entering the carriage on my own…after you."

"Call me James, and very well." He moved past her and climbed into the carriage.

She surveyed the big ships, the sea, the vast array of water meeting sky, and knowing she'd never be able to return home, followed him inside.

# CHAPTER TWO

Tsura waited in the large, well-furnished sitting room for her stepbrothers to appear. After arriving at the plantation, James had led her down a wide hallway where the walls were decorated with lavish paintings and flowered wallpapers to a room off of the library with instructions to wait. He needed to fetch Miles from the fields. The hairs on her neck stood, bumps formed on her arms, and she shivered. She despised being told what to do and would wait a few minutes longer before going to find him herself.

What could they possibly want to discuss with her? She hardly knew her relatives. Living in Bristol most of her life, she'd only met them once when Hiram had come to visit. She was thirteen, a gifted child who delighted in showing them the many talents she'd had. They'd been fascinated by the magick and would beg to see more. Only a few years younger than her, James and Miles had held a special place in her heart. They'd be sad to see she'd changed, no longer the whimsical girl, but instead an empty shell with little regard for magick—or the child she once was.

"It is good to see you, Tsura." Miles Monroe walked into the room, an identical image of his brother James. She stared at them both, wondering how Hiram ever distinguished one from the other. She'd had a difficult time of it when she'd seen them last and remembered them playing her one for the other.

James sat on the chair across from her, and tapped his foot. The air grew thick, and she stiffened.

"What is it you wish to discuss?" she asked. The flat tone to her voice couldn't be helped. Something was amiss. She sensed it in the set of Miles' shoulders, and James's restless tapping. She set herself away from them, pushing into the sofa where she sat.

"It is father," Miles said. "He is not well."

"What is wrong with him?"

"His heart. The doctor feels he hasn't much time."

She blinked unable to believe what they were saying. She hadn't known Hiram was ill. No one had told her.

"How long has he been sick?"

"A little over a year."

"Why did you not send for me earlier?"

"We tried, but our letters went unanswered," James said.

She remembered the letters coming, the flowers, the food, the gifts...she didn't touch any of them. On Micah's insistence four months ago she'd written Hiram to tell him she was coming for an extended stay. She had no idea it would be the last time she'd see him.

"There is nothing that can be done?" she asked.

The brothers looked at each other, and she clasped her hands tightly together.

"We remember the magick...of the things you can do," Miles whispered.

She thinned her lips and held her shoulders higher.

"I no longer practice such things."

"Surely you will reconsider for him?" James asked.

"No." Her hands shook. The bread and cheese she'd eaten this morning turned in her stomach.

"He is your father, and you have the ability to save him," Miles all but shouted.

Tsura stood.

"I no longer use my gift. It lives within me no more. You will need to respect this."

"I respect nothing!" Miles came toward her, anger shadowing his face. "You hold his life within your hands and you refuse to act."

"Brother, calm yourself," James said.

Miles paced the length of the room, his face red. She watched as his lips moved but no sound exited them.

"Tsura, please, you must help us," James begged.

She turned from him unable to see the desperation within his blue eyes. She understood all too well what he was feeling. She too had experienced the hopelessness, the despair, the agony, and the bleakness. Her throat ached with the memories, the guilt, and the horror. She spun around.

"I cannot," she said.

James hung his head, and she looked away not wanting to see his tears.

"How can you be so cruel?" Miles asked.

She heard his words and the cry for help that came with them, but she could not bring herself to pity the brothers. She was no longer the girl they'd known. The child with the kind smile, light touch, and mischievous green eyes had died along with her heart.

"You have no idea what cruel is," she snarled. Anger brewed inside of her to taunt the power. Her body heated as she fought to control it. Fear crept up her neck to wrap around her throat, and she gasped. The last time fury took hold of her she'd been blinded by it, seeing nothing but hate and revenge. She'd not do it again.

"Tsura? Tsura, are you all right?" James asked, standing beside her, his hand upon her shoulder.

He was blurry within her vision, and she tried to focus as she fought with herself, desperate to expel the urge from her body. The room was silent. Miles and James stared at her, eyes big with concern. She could not stay here. They needed her help, and she'd refused. Her palms grew warm. The fingers itched…the magick wanted out. She clenched her hands into tight fists and forced it from her body. Tsura observed her stepbrothers and inhaled a long, deep breath. She pushed the air into her lungs, letting it rest there before expelling it from her mouth.

"I am sorry, but I cannot assist you," she said.

Remorse flooded her senses, and she bit the inside of her cheek until she tasted blood. She replaced the regret with determination, allowing the anger to once again overwhelm her. She took comfort in her frustrations, in the shame that consumed her until she no longer felt the pity, the sadness, and the hopelessness.

"I'd like to see him," she said.

James stood and walked out of the room. She followed, leaving Miles behind them.

The stale odor accosted her when James opened the door into Hiram's chambers. She knew little about how to comfort someone who was so ill. She stood back from the bed, not yet ready to come closer.

"He caught consumption last year and never fully recovered from it. He's been at death's door several times since then, but I fear now his time has come."

"How long has he been bedridden?"

"A few months. With the times before he'd recover enough to get out of bed, but he couldn't go far. We found a midwife to come and care for him, as we cannot working in the fields."

"I see." And she did. Death was coming. She could sense it.

Visions accosted her—the house on fire, the smell of death, the emptiness that followed. Her eyes watered, and she blinked the moisture from them. She'd not submit to the ache—not today.

She stepped closer to the bed. The midwife, an older woman with long deep wrinkles on her face that pulled her cheeks down to hang past her chin, finished bathing her father's face and left the room.

Hiram's peruke sat on the mantel. The hairpiece resembled a matted rat. It hadn't been combed in months. She looked at him. His face was thin and gaunt, and a yellow complexion marred his skin. He was no longer the strapping man she remembered. Her hands throbbed, and she clasped them in front of her.

"Father," James gently shook Hiram, "Tsura has come to see you."

Hiram opened his eyes the blue within them was faded and worn.

"Daughter, it is good to see you," he said in a breathy whisper.

"You're not well. I am sorry," she said, coming to his side.

He reached for her hand, and she stepped back. His eyes searched hers.

"I cannot—"

The corners of his mouth lifted into a weak smile.

"I do not want you to heal me, my dear."

Tsura nodded. He wanted to go, to pass on. Her chest felt a little lighter.

"Father, she is the only one who can make you well. Please, ask her to do this," James begged.

"Son, I do not wish to live much longer. I am tired, and I long to be with your mother again."

Tsura turned from them as a wave of agony washed over her. She gnashed her teeth together to stop the sorrow as it swelled to constrict her heart. She needed to say goodbye, and the thought brought a wave of emotions to settle in her throat. She swallowed loudly before going back to Hiram. She leaned down and placed a light kiss to his cheek.

"I will never forget you, Father," she whispered. She opened her mouth to say more, to let him know of her love, but the words wouldn't come. Her eyes filled with tears.

He reached for her hand, grasping it before she had a chance to pull it away. His eyes met hers, and she saw understanding within them.

"You will heal," Hiram whispered.

She'd not spoken of her past to anyone, and in her letter she'd been very vague as to why she was coming for a visit. He was wrong. She'd never find the happiness she'd once had. Her eyes searched his. She pried her hand from his and placed her fingers to her quivering lips.

"I love you," Hiram wheezed.

A tear slipped from her lashes, and she opened her mouth but could not bring herself to form the words. Any love she'd had died the day her life had been ripped apart. She gazed at him one final time, before leaving the room, the mansion, and the Monroes behind her.

# CHAPTER THREE

*Appalachian Mountains*

Emine Renoldi gazed into the cauldron. She was here. The girl had finally returned. She'd waited seventeen long years for the Branded One to walk upon this land once more—to avenge the slaughter of her family.

She could hardly believe what she saw. The liquid bubbled and hissed, showing a clear image of a young woman with ebony hair and green eyes. She stepped onto the dock in Jamestown, the ruby pendant glowing as it rested upon her chest. Emine flexed her fingers. Soon she'd have the powerful gem, breaking the Chuvani lineage forever.

Once the talisman was hers, she'd have the power to end the Peddler child once and for all. Her lips curved into an evil grin. She reached for her shawl, threw it around her thin shoulders, and raced out the door of her cabin.

The Renoldis had withstood many hardships in the time of the girl's disappearance from this land. It'd taken the clan years to rebuild after the attack and death of her sister and father. Emine's eyes narrowed, and her heart grew darker when she thought of the Peddlers. The girl's mother, Pril, had ended Emine's kinfolk, and she would have her revenge.

It took hard work and dedication to re-establish the land the Renoldis called home. Now, it flourished. Gardens overflowed with vegetables, livestock grazed in fenced pens, and the vardos had been made into wooden lodges. The Monroes were no longer a threat. There had been no reason for the Renoldis to move.

Emine was the leader of this clan and powerful in her own right. The gypsy lineage passed onto her from her mother, the second born daughter to a Chuvani. Not as strong as the Branded One, she had taken time to study over the years and ready herself for the return of the Chuvani and kill her.

She ruled the Renoldis with a hard heart, controlling what exports went from the village to be sold. The men were talented woodworkers, creating new and beautiful pieces that were sold to other towns and some Cherokee tribes. The women utilized their way of life creating homemade remedies from the ground and plants within the forest surrounding their village.

She walked past children playing a game of rocks on the ground and skipped to avoid being hit by one. She hadn't felt this light on her feet in years. All was coming to fruition. Soon they'd have their revenge.

She headed toward Magda's cabin, passing members of her clan along the way. The Renoldis had grown from a small clan to one that had manifested into other gypsy clans coming to join them.

She came to Magda's door and instead of knocking, simply opened it and entered. The smell of rosemary surrounded her. The women were brewing up something. Did they know? She shook her head. Impossible. She was the only one with the gift of spells and magick. Magda held no such favors. Sorina, like her sister, Sabella, was good with the ways of the earth, concocting healing balms and remedies from the ground, but neither held any sort of power.

"What have you seen?" Sorina asked, jumping up from her rocking chair. Sabella placed her sewing aside. The poor woman hadn't spoken a word since the Monroes attacked her clan years before. They'd been looking for the child, killing anyone who got in their way.

"She is here," Emine said, rubbing her weathered hands together.

Magda flew out of her chair. Her long black hair, woven with grey strands and braided with blue ribbon, whipped around her shoulder.

"You are sure?" she asked.

Emine nodded.

"As I've done every day since the girl's disappearance I've cast the spell to find her, and today a vision appeared. She is here."

Magda and Sorina turned toward each other and squealed. Wide smiles spread across their faces. Aside from their height, build, and ages—both in their early forties—the two women had little in common. Magda's face had aged beyond her years, the skin weathered and wrinkled, while Sorina still held the beauty of her youth.

"What shall we do?" Sorina asked.

Emine sat down in one of the two chairs around the small table.

"We must find her and lure her here."

"But how?" Magda asked.

"We will offer her something she cannot refuse."

Both women stared at her and waited for her to reveal her plan. Their weakness wore on her. Neither woman could make a decision without

Emine's guidance or instruction. She grew tired of their insistent questions and lack of direction. She frowned, giving way to the ice in her veins as it spread into her heart. She was their leader, and she'd see that everything fell into place.

# CHAPTER FOUR

The docks of Jamestown were lined with merchants, scalawags and rich portly fellows. Each had their own reasons for lingering on the wharf. Some sold wares while others stole them, and the wealthy sized up the slaves chained together near the water.

She paused before leaving the dock to stare out at the sea. The waves were low today, and she watched them roll and crash into the harbor. She searched the merchant ships for the *Jade* but did not see the three white sails waving in the breeze.

She tipped her head and weaved through the crowd, leaving the smell of rotten fish, lice infested perukes, and loud guffaws behind her. James had told her the wharf was no place for a lady and she'd do well to keep from being near it. At her insistence he'd brought her back to the very spot he'd found her two days before. Hiram had grown worse through the night, and when she'd been called to his bedside, she'd refused.

The thought of watching him take his last breath made her ill. She'd seen enough death, the memories forever embedded into her mind. Her hands shook, and she wrapped her arms around her middle. The ache penetrated her spine until she was forced to lean forward to ease the pressure. The scream scratched its way up her throat, wanting to expel the misery from her lips. Why was she here—alive—when all she wanted to do was die?

She stepped in between two buildings and held out her arm to lean against a wooden wall. Her forehead was moist, and she licked her lips, tasting salt. The breath did not want to release from her lungs, and she wheezed, feeling winded.

The side door swung open and two men rolled to the ground in front of her. She jumped back away from them as they began fighting.

It seemed the larger of the two men had an advantage, however his opponent was doing a fair job of holding him off. He was an inch shorter and not as thick as the brute he fought yet his skills were impeccable. His long black hair whipped around, hiding his face from her view as he dodged fists, and at one point a knife.

She inched backward until there was nowhere left to go, and her spine pressed against the wall of the building.

The longhaired man landed a stunning blow to the bigger man's nose, and Tsura watched horrified as blood sprayed from the nostrils. The ogre laughed while running his forearm across his face.

"That yer best is it?" he slurred.

The other man straightened his shoulders, but Tsura still could not see his face for the long black hair covering it.

The beefier man pulled a pistol from his trousers, and laughing, aimed it at his opponent. A tanned arm darted out, knocking the gun from the man's hand before he smashed his large fist into the ogre's chin. She heard the loud crunch as teeth crushed together and winced when the man crumbled to the ground.

The dark haired man had won. His back to her, she pushed herself from the wall to leave, lest she be his next victim. But when he turned his black eyes locked with hers, and the breath she'd been holding blew from her lungs explosively.

Red Wolf stood before her, tall, fierce and angry as hell. Clad in tanned slacks and a white shirt, his long black hair fell past his shoulders with one red feather tied to the right side behind his ear. The corner of his mouth dripped blood, and he made no attempt to wipe it away as his deadly eyes pierced her own.

She had not seen him in years and could not keep the shock from her face as he stood before her now.

"To what do I owe this pleasure?" he asked, his lips quirked into a vile grin.

She snapped back into herself and stood taller. The fury and resentment she'd felt toward him filled her already cold heart, and she gave him a scathing glare of her own.

"You have no words?" he taunted. "As I recall you were never without them."

She had turned to leave when his hand caught her arm, and he yanked her back toward him. He was quick. She wasn't surprised. Red Wolf had many talents—a skilled fighter and deft quickness were just a few of them.

"Where might your husband be?" he asked, peering around her.

She jerked her arm from his grasp but did not answer him.

He glanced at the doors of the brothel.

"Ah, I see. The Baron has left you to your own defenses has he?"

"I am quite capable of caring for myself."

"What brings the Baroness of Lithshire here, to Jamestown, and without the chaperone of her pompous husband?"

"That is none of your concern."

"It sure as hell is. The bastard should be hung for letting you wander the wharf by yourself while he wets his lips on cheap ale and probably cheaper women."

The comment stung, but she refused to allow the emotion to change her rigid features.

His black eyes slanted, and his lip curled.

"The man should be shackled and beat with clubs."

"The man is dead!" she hissed. It was too late to take back the words she did not want him to hear, and so she settled for giving him a shove.


Red Wolf hardly felt her touch. Morgan Harris was dead? How? Where? And bloody hell, when?

She turned to walk away, but he stepped in front of her. He thought he'd never set sight on her again, but fate, or some evil being had brought them together, and he wanted to know why.

"When did he die?"

He watched as her cheeks grew red, and her lips strained against her creamy skin.

"It does not matter."

"Answer the damn question, Tsura."

"Go to hell," she snapped.

"Do Pril and Kade know?" he asked. It'd been three years since he'd seen the couple that took him along to England, and he missed them very much. He'd left without warning, without telling anyone where he'd gone.

Seeing Tsura, now in front of him, brought a rush of emotions he was not ready to deal with. She was different. He could see it now clear as day. The girl he'd left behind with the beautiful emerald eyes and impish grin was gone. Before him stood a stone-faced woman with hard lines.

She nodded and averted her eyes from his.

"Micah?"

"I came on the *Jade*. Are you finished berating me?"

Micah was a merchant like Kade and Red Wolf. It had been the family business with Kade commanding the S.S.W after his father, Samuel Walker. He was baffled as to why Micah hadn't mentioned Tsura's presence in

Jamestown when he'd seen him yesterday. The bastard hadn't said Morgan had died either. Red Wolf didn't ask, and he supposed the past was better left there. Micah wasn't one to meddle and knew it was a sensitive subject to broach. They'd shared a pint and some good laughs before he sailed out this morning. Red Wolf should've set sail as well, but he'd been inclined to lap up more whiskey and the blonde who kept calling his name from across the brothel.

"Why did you not sail with Micah when he departed this morning?"

"Release me at once."

"Why are you here?" he asked.

Her green eyes flashed, and he let go of her arm. A warning. He waited for it, but nothing happened. No magick flowed through her body. No beam struck him, causing his breath to still and his chest to ache. She was not the same...not the same at all.

"Let me pass." She moved to walk around him.

He followed. Her short legs moved quickly, the long skirt swishing as she walked. He didn't have to place too much effort into keeping up as his legs were much longer than hers.

"Why have you come back?"

She knew of the danger. Pril and Kade had told her of the Renoldi clan. Hell, he even relayed a few stories and made her promise to never step foot on this land again. Yet, she stood before him now.

She tipped her chin another notch. He reached for her hand. His palm singed from the heat of her flesh. She withheld the magick. It burned inside of her now, yet she did not release it. Why?

"Leave me," she hissed.

He slowed his steps and watched her walk away. He examined his hand, stared at the two blisters that formed on the palm. He never thought to see her again—to set sight on her beautiful face. The betrayal she'd dealt him crashed down upon him like the waves on the dock, and anger took hold of his heart. She'd killed his soul. He ground his teeth. He'd never forgive her for it.

He swiveled on his heel and walked back inside the brothel to drown his memories in a pint of ale.

# CHAPTER FIVE

Red Wolf clutched the fifth glass of cider ale close to his chest and threw in two coins. "I'll take the one with the blue ribbon tied to his leg," he said to the reedy fellow taking the bets.

Men gathered close to the makeshift circle, and he felt an overwhelming urge to punch his way out of the crowd. He should've sailed yesterday, but seeing Tsura had kept him from sleep and placed him in a constant vigil on a stool at the tavern. His mates had been in and out a few times to inquire when they were departing, and he had yet to give them an answer. He was too busy drowning any memory he had of Tsura in glass after glass of ale.

He needed to sail soon if he was to meet the ports and make any money, but something held him here, in Jamestown, and this damn saloon.

"Which one ye be bettin' on, Ol' boy?" Mack, his first mate, asked, slapping him on the shoulder and spilling half his ale all over the front of his shirt.

"The one in the blue," he answered before taking a long drink.

"Aye, it will win."

Red Wolf frowned.

"I have me wits and know these cocks. Yers will win, be sure of it."

Mack's short slacks, always worn cut at the shin, were black from dirt and many days without a wash. His shirt, once white, now resembled filth at its finest.

"When was the last time you bathed?"

Mack's round face turned upward. His long white beard did little to hide the toothy grin. "Been a while it has."

Red Wolf tossed him two bits.

"Go find a whore to clean you up."

The portly man lingered, and Red Wolf knew he had something else he needed to discuss.

"Speak your mind, Mack."

"Aye, Captain."

He turned to face him and waited.

"The mates, they're gettin' an itch to be leavin' 'ere."

He sighed.

"We be behind two days already."

It was the truth, and mainly due to Red Wolf's new addiction to cider ale.

"Very well, we will sail at dusk."

"Aye, Captain. This evenin' then?"

Red Wolf nodded. He needed to depart, whether he wanted to or not.

"Ready the men and the ship."

"Aye, that I will." Mack hesitated before continuing. "Somethin' botherin' ye, lad?"

"Nay. Now go old man before I throw you to the cocks."

Mack stared at him for a long while, but Red Wolf refused to divulge his thoughts especially when he was unsure of what they were.

"Aye. That's the way of it then."

Red Wolf turned away. He wanted to be alone. He heard Mack leave, and only when he knew the man was gone did he turn back around. He lifted his hand to summon the barkeep for another glass and sat with his back leaning against the bar. He learned long ago to always face the crowd. It allowed him an advantage to watch for trouble. Today he hoped for it. He fisted his hands, holding the tension he'd felt since yesterday within them.

Tsura was here.

Why had she come back to Jamestown? He knew Hiram Monroe lived here, and that may be the very reason for her arrival, but something told him it wasn't. Danger lurked on this land, not just within the Renoldi clan, but also in the rogues lurking the damn wharf where he'd found her. He should've thrown her over his shoulder and dumped her on the first ship sailing back to England.

He growled.

Nay! She could go to the dogs. She was a vixen that lavished in toying with one's emotions only to destroy them with a devious smile. The wretch! Tsura could burn for all he cared.

He remembered the hard lines of her face. The once smooth skin now shadowed with something he couldn't quite place. He shrugged. She was in mourning, a reason for her sour appearance. So why had she come? Hadn't

Morgan given her everything she'd asked for? She married a Baron, damn it. She got the life she wanted, an extravagant home with servants and prestige. He frowned. All she cared for were riches and fineries, and Morgan gave them to her.

Why come to a land that could offer her nothing but heartache and possible death? None of it made sense, and his head began to ache. He closed his eyes and rubbed the lids with his finger and thumb.

Bitterness rose to the back of his throat as fantasies of the life he'd thought were once his had become nothing more than a lie. He downed the ale, letting the liquid escape through the corners of his mouth to dribble down his chin. He ran his forearm across his mouth to wipe the remnants away. A loud belch blew from his lips at the same time as the brothel erupted in cheers and handshakes.

The blue cock had won.

He walked toward the circle and peered over shoulders to get a closer look. The other cock lay bloody and limp on the ground. Pecked to death by the more vicious of the two. A shame. He'd hoped for a loss, for a reason to brawl. He watched the man hand out money to the men who'd won. Not in the mood to thrash his way through the crowd, he went back to his seat at the bar. He slapped a coin on the counter.

"Another glass," he yelled to the barkeep, a stocky man with long scraggly silver hair.

A foamy mug was placed in front of him, and he took a swig almost choking on the airy liquid at the top. He squinted as the door opened and light from outside shone through the hazy room. The dust sparkled like stars, and he thought of the clear night he'd left England three years before. His heart heavy, his dreams shattered.

The room grew quiet. Red Wolf watched as men stepped aside, parting for someone he could not see. Low murmurs hummed around the room, but his attention was on the visitor who'd just walked in.

The men in front of him stepped aside and Red Wolf recognized Romulus Black, the most ruthless bandit of the seas. A Corsair, he sailed the waters off the coasts of England and Africa stealing and bartering for slaves.

If the law found him they'd lynch him sure as the sea was blue. He was wanted on both sides of the water from here to England for theft, treason, and murder. A sailor himself with a love for gambling, Romulus relished in delivering the consequences of unpaid debts owed to him. He never walked away from conflict of any kind. Devious by nature, Romulus was a liar, a cheat, and as corrupt as they came.

Red Wolf had met the notorious outlaw a few times over the years, but nothing ever came of their encounters. Other merchants hadn't been so lucky. The bastard of the sea had little regard for consequence or the lives he stole.

He remained seated as Romulus came toward him. The Corsair limped, favoring his right leg. He'd not noticed this trait before and wondered if it was a recent injury. He had the face of a rat, small and pointed. His long hair and beard did nothing to hide the jagged edges of his cheeks and chin.

"Ah, if it isn't Red Wolf, Captain of the *Falcon*," he said with a leering smile as he pulled out the seat beside him and sat down.

Red Wolf swayed. He probably shouldn't have drunk the last four glasses of cider ale.

Two burly men with shoulders twice the width of his own stood behind Romulus. Gaspard and Meril were the Corsair's henchmen. They did whatever their captain commanded without question.

Gaspard's left eye stared off to the side while the other remained straight, and his mouth drooped downward. The man's hands were large enough to wrap around Red Wolf's head and crush it.

"Romulus." He lifted his mug.

The barkeep placed a jug of rum onto the counter. The sweet smell turned Red Wolf's stomach, and he swallowed back the urge to vomit.

"How have the waters been to you?" Romulus asked before he took a long drink from the pitcher.

"Well enough. How is it you are not shackled and chained by now?"

The rogue laughed. "Ah, that is because I am always one step ahead, my friend."

"I am not your friend."

No longer in the mood to drink, Red Wolf stood trying to catch himself on the stool before he fell over. The ground was remarkably soft considering it was littered with broken bottles and mugs.

"A bit too much?" Romulus asked.

He smiled a lopsided grin as he stood. He'd had too much hours ago.

"I was sure savages weren't fit to mingle with the civilized."

The insult shouldn't have bothered him, he'd heard worse, but before he could stop himself his left hand grabbed hold of the slimy bastard's throat. Gaspard and Meril were on him within seconds. Red Wolf was thrown against the table behind him, knocking it over and all the drinks that were upon it.

"Take him outside," Romulus said, grabbing the jug of rum from the counter to bring with him.

The room swayed and dipped as Red Wolf was ushered out into the afternoon sunlight. He squinted, the brightness blinding him. Gaspard held his arms crushed between the large man's stomach and Red Wolf's back.

He didn't bother trying to escape. He was much too drunk. And even sober he wasn't sure he could beat the giant.

"I hate to be such a bother, but I am inclined to know a few things," Romulus said as he walked closer.

"And what might they be?"

"You hail from Bristol?"

"I did." What the hell did he want to know about that for? They'd never had any bad dealings. In fact, he'd never dealt with the bastard because of his horrid reputation.

"How is it a savage such as yourself lived a lavish life in England?"

Red Wolf's nostrils flared.

"You were raised by the merchant Kade Walker?"

Every muscle within him tensed. Kade and Pril had taken him in when he was twelve. He loved them more than anything.

"What do you want?"

Romulus nodded to Meril, who drove his fist into Red Wolf's stomach. The air flew from his lungs. Winded, he hunched forward.

Gaspard yanked him back up.

"Yes or no?" Romulus asked.

Red Wolf refused to answer.

Another blow to the midsection brought up the last three glasses of ale.

The Corsair came closer. Red Wolf stared at his brown boots through a haze of drunkenness and pain. He was pulled up yet again to face the rogue.

"A simple yes or no will suffice."

"I hardly think my answer will suffice to a bastard such as yourself."

This time he tightened his muscles ready for the punch to his stomach, but instead Meril's fist clipped the edge of his jaw. His teeth jammed upward, cutting the skin on the inside of his lip, and vibrated up to the skull. Bloody hell, the bastard could hit. He struggled against Gaspard's hold, but the thug didn't move.

Red Wolf would not yield. Romulus wanted something and it had to do with the people he loved.

"Your resistance speaks volumes," he said as he cupped Red Wolf's chin and inspected the wound.

"The woman with the ebony colored hair and emerald eyes, widow to Baron Harris of Lithshire."

Tsura. He was talking about Tsura.

"Where is she?"

"I know of no such woman," he said, keeping his face straight.

Meril stepped toward him, and Red Wolf kicked out his leg, catching the bastard in the stomach. He laughed as the portly man stumbled backward.

Probably not the best reaction, but damn it to hell with them. He would not yield.

Gaspard's grip tightened and he pulled Red Wolf's arms further back behind him. It was getting more and more difficult to breathe. Meril's fist came out of nowhere and found yet another piece of Red Wolf's cheek, this time closer to the eye.

His knees buckled. Son of a bitch that one hurt. He was sure his cheek was split in two. The whole side of his face throbbed.

Two more punches to his chin and one to his eye followed. The lid began to swell—the skin covered most of the eye and blocked his vision. He tasted blood upon his tongue and let the spittle drip from his mouth. He hung from Gaspard's arms unable to pull himself back up.

Romulus grabbed his head and tipped it upward. "Where is she?"

Red Wolf spat into the rogue's face.

Gaspard held his arms up, pulling them behind his neck to wrap with his own in a vise-like grip.

He gasped, trying to draw in air, but was only held tighter. He saw a glimpse of the blade before Romulus dug the tip into his armpit.

Red Wolf groaned. He refused to scream, even though he wanted to. He slammed his jaw closed and ground the back teeth together. The knife moved slowly along his side. Bile rose to his throat to tempt evulsion, while his muscles clenched and his head spun. He blinked against the fog that surrounded him, and tried to stay conscious. Romulus intended to kill him, and he'd succeed, but Tsura's name would not pass through Red Wolf's lips.

Voices came from the streets.

"'Tis the county sheriff."

He was dropped to the ground before he blacked out.

# CHAPTER SIX

Tsura removed the petticoat from her reticule. The shift, a gift from her mother when she was sixteen, still looked new. She fingered the small pink flowers embroidered on the hemline. It took her weeks to finish the undergarment, and Tsura remembered the joy in her eyes when she'd given it to her.

Her mother had been a constant pillar of strength in her life. From the time she was a little girl and the betrayal of their clan, to teaching her the ways of their people. She was a Chuvani and with that came great power. Born with a gift to do remarkable things, but if not careful it could cost her deeply. Her mother had instructed her on how the spells worked—the right words to say and when. She warned of magick while angry. *One cannot control the words if the mind is fogged by rage.* Tsura studied hard throughout her years growing up in Bristol. While Kade was away at sea, her mother took hours teaching her their way of life.

The counting of the spells and ability to raise the dead were just a few of the gifts Tsura had been blessed with. Vodama, her blood mother and Pril's sister, had been a very powerful Chuvani within the Renoldi clan. She'd overturned many rules, which resulted in her hanging while burned when Tsura was a baby.

She glanced at her hands, turning the palms upward to face her. She'd done many wonderful things with the gift she'd been given…and she'd done some awful ones too, but it was what she could *not* do that she'd never forget.

She shook her head. None of it mattered anymore. She didn't use the gifts, hadn't in almost a year. Her hands were useless when it came to doing anything of significance…like saving a life. She hung her head and waited for the wave of despair to wash over her. She swayed as it covered her in revulsion and disgust. No remorse lurked within its shadow, only detestation and bitterness for the life she was left to live alone. She allowed one tear to slip past her black lashes and fall onto her cheek.

Tsura knew she'd never be the same again, and she wanted nothing more than to go back to that day, to stop the horrible things from happening, but she could not. Time would not allow it, and she'd been left to wonder why for the rest of her miserable life.

She sat on the end of the bed and removed the pins holding the thick knot of hair at the base of her neck. She massaged the scalp, releasing the tension it held. The door to her room burst open, and Red Wolf fell to the floor. Tsura jumped, took a step back, and stared at him. Her body grew cold. The smell of blood filled her nostrils, and she sensed danger. Her stomach dipped, and she began to perspire. Her hands restless, she flexed them.

No magick.

She walked around him to peek out into the hall, but no one was there. She closed the door and slid the chain across to lock it.

"Red Wolf." She nudged him with the tip of her toe.

He was still.

Panic shot up her throat and lodged there. She knelt beside him, careful not to touch his flesh, and rolled him onto his back. There was so much blood. The shirt he wore was soaked in it. His face was covered with cuts and bruises. The tingling in her fingers started, and she ignored the need. She stripped him of his shirt and gasped when she saw the long gash from his armpit to just above the hipbone. He'd need more than the mere beeswax and yarrow she kept in her bag.

He'd need a spell.

Tsura stood and stepped away from him. Her lips moved desperate to utter the words, but no sound came from them. She inhaled a deep breath waiting for the notion to pass, and the demand to speak the words left her body. There would be no magick, no spell, and no hands to heal. She repeated this silently until she felt the urge leave her.

She set her face and placed the walls around her heart once more. A thick strand of hair fell across her forehead, and she fastened the heavy tresses with a leather twine before she pulled her bag from the armoire to dig through for the yarrow and beeswax. She placed the jars beside Red Wolf on the floor. The basin of water sat on the dressing table, and she positioned it close by.

She cleaned the wound, careful again not to touch the cut with her fingers. She used the cloth to pull the skin apart. The gash was deep and he would need to be stitched.

She surveyed the room, unprepared for such an endeavor. She had no needle or thread. Tapping her finger to her lips, she remembered Red Wolf carried a small satchel of these things on him. He'd shown her on a warm day while they'd sat under the tree. She swallowed past the dryness in her throat. She blocked the memory from her mind and went about searching his person for the small leather sack he carried.

She found it attached to the sheath he wore around his thigh to hold his knife. Inside were a needle, thread, and something else wrapped in thin velum. Curious she unfolded the calfskin to reveal a dried orange and yellow flower with over a dozen petals. She touched trembling fingers to her lips. The Immortelle blossom, she'd given it to him years before. Her eyes welled with tears. She shook her head and growled low in her throat.

He was the very reason she'd been subjected to the horrors that had become her life. She flattened her lips. The muscles in her neck tightened. She despised him. She crushed the flower within her hand, letting the dust fall from her palm onto the floor next to him. Bah! He could go to hades.


An hour later she placed the last stitch into his side, pulling the thread into a triple knot before she removed the needle. She took the yarrow and broke it into small bits before mixing it with the beeswax to smooth over his cut.

She lathered the mixture and covered each of the lesions on his face. Her finger trailed the curve of his lips and angle of his high cheekbones. There had been a time he'd been all she ever wanted. She'd built her dreams around the promises he'd made to her. She straightened. But it had all been a ruse. He'd lied, left her. Tsura's eyes misted. She clenched her teeth and released an aggravated groan.

She stood and stared down at him. The hardness overcame her once more. Red Wolf would either get better or die, but she'd not watch either. She reached for her reticule, took one last look at him then left the room, closing the door softly behind her.

# CHAPTER SEVEN

Red Wolf leaned against the wall of the livery. His side pulsed, the skin tight and hot where his wound was. It'd been two days since Mack found him in a room above the tobacco store. Injured and running a fever, his first mate had tended him until he could stay conscious enough to remember Romulus Black hunted Tsura.

Against Mack's advice, Red Wolf insisted upon leaving the cozy room and warm bed to search for her. Desperate to make sure she hadn't been harmed by the foul merchant and his men he'd scoured the streets for hours.

He commanded Mack take charge of the *Falcon*. The first mate was to sail it on the only run Red Wolf had not made. He trusted his men would have a successful trip and come back safe. They were all he had, the family he'd grown to love aside from the one he'd left behind. The life he'd led with Tsura was muddled in the back of his mind, and the memories were more of a nightmare that haunted him when he least expected.

He'd searched for her for two days, keeping from the main roads and popular taverns. Luck had finally shown him some kindness when he questioned the gangly girl working the counter at the mercantile. She'd said the woman with the green eyes and midnight hair had gone into the livery not long ago.

Careful not to draw any attention, he made his way to the large barn at the end of the street. He tipped his chin and scanned the road and buildings for any sign of trouble. The air was hot and humid and reeked of fish from the harbor.

Romulus was close. He could feel it. Had the Corsair wanted Tsura to sell as one of his slaves? He'd bet she'd make a good bartering tool with such exotic features. Her beauty had often amazed even him. She'd bring a heavy ransom if Romulus wanted to steal her for money too. Kade and Pril would pay any amount for her return.

The Corsair's sole purpose in life was the acquisition of money and liquor. Had he found out she was also a Monroe? Red Wolf shook his head. How had Tsura gotten acquainted with such a scoundrel? Surely she knew of the consequences if she crossed him.

He glanced at the wide doors of the livery. The answers would be found in there with her. He pushed himself from the wall. His side was still sore and throbbed from any sudden movement of his muscles. He'd learned to ignore the pain or grimace through it, but today the wound seemed irritated, hot and uncomfortable. The sack of medicine Mack had given him appeared to be helping, but he hadn't applied the plant since yesterday. What he needed was a drink. A glass of cider ale to ease the pain and drown his memories. Instead he stood outside in the stark heat with aching ribs determined to help a woman who he'd rather forget.

He walked through the wide entrance. The sweet smell of hay surrounded him. Eight stalls lined the sides against the wall. Each housed a horse, or two. He spotted Tsura standing at the end of the barn. She was speaking to the livery master and by the disgruntled expression on her face the conversation wasn't going her way.

"Sir, I want your finest horse to buy not to rent," she demanded.

The man scratched his head of uncombed hair. "Ma'am, this one is not for sale."

"Is he the best one you have?" She pointed to the brown appaloosa lingering beside them.

"Yes, Ma'am, but like I said before, Baron is not for sale."

"That is his name?" Her cheeks paled.

The man nodded.

"That will not do."

"I think it is rather fitting," Red Wolf said as he walked toward her.

He watched as the surprised expression left her face followed by angled brows and green eyes that spit fire at him.

"I care not for your opinion," she replied, turning away from him. "What else do you have, sir?"

"I've only got one for sale, but I won't sell him to you."

Tsura bristled. "Why ever not?"

"Caesar is mean. He'll throw a pretty thing like you within seconds."

Red Wolf looked behind him to the black stallion with a patch of white hair between his eyes.

"How much do you want for him?" he asked.

The man eyed Red Wolf, taking in his cut lip, blackened eye, and bruised cheek.

"Four pounds."

"On account of he's mean and selling him will be difficult, I'll give you half of that."

"Nay, four pounds on account you're a savage."

The man had gall. Red Wolf wasn't in the mood, nor did he have the time to barter with him. He reached inside his pocket and pulled out his leather pouch. He counted out five pounds and handed it to the man.

"I've given you one extra for the lady's horse."

"I do not need your charity. I can make do on my own." Tsura stepped in between the men.

Red Wolf ignored her.

The livery owner took the money. "I've got nothing to sell the lady."

"I'll rent the mare two stalls down for her."

Knowing Red Wolf had paid too much for the mare, the man smiled and showed his the gap where his missing front teeth had been.

"This is absurd," Tsura demanded. "I'll not ride a horse I have not chosen for myself, and I'll not be indebted to a filthy bugger such as yourself."

"She is a Baroness and isn't used to being told what to do," Red Wolf whispered to the man, who nodded in understanding.

Tsura's gasp brought a smile to his lips, and he disregarded the pain that came with it from stretching the lips to pull on his cut.

"I no longer hold such a title, and I am my own person who, may I remind you, can and will pay for my own steed."

"Very well. Give the man a pound so we can be on our way," Red Wolf said to her.

"I'll not be going anywhere with you." She reached inside of her purse hanging by a thin leather handle from her wrist and pulled out the coin. "One pound, but I'll take that one," she said, pointing to the brown gelding behind the man. It was the first horse she'd wanted, the finest in the livery.

"He is three pounds," the man said.

Red Wolf knew the man was full of it and was trying to pull in as much money from the Baroness as he could. The horse wasn't worth more than one pound to rent.

"I will not pay that," she said.

The man walked over to the stall that held the spotted mare Red Wolf had rented for her earlier and with gentle hands, pulled the horse from the stall. He handed her the reins and her coin.

"Seven days you are to return her."

Red Wolf peered outside wary of anyone passing by. They needed to be going.

Tsura crossed her arms and shook her head. The black curls were braided down her back, but a few stray strands had escaped to frame her porcelain face. He wondered if they were as soft as he remembered.

He spotted Gaspard across the street and knew their time had run out.

"Take the damn horse," he said and opened the gate holding the wild stallion inside.

"I'll not take orders from the likes of you," she spouted.

He heard her words, but was too busy familiarizing himself with Caesar. The horse shifted to the left, and Red Wolf placed his palm out to let the animal smell his scent. The horse jumped back and reared up, kicking his hooves high into the air. He tightened the quiver around his chest. This was going to hurt like the blazes.

Red Wolf grabbed hold of the mane and leapt onto the horse's back. It almost bloody killed him to do so. The stab in his side a reminder he'd not yet healed. He was about to say a prayer the wild beast didn't buck or throw him when Caesar did just that. The stallion kicked and swung around, knocking into the wooden fence he was penned in.

Red Wolf was in hell. He ground his teeth against the sharp pain in his side. His stomach turned offering no reprieve from the sweat on his forehead. With no other choice but to ride it out, he leaned down and rested his chest on the stallion's neck.

"Unalii, shush. Friend, shush," he whispered, "I will not hurt you."

The horse shook his head, stomped his front hooves a few more times before he settled and stood still awaiting Red Wolf's command.

The livery owner stared with his mouth open and his eyes wide.

"Sir, I would like another steed," Tsura said.

Red Wolf walked Caesar toward her when he spotted Gaspard and Meril at the entrance of the livery.

"Get on the damn horse," he growled, watching the men come toward them.

"Leave me at once!" She glared at him.

He glanced at Gaspard and Meril again.

"Ah hell." He leaned down, wrapped his arm around her tiny waist, and yanked her up to lie across the horse. He ran his molars together and growled low in his throat from the shock of torture that surged through his side. Tsura's rump in the air, he held onto her, swung the stallion around, and stabbed his boots into Caesar's sides.

Gaspard's large hand grabbed hold of the horse's tail, and Red Wolf watched amused as the stallion kicked his hind legs out to slam the giant in the shoulder and send him sailing through the air.

"Get going!" he shouted.

Caesar bolted out the wide doors of the livery and onto the street. Red Wolf spotted Romulus and slapped the reins, urging the stallion to run faster. Tsura screamed in front of him. Her bag dangled from her hand, and for a moment he felt sorry for the position he'd placed her in on top of the horse. It had to be rather uncomfortable. The sound of a pistol echoed behind him, and his conscience dismissed any guilt he'd had before. The dust kicked up around them as he steered the horse out of town.

# CHAPTER EIGHT

"What in bloody blazes is the matter with you?" Tsura asked, swiping the dirt from her skirt. They'd ridden with her swung across his lap for the better part of an hour before Red Wolf had all but dropped her onto the ground. Her head swam as she tried to steady herself from being hung upside down for such a long time.

He ran his hand along the animal's coat, speaking to the horse in Cherokee, words she could not understand. Caesar nuzzled his snout into Red Wolf's palm.

"We were being chased."

"By whom?" she demanded.

"You tell me?" He pulled his quiver from his back, winced from the pang in his side, and placed it onto the ground.

"What are you speaking about? Take me back to town at once." She went to the animal to try and climb up, but the horse walked away from her.

"He does not trust you."

"Nonsense! I have a way with animals." She walked toward Caesar again, placed her hand on his side, and stroked the soft hair. "There, see?"

Caesar's hind legs bucked high into the air, and Tsura didn't get a chance to move away before Red Wolf tackled her to the ground. Her chest expanded. She could not draw air, and she gasped. Unable to move until the breath had been restored to her lungs, she lay there staring up at the blue sky, trying to control the urge—the need to throw Red Wolf from her body.

"Remove yourself at once," she said carefully.

"I'd rather stay here for a minute or two if you don't mind." He smirked.

"Get off of me!" she shrieked. Her body heated, and she was past the point of any control. Damn him and his blasted words. She hated being touched—hadn't prepared herself, couldn't stop the magick from taking over.

Red Wolf yelped as her body burned him, singeing his shirt and leaving a red welt where his skin had touched hers.

"I see you still have the gift," he said, giving her a sideways glance as he inspected his clothes.

She ignored him and stood, making an effort to place some distance between them.

"When did you stop using it?"

"My life is none of your concern." She placed her eyes on him. "Take me back to town at once."

He tied Caesar to a tree before he went about picking up dried leaves and broken branches. She noticed he limped and was favoring his left side. He was still in pain from the attack on him days before. She set her chin and refused to let the feelings from the past affect her. She'd not pity him in the least for he didn't deserve it. She'd not pity him.

"Were you always this rude?" she asked.

He dropped the armload of branches he carried onto the ground and stared at her. His long black hair pushed off of his face to hang past his shoulders. The bruises on his cheeks and around his eye reflected in the sun.

"The time past has hardened me. You however, were always a pretentious wench."

She had opened her mouth to blast him when he held up his hand to stop her.

"Honestly, when I think of that time so long ago my stomach turns, and quite frankly, I feel the need to expel all that is in it."

"I hold the same sentiment. So give me the steed, and I will be on my way."

He shook his head.

"I own the horse."

"I should've left you to die." She marched past him. She would walk back to Jamestown.

"Left me to die?" he echoed. He grabbed her arm and swung her around. "It was you who mended my wound?"

She tipped her chin. "Do not flatter yourself. I was merely doing the innkeeper a favor."

She needed to be rid of him—of the memories that invaded her mind when he was near. Damn it. She'd never thought their paths would cross again and yet, here they were in the middle of a blasted forest, she with no steed of her own to escape him.

He cleared his throat, and she watched him. He was stronger, wider, and held an air about him she had not noticed before. She almost laughed out loud at her thoughts. What did any of it matter he was her enemy, and she'd not be fooled by him again.

He stepped toward her, and regret flickered within his dark eyes.

Before she could conjure up another reason to hate him memories smashed her resolve. The anguish swelled inside of her stomach and pressed its way up into her heart. She blinked, praying for it to cease, for the pain she knew would come to halt. The fear crept up when she was tired, angry, or on the verge of weakness. Most times she'd breathe through it and force her mind onto something else until it dissolved. Not today…not now. It trapped her, bound her like shackles and chains, and it was all because he was here.

She closed her eyes to stop the images from invading her mind. She inhaled the putrid smell of wood, burned flesh, and no, please no, not death. It was all too much. Frantic, she'd searched, tried to bring him back. Tsura's heart raced. Her eyes flew open. Her throat dry, she grabbed at her chest and rubbed trying to rid the ache from her body, desperate to catch her breath.

"Tsura?"

She heard his voice—it seemed so far away. His hand still on her arm loosened, and she pulled herself away from him. She had to go. No idea now what direction she headed, she continued to walk. Distance. She needed distance.

"Wait. You cannot go off on your own." He was beside her again.

"Leave me." She did not recognize her own voice. The breath would not come, and her throat burned.

"You keep asking it of me and yet, I find myself not obeying you."

She halted and turned pointed eyes toward him. "I despise you."

He laughed.

She straightened.

"Wonderful. I detest you as well. We will get along famously."

"I see nothing humorous about this situation." Her chest eased, and the rigid set of her shoulders sagged once more allowing her lungs to expand.

"Nor do I. However, we are stuck with one another, and so we must make the best of things."

"I am not, nor will I ever be *stuck* with you. Now, let me pass."

"I cannot do that."

She sighed and threw her hands into the air. He ducked and for a moment she had no idea what he was doing.

"I am not familiar with the lack of interest you have in wanting to use your gifts." He stood taller.

"I told you they are not a part of me any longer." She reached for her reticule lying on the ground.

"Why is Romulus Black after you?"

She knew the rouge but remained indifferent to his question.

"I do not know this man."

"I say you do."

She turned from him, and busied herself with searching through her bag.

"We may have parted ways three years before, but some things remain, and I can still tell when you are fibbing."

"Yes, well I do not care."

"What does he want with you?"

She shrugged.

"He is not someone you toy with, Tsura. Romulus will kill you and enjoy doing so."

She averted her eyes.

He reached for her, and she evaded him by sidestepping his hand.

"Who do you think cut me?"

She did not reply.

"I can assure you he will do worse to you than a mere swipe of his blade."

She stepped toward him, her eyes blazing bright green with rage.

"I care not what the rogue wants from me. In fact he can bloody well have me."

Red Wolf stared at the woman he once knew so well. No ounce of kindness showed on her face. He wondered when the last time was she'd laughed. Morgan's death must've done her in. His chest constricted. Had she loved her husband so much she no longer wanted to live?

He couldn't stand back and watch her surrender to the bastard Romulus. They may despise each other, but she was Pril and Kade's daughter, and because he loved them—and nothing else—he'd keep Tsura safe…even if it killed him.

"I cannot in good conscience allow you to return," he said.

"When did you acquire a conscience?" she snarled.

"Do not mistake my duty of conscience for any type of affection I may have for you. I can assure you there is none."

"Duty? I need not your duty."

"You are correct. Nor do you deserve it. However, Kade and Pril do, and I love them."

"You do not know what love is."

"Ah, that is where you're wrong. I've loved many a bosom and nestled plenty of plush asses in my day." He winked.

"That is lust, you fool."

"I am not so sure. I loved every minute of it."

"Bah!" She threw her hands up and walked back toward the horse.

He let her go. He hadn't the energy to fight with her. His side pounded relentlessly, the skin on fire, and he was sure the insistent ache would never go away. Red Wolf went to the thatch of sticks he'd dropped on the ground earlier. He pulled out his flint and steel, knelt and struck a spark, lighting the fire. He needed to rest and allow the heat to penetrate his sore body.

Red Wolf lay with his head resting on his forearm. The glow from the fire cast the trees in tall shadows that loomed over them. Tsura had nibbled on the small rabbit he'd been able to kill with his bow and arrow, before laying down across the fire from him and going to sleep.

He'd bet the *Falcon* she wasn't sleeping any more than he was, but he was reluctant to speak with her. Long black hair framed her pale face in bouncy curls. No color graced her cheeks, only the simplest pink hue shaded her full lips.

He let his mind wander to the girl he once knew so well. Whimsical, bright, and alluring, Tsura could hold him captive with one smile. From the moment he'd met her on this very land, he'd known she was special.

Aside from her gifts, which were impeccable and impossible to believe if you hadn't seen them for yourself, Tsura was kind and compassionate. She loved to laugh. He closed his eyes and summoned the sound within his mind. He hadn't forgotten. It played in his dreams, haunted his sleep and pulled at his sanity. There were times he was sure he'd go crazy.

The past came back like a vicious storm, catapulting his heart and seizing his mind. Nothing had seemed to touch him then. His life had been wonderful. He had a future to look forward to and a woman to share it with. They loved one another, or so he'd thought. She'd taken his love and stomped on it. How had he been so blind? Why hadn't he seen she was fooling him all along?

Mack had told him once that love was a trick the heart played on the soul. The passion had killed many he was sure, leaving in its wake desolate shells with little regard to life afterward.

Tsura had broken him—cut his heart in two without so much as a care.

There had been a time Red Wolf thought he'd die because of it. He wandered for months from one place to the next, searching for what he once had.

He blew out an exasperated breath and closed his eyes. He'd accepted long ago that he'd live with half of himself. He closed off all feelings for Tsura he'd had, or so he thought. Seeing her in the flesh hurt worse than any torment Romulus and his men could inflict upon him. The Corsair wouldn't stop until he had Tsura. Red Wolf was sure of it. They couldn't run forever. He needed to take her somewhere safe, to someone he trusted.

# CHAPTER NINE

Tsura sat up, her back ached from the uncomfortable ride yesterday. She stretched her arms high above her head. Her ribs expanded and with each inhale pushed the stiffness from her bones. The reticule hadn't been the soft pillow she was used to resting her head upon. Instead, it was hard and lumpy. Her neck had been bent awkwardly throughout the night, and any movement sent a piercing pain down her back. She slowly moved her head from side to side in an effort to loosen the sore muscles.

The fire had burned down to ashes and smoldered, leaving the scent of charred wood in the air. Red Wolf's pack was rolled and lay on the ground a few feet from the fire. She blew out a long sigh and did a quick survey of their meager camp for him. He must've gone hunting. She stood and tossed the long braid behind her shoulder. Her stomach growled, but she ignored the hunger and walked quickly to where Caesar grazed.

She secured the reticule around the horse's neck. This would be a challenge. The animal was huge, and without riding slacks, she'd have to hike the skirt up past her waist or find something to stand on to mount him. Red Wolf could come back at any moment, so with no time to spare, she bunched the skirt, petticoat, and bustle under her left arm as best she could. The hoop, which fell just below her hips, was difficult to maneuver, but after a few minutes of struggling with it she'd secured the short bustle under her arm with the others. She clutched the reticule tightly within her hand.

The cool morning air chilled her bare thighs where the long green stockings hadn't reached. The motion of getting one's leg over the massive beast proved to be a trial. She scrunched the fabric tighter within her arm as determination pursed her lips.

Tsura held onto the thick mane of the horse with her right hand and swung her leg up, knocking it into the animal's side. Caesar was too tall.

She'd need to jump while hoisting her leg over. She repositioned herself, squeezed the skirt within her arm, and jumped while kicking her leg high into the air. Caesar stepped to the side, and she landed on the ground in a heap of hoops, linen, and wool.

"Blast!" She slammed her hands onto the ground, squishing the dirt between her fingers, and sat up. She needed the horse if she was to get back to Jamestown and avoid Red Wolf all together. His tracking skills were impeccable. She didn't doubt he'd find her within minutes if she left on foot.

She stood, picked up her bag, gathered her skirts, and grabbed Caesar's mane. She threw her leg up again. Her foot caught on the animal's back. Hallelujah! Now she just needed to pull herself into a seated position and she'd be on her way. It seemed to take forever. Her bodily strength wasn't what it used to be when she was young.

She clamped her jaw closed, ground her molars, and pulled. Inch by inch she hoisted herself up. She was almost there. Tsura let go of the skirt, feeling the layers fall down her leg.

"What are you doing?" Red Wolf's voice came from behind her.

Tsura refused to stop now. She was getting on the damn horse whether he stood there or not. Using all of her strength, she shimmied closer to the top.

"Asiu, asiu," Red Wolf said.

Caesar walked toward Red Wolf. The motion caused Tsura to lose her balance and fall to the ground again.

"Bloody unbelievable," she growled low in her throat and stood. While she brushed the dirt and leaves from her skirt, she watched him through her lashes.

He spoke in his native tongue to Caesar while running his fingers through the black mane.

"What did you say to the horse?"

He glanced at her over the animal's back. "Walk."

Her mouth gaped open. "How does the animal understand Cherokee?"

"When we were in the livery I spoke it to him, and he understood me. I knew he was one of my people's horses."

Frustrated she threw her hands into the air.

"I do not see why you're so angry. It isn't Caesar's fault you cannot mount a horse properly."

"I can ride just fine. The blasted animal is at your mercy. I see it now. I never had a chance."

He smiled.

"Actually you did."

She gaped at him.

"Had you used the stump I placed on the other side this morning you'd have been well on your way. I, on the other hand, would've missed seeing your bare legs and plump ass in the air greeting me this fine morning."

Her face heated.

"You're a lout." She grasped at whatever reason she could use to force him to take her back. "You've compromised me. Take me to Jamestown at once."

He laughed and his eyes grew two shades darker.

"I believe you were compromised long ago." There was a warning to his voice, but she refused to heed it and continued.

"You bastard, I am no whore." Anger was her enemy when it came to the things she could do. Her fingers twitched and her veins heated. She balled her hands into tight fists cutting off the magick.

"I never said that. A prominence seeking wench is better suited."

"Go to hell."

"I've been there thanks to you." He grabbed his quiver and bow. "Gather your things. We are leaving."

"I'll not be going anywhere with you."

He walked toward her. She forced herself to stay rooted. His height and menacing stare were enough to make anyone run in fear, but she wasn't afraid of him.

"Get your bag and get on the damn horse."

He was so close she could smell the forest on his skin. Memories of his lips upon hers scratched her mind, and she stiffened. He grabbed hold of her arm, and she shook him off along with the recollections of the past.

"Do not touch me," she hissed.

"Believe me, touching you is the last thing I want to do."

His words smarted, but she could not allow them to affect her. She let her face fall into the comfortable slant and rigid features she honed so well.

"I will walk."

He shrugged, kicked dirt over the smoldering fire, and climbed atop of Caesar. "You will walk beside me and not behind. Do you understand?"

"I take orders from no one. I will walk where I want."

He leaned down so that he was a few inches above her. "I care not where you walk but only for your safety. If you walk behind you risk a kick to the head from the horse." He muttered something else in Cherokee and by the look of disgust on his face she didn't care to hear it.

Tsura had walked for hours without so much as a break. Her feet throbbed and the muscles in her lower back ached from the uneven terrain.

"Where are we going?" It was the third time she'd asked him and the third time he didn't respond. She stopped, anger pressed on her forehead to fold the brow.

He halted Caesar and stared back at her.

"Are you going to continue to ignore me?"

"To my people."

His people? He did not know his tribe. He'd been orphaned and left as a slave when her mother and Kade had found him.

"What people do you speak of?" She was not moving until he gave her answers she could understand.

"The Ama tribe."

"Who are they?"

He walked Caesar to where she stood and reached his hand down for her. "You are tired. Sit atop the horse for a while."

She refused his hand.

He sighed, and his long black hair fell over his face. The thick mass of hair reminded her of the velvet curtains that hung in her sitting room back home. She blinked. She didn't have a home anymore. Her life had changed—serenity was no longer a part of her disposition. She did not know what happiness felt like. She'd cut off any recollection of the emotion. Instead, she was full of contempt, anger, and guilt. There was nothing to go back to. The house, the yard...all of it was gone. She swallowed. And even if it wasn't could she live there without him?

Red Wolf swatted at the veil of black hair, tossing it from his face. He placed his almond colored eyes on hers, and she compressed the past deep down inside her soul.

"The Ama tribe is a day's ride west. There we will find shelter and food."

"How can you be sure they won't want to kill us?"

"I did not think you cared of such things."

It was true she did not, but she was curious and needed something to keep her mind off of the memories.

"After I left Bristol I came here and found some of my tribe. They are the Ama. They will assist us."

"I do not need assistance."

He blew out a long breath before saying, "You are grating, similar to a whining mule, and if you weren't a woman I'd have shot you long ago."

She lifted her chin. "Rotten bugger."

"You are in danger, not just from Romulus and his men, but from the gypsies, or have you forgotten about them?"

In truth she'd not thought about the Renoldi clan in a long time, and when Micah suggested going to Jamestown, they never crossed her mind.

She shrugged.

"I cannot begin to understand you, nor do I care to. But I will not hurt Kade and Pril."

"You haven't seen them in years. It was quite clear you cared not for them when you left without any goodbye."

He was silent.

"Oh, the merchant has no words? No sly comment?"

"You are a witch, incapable of one kind thought," he growled.

"Correct."

His head snapped back toward her.

"You admit this?"

"I do. I care not what anyone thinks of me…I care not for anything."

"But why?"

She allowed the anger to overcome her stature. She glared at him, and her bottom lip trembled.

"Give me your hand. Rest upon Caesar."

She was tired, but she'd die before she'd allow him to help her anymore than he felt compelled to.

"I will continue on foot."

"Very well, keep up. I want to be atop that hill before night fall."

Tsura stared at the massive hill on the other side of the wide meadow. She kept the groan she wanted to release inside. It'd take hours to get there. She took a step and the pain in her heels sent a jolt up her calves.

"Stubborn is a poor quality to behold," he said.

"Since I am not in the market for a husband, I care not for this quality."

"One was enough was it?"

She remained silent. She'd not engage in conversation with him. The less he knew about her marriage to Morgan the better.


Red Wolf walked Caesar beside Tsura. He was tired of her constant determination to leave and return to Jamestown. Her resistance to listen to his warnings of Romulus and the Renoldi wore on him. She was careless to who hunted her, and he had no idea as to why.

The only reason he could conjure for the behavior she displayed was she'd cared for Morgan beyond anything he was able to comprehend. The thought that she'd been happy with the arrogant Baron had cut away at his insides.

He flexed his jaw and stared out at the valley before them. Red winged cardinals flew past toward the forest. Crickets chirruping and the light rustle of leaves as the faint breeze blew from the west surrounded them. He could stay in this beauty, staring at the landscape before him and remain content. He'd always yearn for the sea, but it was here, in the forest and among the animals, where his heart resided…his first home.

Over the years as Kade's student Red Wolf had grown fond of the blue-green waters, the white-capped waves, the smell of fish, and the salt upon his lips. But he'd never forgotten where he'd come from, and the lushness of the land on which he once lived.

Tsura groaned.

He glanced down at her, limping now from the pain in her feet. He'd not ask her again if she'd like to sit atop of Caesar. Her mulishness was irritating. Had she been anyone else he'd have left long ago.

There were things about Tsura he knew had changed. The magick and the anger were the two most prominent features that were different. He still did not know why she refused to use her gift, and he wasn't compelled to berate her for an answer.

The gift and her rare beauty separated her from everyone else. He didn't doubt she'd be able to protect herself against Romulus and his men, but if she didn't use the power, she was defenseless against them.

The gypsies were another problem altogether. They had certain powers he knew nothing about, other than his time as a captive within their camp when he was twelve winters. He recalled the spells and the way they used the earth to strengthen the curses. The Renoldi were a danger even Red Wolf was unsure of.

Tsura knew most spells, but was gifted in many other ways. The ability to touch her skin to yours allowed her to see if you were good or evil. It was remarkable. But it was her gift of healing with her hands that he still had a difficult time accepting. He'd seen her do it with Hiram Monroe when he'd been fatally wounded. She'd mended his flesh by placing her hands upon the injury. The skin closed, healing all that had been wronged. Afterward Tsura vomited, expelling the grievance.

How was she able to control her body from using the magick? Her determination to rid herself of that part of her life left him confused.

She kicked a rock with her toe, and his attention was once again on her lovely features. Chin tipped, shoulders back, eyes cold. She held herself like a Baroness, not the careless girl he knew before. He wasn't used to her haughty behavior or the anger that seemed to be at the tip of her tongue whenever she opened her mouth.

His fingers tingled with the need to touch her cheek—to see if the skin was as soft as he remembered. He grimaced and chastised himself for being a fool.

They'd shared a love he thought to last forever, until Morgan Harris entered their lives. Red Wolf despised the Baron of Lithshire, not just for taking Tsura from him, but for the greed and lust he'd displayed many times in the gaming halls. How could Tsura love a man like him? How had she not seen him for what he was, a thief and a liar?

He closed his eyes, inhaled, and set his shoulders. There was nothing about her he cared for. She was a fraud. She'd toyed with him until something better came along. He grit his teeth. Thinking of the past hurled him into a bitter mood.

Once they reached Soaring Eagle's tribe, he'd leave her there, kill Romulus, send for Micah, and never return. The Renoldi clan wouldn't think to look for her in the Ama tribe, and she'd be safe until Micah came for her. Now that he had a plan, his shoulders settled lower. He'd leave Tsura behind and make sure they never saw one another again.

# CHAPTER TEN

Emine pressed her palms into the table. Something was wrong. The spell she'd been working on—the one she planned to use against the Branded One—would not work. She flipped through the pages of her spell book and re-read every word. The ingredients were correct—one stem of a withered rose, a dash of salt, and a drop of Emine's blood.

"Stir together to meld as one, give me the power of control with the pass of my tongue."

She'd done it right, but each time she tried it on Magda the woman did not obey Emine's commands. When the tea was ingested the person was supposed to become compliant to whoever spoke.

She slammed her hand onto the table. Frustration thinned her lips, and she clenched her teeth together. Her jaw slipped and a jolting pain went up the side of her face. She reached for the bowl of cloves, placed three into her mouth, and waited for the pain to subside. A small lump remained on her cheek, and she smiled lopsided. Anger brewed inside of her at the child's mother. It was because of her Emine's face sat crooked.

She needed the bloody pendant!

She glanced at the book again. Time was running out. She was desperate to complete this last spell before the girl had been captured. A light rap on the door tore Emine from the pages before her.

"Enter."

The door opened slowly accompanied by a low, sorrowful whine. A blond head peeked into the room.

"You asked to see me, my mistress," Darius asked.

"Yes, I need you to fulfill a task," she walked around the table to stand in front of him, "and if completed properly, I will give you whatever you wish."

The young man's face lit up. Darius was ten years younger than Emine, and without the spell she'd placed over him he'd not think to even look at her much less lay with her. She used him to do her bidding and satisfy her carnal desires. She knew how she appeared, how people saw her, and so she thought nothing wrong with using her magick to get what she wanted.

"All I ask is for my creations to be taken with the other furnishings chosen into the towns and sold," he said.

As the leader of the clan, Emine decided who and what was taken into the towns to sell. Up until now she had not chosen Darius's unique creations because they were too good. If she'd taken them to town, he'd see a future without the clan, and she could not allow it. As it was she'd had to strengthen the spell to keep him from leaving her.

All Renoldi must be dependent upon the clan and remain within the trees surrounding their village. Darius had done her bidding for years, all while sharing her bed. Yet, she had not given him any inclination to her feelings toward him. She had none. He was merely a distraction, and she'd not hesitate to kill him if the need arose.

She went to him and placed a long fingernail to his whiskered cheek.

"Yes, my pet. It will be so."

Darius's thick lips spread into a broad smile.

Emine hooked her finger into his hair, brought him close, and whispered, "But if you fail..."

"I'll not fail, Mistress."

# CHAPTER ELEVEN

Tsura slipped her shoes off. Her green stockings stuck to the bloodied toes and heel. The shoe had rubbed at the limbs and caused the skin to break. The silk-heeled footwear was popular back home, but here in the uneven terrain of the hills and nature, she'd rather wear Micah's sailing boots. Her feet ached. She rubbed the swollen toes careful of the open wounds.

"You need a salve," Red Wolf said as he laid his quiver and bow onto the ground.

"I have some in my…" She'd used all of the balm on Red Wolf's injury five days before.

He stood over her waiting.

"I'll…I'll be fine."

He flexed his jaw, turned from her, and walked into the forest.

She winced when her finger touched the cut on her heel. She had no idea where he'd gone, nor did she care.

Water was what she needed. Cool, refreshing water. The leather pouch he'd carried had gone dry hours ago, and she was parched. But more so, she wanted to soak her feet. Tall elm and pine trees surrounded the small spot where Red Wolf had stopped for the night. The sun descended from the sky casting the hills in shades of green and gold splendor.

She stared at the vista before her for longer than anticipated. Her throat worked as she fought the tears. She closed her eyes against the countryside, refusing to relish in the brilliance that lay ahead. She couldn't afford to let herself succumb to the beauty. There was nothing beautiful about her life now. It was a dark endless pit of despair, and if not careful, if she let herself yearn for colorful things, she'd surely fall apart.

Tsura lifted her chin. There wasn't time for such foolishness. What could she gain from being weak? In the end she'd remember what she had lost—and was never to regain.

She stood, unsure of where Red Wolf had gone, and went in search of a stream. He was wise and would not have made their camp too far away from water. Not wanting to see him, she ventured in the opposite direction he had gone.

The forest floor was littered with branches, moss, and knurled roots. She should've put her shoes back on. She sidestepped a downed tree and walked on tiptoes to save herself from more pain.

She used the tree trunks as an anchor to keep her balance while walking through the treed area. Why had she let Micah persuade her to come here? She should've stayed in Bristol and waited for Romulus to kill her. There would've been no magick, no spells, no power, and one stab of his dagger to her heart would've ended the misery she lived in every day.

It hadn't been so, and now the rogue had followed her to the colonies. She hadn't seen him or his men while in Jamestown, but Red Wolf was certain he was there. She didn't doubt he'd spoken the truth regarding the wound on his side and who had given it to him.

Tsura brushed a branch away from her shoulder. She stepped to the side to avoid another low hanging limb. The forest opened up into a decedent clearing with wild violets and the tall stalks of lupine. Green grass spread before her like a lavish rug, soft beneath her bare feet. The pine scented air mingled with hints of sweetness from the violets to accost her senses. She inhaled, tasting the earth upon her tongue. The trickling of water rang in her ears, and she walked toward the sound. The creek flowed lazily over the rocks and disappeared down the hill.

She plopped onto her bottom without thinking of propriety or rules and yanked her skirt up past her ankles. The tops of her feet floated above the water, and she waited several seconds before immersing them. She bit her lip to stop the screech from escaping past her quivering lips. Blast, it was cold.

The creek was refreshing and livened up her tired and sore feet. She wiggled her toes, stretching the skin where her wounds were to try and clean them. Her shoulders sagged, and she closed her eyes. The silence of the countryside surrounded her. Too quiet for her liking, she moved her feet, splashing them in the water. Not used to the silence that was now her life, she slapped her feet harder not caring of the pain it caused.

The stillness enticed the misery—the agony—forcing her to confront what might have been. *I should've been there.* The demand screamed in her mind. She held out her hands. Within them laid a power she had always known, a gift that was hers since birth, and yet, she could not save him.

Would she ever find fulfillment again? A single tear slipped from her lashes to fall into her cheek. She had no purpose, no reason to wake each day.

Her mother tried to help. She offered words of comfort, a warm embrace…but it was not enough. Tsura still had not cried. She'd not grieved, too afraid to give in to the anguish inside of her soul for fear of accepting the truth. Hatred was her only power. It offered a refuge from the things she could not forget.

She leaned forward and placed her hands into the water. The pendant she wore around her neck felt heavy. She hadn't taken it off in years, promising her mother she'd never lose it or release it to the wrong person. She was to protect the talisman and the power it held. But Tsura did not want anything to do with it. She cursed any magick she'd ever known and banished it from her life forever.

Her mother made it a priority to give Tsura a happy childhood while explaining the family lineage and how the magick worked. The family bond she grew up with was strong, and Kade Walker had shown her an instant love. He embraced Red Wolf as his own while teaching him the merchant life. She cared for both of her parents, and that was why she'd left with Micah.

A loud screech came from across the creek. She jumped. Her feet splashed and the water doused the hem of her skirt. The bushes moved, and she watched immobile as the leaves shook and the large head of a golden cat emerged. The wild animal crouched, keeping its legs low to the ground and its back hunched.

He was hunting…and she was his prey.

Tsura's heart thudded loudly in her chest. Sweat formed on her brow and between her breasts. She sat, feet still immersed in the water, skirt damp, hands planted at her sides pressed into the grass.

The need surged down her arms and through to her fingertips. She clenched her hands pulling out the weed beneath them. No. She'd not submit. Tsura knew that with one swipe of her hand, with one spell uttered from her lips, the large beast would cease its hunt and turn from her. She rebuked the power. Tossed it out of her mind as if it were not meant to be there.

The cat hissed, showing large white fangs. He stepped closer to the water's edge. She remained still. If she were to die, she'd not protect herself from it. Would it be quick? The animal's long teeth sinking into her flesh to kill her instantly, or would he toy with her, tossing her body like a rag doll? She couldn't stop the shudder as it passed through her.

She trained her eyes on the cat, watching him as he crouched lower. He was readying himself to lunge at her. She sat taller, planted her feet on the rocky bottom of the creek, and spread her chest.

Red Wolf came back from the woods with the sticky sap from the pine tree cupped in his palm. He'd left Tsura to search for the syrup that dripped from the pines bark. It was a good remedy for open cuts, and would aid in the healing of her heels and toes.

Where was she? The camp was empty. Caesar stood chewing on the grass, and Tsura's bag lay on the ground nearby. He scanned the surrounding forest for any sight of her. The scream of a mountain cat carried across the tops of the trees and covered Red Wolf's body with terror. He pulled the cotton handkerchief from his pocket and rubbed the sap from his palm into the cloth before tucking it away. He ran toward his bow and quiver leaning against the trunk of a tree. He scooped them up and took off in the direction he'd heard the wild animal.

Branches struck his face and cutting his cheek. He continued to run. He ignored the pain in his side as he leapt over roots and foliage to get to Tsura. Why had she left? Was the cat attacking her? His mind raced with all sorts of possibilities as he jumped across a downed tree. He could see the brightness from the sun as it peeked through the forest. He was close.

Another screech. The hairs on his arms stood. Red Wolf broke through the trees. Tsura sat on the edge of a creek, her feet in the water, arms spread wide. What was she doing? He saw the cat, ready to lunge.

Red Wolf pulled the arrow from the quiver on his back. He positioned the wooden shaft in the bow and pointed the stick toward the cat. The animal jumped. He released the string, and the arrow flew through the air. He could hear his own heart as it beat in his ears, the fear for Tsura deafening. He blinked. The cat lay in the creek, Red Wolf's arrow lodged in his throat.

The bow still clutched in his hand shook against his leg, as the impact of what could've happened flowed through his veins. He inhaled deep to calm his nerves. He took two more breaths before his eyes sought out Tsura. She sat in the same spot she'd been in before the cat attacked.

Red Wolf couldn't contain the anger stirring in his gut. She could've been killed. Ripped apart by the animal's sharp nails. Why hadn't she rescued herself? He growled low in his throat and stalked toward her.

"What in hell were you doing?"

She didn't answer him instead stared at the large cat laying with its body half in the water, blood seeping from the wound on his neck.

He shoved her. "Do you have a death wish?"

When she lifted her eyes to his he stepped back. The contempt he saw within the green pits was not what he'd expected. She had wished to die, to have the animal rip her apart.

"You care not for your own life?" he asked, astounded at what he'd just witnessed.

"I care not for anything," she whispered.

Rage filled him and his chest expanded.

"What of your mother, or Kade?" He couldn't contain the irritation as it swelled within him. He grabbed her arm and yanked her up to stand.

"Take your hands off of me!" The fire he'd seen in her eyes many times before returned.

"You need a damn good whipping."

"You place one hand on me and I'll—"

"You will do nothing. I am not afraid of your magick, and frankly I've long given up wondering why you won't use it. You could've died—been marred by the cat's teeth." He didn't miss her shudder, and he used her reaction as his leverage. "Morgan was a bastard. I am sickened that you'd end your own life because of his demise."

"You know nothing of my marriage."

"I have no need to know. It exudes from your face."

"Leave me."

"I'll not stand by and watch you throw yourself into harm's way."

"I care not what you do."

"The time will come when we never have to see one another again, and believe me when I say I cannot bloody well wait, but until I know you're safe from Romulus and his men, I'll not leave you to your own madness."

"Madness? I can assure you, I am not mad."

"Your actions dictate you are far worse off."

"How dare you!"

He leaned in. "I dare say Morgan is the lucky one. Gone from your lunacy and deception."

She slapped him. His cheek throbbed from the blow. The contact did little to stifle the bitterness he felt for her.

"Know this, I want nothing from you, including your damn protection," she hissed.

He was sure he'd seen tears in her eyes, but the malice in her voice—the distance it spewed—fed his rage and blinded him to her insecurities. He watched her march back up the hill to disappear into the woods. He ran his hand down his face and stared at the animal. The Cherokee never left anything to waste, and he couldn't in good conscience leave the animal there. He dropped his bow onto the ground and waded into the creek. He needed something to take his mind off of seeing Tsura use herself as a sacrifice and this would work.

"Well done, Cousin."

Red Wolf recognized the voice to be Soaring Eagle's. A skilled tracker, he could appear without warning. A trait Red Wolf wished to acquire. It had been almost a year since he'd seen him last. Life at sea forced him to travel from one port to the next, and the trek across the waters took months.

He and Soaring Eagle had been inseparable when they were young. Cousins, they had treated each other more like brothers, until he'd been captured and used as a slave by the white eyes. Red Wolf thought he'd never see his family again.

When Tsura cast him from her life, he deserted all that was in Bristol and came back to the very place he'd left sixteen years before. Not expecting to find anyone from his tribe, he wandered the countryside brokenhearted for months before Soaring Eagle had found him.

He took Red Wolf to his tribe, where he was reunited for the first time with his aunt and cousins. He never knew what had happened to his mother after his father had been killed and he was captured. Soaring Eagle had told him she'd perished shortly after he'd been taken.

"You are much better than when I saw you last?" Soaring Eagle asked after he dismounted.

Red Wolf shook off the memories and the desolation that came with them. He smiled. Leaving the cat in the water, he went to his cousin and embraced him in a rough hug.

"I no longer wallow in self pity," he said in Cherokee.

Soaring Eagle laughed, creasing the white paint that covered his face. "This is good. You are complete once more?"

He'd never be the same, but his cousin didn't need to know that.

"I am."

Two warriors exited the trees to the west and walked their horses toward them.

Red Wolf knew them both. White Owl and Running Bear were some of the Ama tribe's most skilled warriors. Why had they left the tribe to accompany Soaring Eagle? He assessed his cousin for the first time. His deerskin breeches were clean and beaded down the sides. He wore no shirt, but the beaded necklaces hanging against his chest spoke volumes.

"You have become chief, Cousin?"

Soaring Eagle's face lit up. His thin lips spread into a proud smile. "Since winter. I am the white chief of the Ama tribe."

The Cherokee chose two chiefs to rule their large clans—a white chief in times of peace and happiness, and a Red one in times of war. Red Wolf couldn't think of a better warrior to lead the Ama than Soaring Eagle. His skills and kind heart would be the success of his tribe.

White Owl had dismounted and knelt on the water's edge, his wide face painted red from the bottom of his nose down to his neck. The face paint indicated the emotions they felt. Red was success, white, peace and happiness. Blue was defeat and black meant death and mourning.

White Owl stared intently at the ground. "What female accompanies you?" he asked.

Red Wolf remembered Tsura and their argument minutes before.

"You have brought a wife?" Soaring Eagle asked, his dark eyes lit with mischief.

Red Wolf sighed. "Not exactly."

All three warriors stared at him confused.

"Come, I shall show you."

"What of the cat?" Running Bear asked.

"You may do with it what you want," Red Wolf answered.

Soaring Eagle spoke to his warriors, telling them to skin and gut the animal. They'd all share in its nourishment tonight and bring the rest of the meat and fur back to the tribe. He watched as White Owl and Running Bear pulled the cat from the water and laid it on the grass.

"Bring me to your woman," Soaring Eagle said.

"She is not my woman," Red Wolf murmured and set off up the hill.

# CHAPTER TWELVE

Tsura sat on the ground still reeling from her confrontation with Red Wolf. If he had let the cat take her, she'd be free of the constant shame and agony that seemed to consume her. Blast him and his duty!

She reached for her stockings. The carefully knitted wool had lost its shape from wear, and she had no others left. When Micah had demanded she come with him to the colonies, she'd taken all she had with her. Which wasn't much. Most of her belongings fit into the small reticule. The mockery of such was she'd come from being a Baroness. She hadn't wanted for anything while married to Morgan. Servants, maids, and butlers were housed in the mansion on the hill—the mansion that no longer stood.

She hadn't been married to Morgan long, nineteen months to be exact, but in that time she'd come to see him for many things. He was kind and loving when it suited, and most of his time was spent at the gaming halls in town. If it hadn't been for her, he'd have lost his title long ago. She kept the finances intact, placing monies away secretly so he didn't gamble it away. Her marriage was not founded on love, but convenience.

She heard voices coming from the forest. The language was not English, but she'd heard it somewhere before. She stood, stocking still in hand, and waited. Red Wolf and an Indian man, dressed in breeches, with white face paint walked from the trees.

A headache began to pound at her temples, and she refrained from rubbing her eyes. She'd need to take out the braid and let her scalp rest—her long tresses were heavy, and often caused headaches.

"My cousin, Soaring Eagle, white chief of the Ama tribe," Red Wolf said to her.

She studied the visitor. He'd shaved his head except for the long piece of hair on top of his head that hung down to the middle of his back in a long braid.

"Hello," she said.

Soaring Eagle's face did not change from the stoned expression he'd given her when Red Wolf introduced them. His dark eyes bore into hers, and she fidgeted under his scrutinizing glare.

She looked at Red Wolf. "Does he not speak English?"

"He does."

"Why does he not answer me?"

Red Wolf glanced at his cousin and smirked. "I do not think he cares for you."

She was sure the Indian could see right into her soul, and having had enough of his intimidation, she met his ominous stare with a scowl of her own.

Soaring Eagle turned from her. "Cousin, is she the one who has poisoned your heart?" he asked in perfect English.

Red Wolf remained silent.

"Poisoned his heart?" she echoed. "Is that what you have told him?"

He shrugged.

"Bah! Your truth is false. You speak with a forked tongue."

"And you continue to twist the truth," Red Wolf growled.

"You are a coward."

"And you, my dear, are a deceiving witch."

"I wish we'd never met."

"The past is gone from my life as is the memory of ever being with you."

She focused on Soaring Eagle. "Believe me when I say if given the chance, I'd bludgeon his black heart."

She turned from them about to lose control. Her body heated, the need strong and feral. She stalked toward an oak tree and sat down. She leaned against the trunk of the tree and gingerly rubbed her feet. The skin was broken where the blisters had formed and was sore to touch.

She watched as Red Wolf searched the outline of the forest for small branches to start a fire. Once he got a good flame going, he sat down beside Soaring Eagle and the two of them began talking. She couldn't understand a word of Cherokee and figured they used their native language so she couldn't hear their conversation. She sighed. It was just as well. Any more insults from him and she was liable to forget her promise to never use the magick. It was always close by, waiting. She had to be careful, stronger than the urge and the wanting. Time would make it easier.

Red Wolf appeared content and happy as he sat with his family. She didn't know how he'd found them, only that it was where he'd disappeared to three years before without an explanation. How could Soaring Eagle think she poisoned Red Wolf's heart? She'd loved him, but sadly it hadn't been enough. Maybe that was why he left. He'd been restless while in Bristol and sailing the *Falcon*, and she had not fulfilled him. The realization that it could've been her, and not his arrogance which caused him to leave without a word, struck her in the chest. She leaned forward to ease the tension there.

Red Wolf laughed from across the lawn, and resentment toiled within her. He was the reason her life had gone so awry—why she could not see past her own anger to grieve for what she'd lost. If he had stayed, like he promised, she'd have remained whole. There would've been no agony, no horror, and no loss. Tsura cast narrowed eyes upon him. Instead she was a broken mess—a pitiful sight.

She once flourished, loved and laughed. Now she had no recollections of those emotions. She stared at the fire. The crackle and hiss of the wood was all she heard. She too was a dying ember, burning inside with rage, hate, and bitterness. Her soul screamed for retribution. She blinked back tears. Even when she'd unleashed her fury, even after she'd killed men...it still had not mattered.

Red Wolf refrained from watching Tsura as he and Soaring Eagle sat around the fire.

"She holds hate within her heart," his cousin said.

"Yes, and I do not know why."

"Could this hate be caused by you?"

Red Wolf turned toward Soaring Eagle and shook his head. "I left because she'd confessed her love for Morgan. So I am not the reason she is so irritable."

"I think you are wrong."

"Morgan died. I feel that is why she is so angry." He stoked the wood with a long branch.

"This bothers you."

"Romulus Black, a vicious Corsair, seeks her life. I am unsure as to why, but I feel it has to do with Morgan somehow."

"And you are protecting her from this Black?"

He nodded.

"Where is the Corsair now?"

"He is in Jamestown, but it is only a matter of time before he gathers men to come and search for her. I cannot fight them on my own."

"You want the Ama to aid you in this?"

"No, I cannot ask that of you."

"What is it you wish me to do?"

"Let me leave Tsura at your village until I can stifle the threat of Romulus."

"I can do this." Soaring Eagle placed his hand on Red Wolf's shoulder. "I promise no harm will come to her."

"Thank you, Cousin."

"Will you return for her?"

"I will send her brother, Micah."

"You cannot run from your heart."

"You see things that are not there."

"I see the truth."

He stood, distancing himself from his cousin and their conversation. He wasn't about to admit any truth to what Soaring Eagle had said. His cousin saw things that no longer existed. There was no love between Tsura and Red Wolf. He certainly could attest to that. He felt nothing for her, other than the need to protect her for Kade and Pril.

White Owl and Running Bear walked into the clearing. The large cat, skinned and gutted, hung over Running Bear's horse. The meat had been placed in the deerskin sacks hanging from the sides of White Owl's horse. He carried a thick piece of meat, in his other hand, for their dinner.

The warriors were intimidating, and he could imagine what Tsura thought of their presence. Their hair was scalped, leaving a long square piece on top of their heads, no emotion showed on their painted faces. Their breechcloths covered their private areas, but their muscular chests and lean legs were still visible.

White Owl placed the meat onto a flat rock beside the fire and worked a long branch through it. He positioned the stick above the flames and turned it slowly. Running Bear left the horses to come and sit beside them. Red Wolf sensed when both braves spotted Tsura. They stared openly at her, and he clenched his jaw. He had to refrain from positioning himself in front of them to block their view of her. The Cherokee believed attraction to be the main component for marrying their mates. It was clear the two warriors found Tsura alluring.

He glanced at her. She sat under the oak tree massaging her feet, and he remembered the salve he'd found for her earlier. He reached inside his pocket for the cloth he'd placed there and walked toward her.

"This will help." He knelt and handed her the light blue handkerchief.

She stared at the cloth, and he was sure he'd seen tears form in her green eyes, but she blinked them away.

"Thank you," she said, her voice scratchy.

"May I look?" He wasn't sure why he'd asked, or why he cared, but the words had come from his lips before he could take them back.

She inched her toes out from underneath her skirt, the skin torn and swollen around the short limbs. It wasn't until she'd shown him the whole foot, that he bit back a curse. Her heels had taken the worst of the shoes. Raw, the skin was oozing yellow puss and several layers of flesh had torn away.

"Why the hell did you not climb on top of Caesar?"

"I need not your assistance," she said.

He watched as she tipped her pert chin, a mannerism she did often when being defiant.

"It is not assistance, Tsura. It is common sense." He was irritated at her for not placing her stubbornness aside long enough to save her toes and heels, but more so he was disgusted with himself for not forcing the issue. "No more walking. You will ride to the Ama tribe in the morning."

"I feel it unnecessary that we travel there." She winced as she rubbed the salve onto the open wounds.

"It is for your safety."

"I am quite capable of caring for myself."

"There will be no discussion. You are going to the Ama."

"And where will you go?" Her eyes met his and they reminded him of a lush valley of rolling hills.

He let his heart soften toward her for a mere moment, remembering how her face lit with joy whenever he'd come near. The memory filled him with nostalgia, but soon he began to drown in the truth and what he'd actually meant to her.

"I will right the wrong." He tore his eyes from hers. "And then you shall never see me again."

"I see." She dismissed him then and concentrated on massaging the sap into her feet.

He left her by the tree and returned to Soaring Eagle and his warriors.

# CHAPTER THIRTEEN

Tsura peeked around Red Wolf's shoulder at the place the Ama tribe called home. Log structures with thatched rooftops were scattered across the field and were sheltered by tall trees and grassy hills. Horses grazed freely on the earth surrounding the Ama homes.

The scene was reminiscent of the time she spent with the Peddlers. The gypsies never stayed in one place for too long and lived within the confines of their well-furnished vardos. Similar to the Ama the Peddlers had a large supply of horses and oxen. They grew their own foods and used the earth to aid in healing the injured or sick.

Tsura shifted her legs away from Red Wolf. She was desperate to keep her distance, but as the horse had jostled on, she'd slid forward into him. Her back was cramped from the awkward position, and she supposed it was due in part to straddling the saddle for most of the day. She wanted nothing more than to stretch her legs.

Caesar halted and Red Wolf climbed down. He glanced at her, and she thought he'd assist her from the horse, but instead he walked away. She'd not have taken his hand anyway.

Tsura bunched her skirt, pulling it tight around her legs, and dismounted. She needed to bathe, wash her clothes, and rid herself of these blasted hoops. She surveyed the people before her. The men of the Ama tribe were clothed much like Soaring Eagle—deerskin pants with no shirt, and half of their faces painted. A few others wore the breechcloths and leggings that White Owl and Running Bear dressed in.

The women shuffled closer in deerskin dresses embroidered with colorful beading, while some fashioned dresses similar to the white woman. High cheekbones and bronzed skin were framed with long black hair that hung to their waists. The Ama women were beautiful.

She stood off to the side and fidgeted, uncomfortable with her unclean appearance and the company of strangers. She'd taken great care into placing herself at a distance from others. This not only suited her, but also protected her from their judgment and curiosity.

Soaring Eagle walked proudly toward a petite woman with clear skin and round brown eyes. She had the longest hair Tsura had ever seen. The black mane went past her knees and when she moved, the sun played on the strands of hair making it glow like the moon on the sea. As Soaring Eagle gazed down at the woman, Tsura did not miss the tenderness in his eyes before he leaned down and embraced her.

Red Wolf had untied her reticule from Caesar and handed it to her. She took it from him without offering a word of thanks. Her insides felt uneasy, and her breath became stifled. She was not supposed to be here. She needed to go back to the life she'd been leading...alone. Not required to hold conversations, smile, and pretend like everything was okay.

Red Wolf's hand touched the inside of her arm as he escorted her toward the woman and Soaring Eagle. She wanted to dig her heels into the soft ground and demand he take her back to Jamestown like she had so many times on this horrible journey. She surveyed the faces staring back at her, not wanting to make a scene. She forced herself to put one foot in front of the other.

"Cousin, you remember my wife, Beautiful Meadow," Soaring Eagle said.

Red Wolf tipped his head, reached for her hand, and kissed the top. "It has been a long while. Good day to you, Beautiful Meadow."

Tsura had to keep from groaning in disgust at Red Wolf's portrayal of a decent human being when in fact he was a fraud.

Beautiful Meadow turned toward her and smiled.

"Good day," had been all she could manage to say. She did not want to be here. She did not belong. She turned pleading eyes toward Red Wolf. "Must we stay?"

He leaned in, his lips barely moving, and whispered, "Can you not find one ounce of courtesy within your titled bones?"

"It is not a matter of courtesy, but merely one of inconvenience."

He raised a dark brow.

"It is not their responsibility to watch over me as you wish, nor is it your duty. Now I want to leave."

"No."

He offered no other words and turned from her to speak with Soaring Eagle in Cherokee.

Tsura's blood rose. She could feel her cheeks heating. She turned from him, but was surrounded by curious Ama faces, most of which were friendly. She did however, see a few elderly women who did not approve of her presence among their tribe.

Two little girls burst from the legs of the people standing around and ran toward Soaring Eagle.

"Edoda, Edoda!" they shouted. Their flushed faces smiled, showing small white teeth.

Soaring Eagle bent and picked them up, cradling the two girls within his strong arms as they kissed his cheeks. Tsura averted her eyes from the scene before her. She blinked away the black dots dancing in her vision and the onset of tears ready to escape past her lashes.

"My daughters, Fawn and Star Dancer," Soaring Eagle announced.

Red Wolf's cheeks spread into a wide smile. He reached his arms out to the girls and they flew into them, shouting something she could not understand.

Tsura was not prepared for the emotions that rose from her belly to stick in her throat at watching Red Wolf with the two girls. She ground her back teeth together at the memories of what they could've had and walked away.


Red Wolf watched Tsura disappear among the crowd. He didn't miss her reaction to the children, nor did he ignore the fact she wanted to leave. He could not place her reasons for separation from anyone, or anything. He simply did not know why she'd chosen to remain alone. Because of his stubbornness, he'd refused to ask. The past was gone from both of their lives and better served as a distant memory.

Star Dancer placed her pudgy arms around his neck and hugged him tight. The last time he'd been at the village the girls were three and four. They'd grown close then, and he treated them as if they were his nieces.

"Your wife does not want to be here?" Beautiful Meadow asked.

"She is not my wife." He pushed the bitterness from his voice and smiled at Soaring Eagle's woman. His cousin had a great love for his wife. It had been the reason he'd left a year ago. The affection they showed for one another tore at his soul, and he'd sunk lower into his own despair for he'd loved Tsura with every part of his being.

"I will see if she is hungry," Beautiful Meadow said, leaving before he could warn her of Tsura's sharp tongue and resistance to kindness.

"My wife will know how to speak with your woman." Soaring Eagle placed his hand on Red Wolf's shoulder.

"She is not my woman, and you will see this when I leave and do not return for her." He was irritated that his cousin insisted Tsura to be his when he'd stated several times it was not so.

Soaring Eagle smiled. The white paint was wearing off of his cheeks and chin, to show the bronzed skin beneath. "You will be back."

Red Wolf groaned. He knelt to place his nieces on the ground and watched as they ran after their mother. Within the Cherokee tribes it was widely known that the women ran the household, teaching their children how to farm, cook, weave, and sew. Women were held with the utmost respect. They were appreciated and often sought out for council among the tribe leaders.

"Come, Cousin, I will walk with you to your lodge. Later we will enjoy the Itse selu" Soaring Eagle ushered Red Wolf through the crowd of men and women who offered him hugs and handshakes of welcome.

The Itse selu was the celebration of the green corn, the tribe's stalk. Today the new corn was ripe and ready to eat. A week before the Ama would send out a messenger to take one stalk from seven of the closest tribes. Once it was determined that the corn was ripe to eat, all of the tribes got together and celebrated the Itse selu.

He scanned the faces for Tsura but did not see her. He knew she was safe here and let his shoulders fall. He brushed his hand through his long dark hair and sighed. It was best they distance themselves from one another. He was tired of the constant bickering, but more so he struggled each day she was near not to hold her in his arms.

The lodge Red Wolf had built with Soaring Eagle while he'd stayed here stood on the east section of the Ama land. The home was small with a thatched roof and no windows. The wicker door opened and two women exited the home. They'd cleaned the lodge for his arrival.

He nodded at them as they passed by. The woman on the left, with the pretty features and shy smile, stopped halfway to turn and stare at him. Red Wolf smiled back at her, a gesture to show his appreciation for what the girls had done.

"Raven is Beautiful Meadow's sister. You do not remember her?" Soaring Eagle asked.

He did not. In the months he'd spent with the Ama, he'd been too absorbed in his own despair to notice anyone unless they made it so. Beautiful Meadow's sister had not spoken or sat next to him in the time he'd been here, and therefore had no recollection of the girl.

"She is waiting for a husband."

Red Wolf nodded. Raven was beautiful, and he didn't foresee her waiting too long. He went inside the lodge and was greeted with memories of the home he'd been taken from so many years before. A small fire burned in the center of the room. Buffalo, cougar, and a bear pelts lay on the floor around the fire. Handmade bowls and utensils sat neatly stacked on the counter that stretched against the wall. His body ached to lie within the fur and sleep for days. The pain in his side had subsided, and now the skin itched where the flesh met. He'd need to remove the sutures soon.

"I will leave you to rest before the celebration," Soaring Eagle said and exited the lodge.

He eased himself down onto the pelts and inhaled the scents of the life he'd left behind. The Ama were a warm welcome to his tampered soul, and a part of him wished he could remain here forever. Red Wolf had traveled most of the last sixteen years of his life. First, with Kade aboard the S.S.W., and then on his own commanding the *Falcon*. He missed Pril and Kade more than he'd allow himself to admit. They'd embraced him as their own, showing him kindness, but more importantly love. He yawned. Contentment settled over his weary bones. Red Wolf closed his eyes and dozed off.

Tsura sat on the ground away from the Ama. The shelter of the trees offered shade from the hot afternoon sun. Her feet throbbed. She gingerly removed her shoes and peeled off her stockings. She had a small amount of the salve Red Wolf had given to her yesterday and pulled the cloth from her reticule.

"Dandelion bath," Beautiful Meadow said as she stood over her.

Tsura hadn't heard the woman approach. Caught off guard, she was unable to prepare herself for the discussion. She cleared her throat. "Yes, dandelion holds many healing elements." She remembered the teachings from her mother.

Beautiful Meadow smiled. The woman was kind and genuine. Tsura could tell without having to lay her hand upon her.

"Yes, that is so. I can get one for you to soak your feet."

Tsura shook her head. "I am fine, thank you."

"Your skin is poisoned. It seeps yellow bile. You must rid the flesh of this."

She glanced at her feet. The other woman was correct, but Tsura couldn't bring herself to care. After all she deserved far worse than this for what she'd done.

"No."

The Ama woman sat down beside her, and Tsura inched herself away.

"Why must you suffer if there is something to ease the pain?" Beautiful Meadow asked.

She held her lips firmly together. How could she tell this kind woman of the things she had done? How could she confess she'd let him die?

Beautiful Meadow's bronzed hand rested upon her own, and Tsura pulled her hand away.

"I will not hurt you."

"I am not concerned with whether you will cause me harm, but rather the opposite."

The other woman's thin black eyebrows scrunched together, and her lips laid flat. "I do not understand."

"It is better for you not to."

She could sense Beautiful Meadow's eyes upon her. Their conversation had ended abruptly by Tsura's harsh reaction to the gentle woman. It wasn't long before Soaring Eagle's wife stood and walked away.

Tsura watched her go, long hair swaying behind her, shoulders back, head held high. Beautiful Meadow had traits Tsura herself once had. She'd loved life and everything it had to offer. She stared at the ground and willed the tears wanting to fall to cease. She'd become the very opposite of the woman she once was, and sadly there was no way she could go back.

The Ama were a gentle tribe, she could tell. However, their willingness to help her made the thought of leaving more appealing. She wiggled her toes, the flesh swollen and purple. Beautiful Meadow was correct. The dandelion bath would banish the infection and take the horrible ache away. There were many earthly remedies that Tsura could use for her ailment. Some healed all on their own, while others needed the words to assist in their abilities.

Beautiful Meadow walked back toward her with a wooden bowl. She knew what was inside, and frowned. The Ama woman had not listened to what she wanted, and she could not help but be perturbed by her actions.

"I have mixed a dandelion bath." The woman placed the bowl down in front of her. Without asking, she lifted Tsura's sore feet and gently laid them in the water.

The surge of the yellow flower mixed with her open flesh placed bubbles upon her toes and heels. All the anger she'd felt minutes before dissolved as the pain in her feet subsided.

Beautiful Meadow smiled.

"I will come back soon with clean clothes so you can bathe in the river."

She nodded. The woman's kindness made her long for her mother and the reassurance she'd always offered. It didn't matter what the circumstance, Pril was always prepared to battle for those she loved. Tsura had spent the first four years of her life on this land, which seemed so foreign to her now. Her mother had fought to protect her from the evil men and women who wanted to do her harm. Her own uncles had deceived them, and the heartache of their betrayal stayed with her mother for many years afterward.

She gazed at the mountains in the distance. The Renoldi clan lived within the canvas of tall elm and pine trees. She wondered how her aunt Magda or the others were faring now that sixteen years had passed. Did they still seek the pendant, and her life? Were they aware she was here, on this soil, so close, and had they planned all this time what they would do to her? Romulus and the Renoldi hunted her, but oddly enough neither frightened her. If she were to die, which in truth was what she pursued, either evil would do. She'd not choose one from the other to end her miserable existence.

# CHAPTER FOURTEEN

Red Wolf stood under the gathering lodge next to White Owl. The large hut had been erected with thick wooden poles in the shape of a circle. The roof came to a point in the center and was covered with strips of bark. When he looked up, he could see the pink sky peek through the thin slits where the bark did not meet. The Ama held council and all celebrations within the great confines of the lodge. Men, women, and children had prepared the tables for the feast of corn.

Soaring Eagle stood in the center, the other chiefs beside him, and reached inside the woven basket brought to him by a young brave. He pulled out a husk of corn and brought it to his nose, inhaling the sweetness. The White Chief's lips creased into a wide smile, and he held the husk high into the air. The tribes cheered.

Red Wolf spotted Tsura off to the side and away from the crowd. He wasn't surprised she'd detached herself from the joyous occasion. Her stance was rigid, and the cold expression upon her face warned those around her not to come near.

He allowed himself more time to assess her appearance. She wore a deerskin dress that hung to just above her ankles. The beads on the front were sewn into shapes of birds while the rest of the dress was plain. It fit her well—the leather hugged her hips and formed a silhouette he'd almost forgotten existed. Coal black hair reflected against the fire burning behind her and hung down her back in long corkscrew curls. He had loved to play with the bouncy ringlets, pulling them straight only to let them go and watch as they sprung back up. The soft as silk tresses smelled of rose water and the many different herbs she'd grown in the garden.

He gazed at her high-sculpted cheeks hinting the slightest shade of pink, emerald eyes filled with secrets shadowed by thick black lashes and plump lips. Red Wolf's heart fluttered, and he looked away. Her lips had tasted of pleasure, of promises, of love. He inhaled the memories, the bits and pieces that had carried him from day to day. He peeked at her, seeing her as she once was, and his heart swelled. But as he drank her in the sorrow of the past struck him in the gut expelling the hope he'd had. Damn it. He'd never forget. He'd never forgive her either. He held back the disgust before it reached his face and turned from the celebration.

Red Wolf walked until all he could hear was the river ahead of him. Tall grass brushed his knees. He plucked a blade and placed it into his mouth. The bitter flavor was a contrast to his heart. Would he ever heal?

He had to get away from her, but he knew the distance would not erase the memory of her in his arms. He ran his hand through his hair and sat down by the rivers edge.

He wished to be upon the *Falcon*, away from Tsura and every feeling she provoked within him. The sea had been his refuge from her dismissal. The salted wind caressed his face. No troubles, no cares, only the vast array of the blue waters. He could leave now, he knew it, and Tsura would be happy to watch him go. The stubborn nit, abolishing her need to stay put, would head back to Jamestown and walk right into Romulus' hand.

He released a heavy sigh. The Corsair needed to be taken care of if Tsura was to ever be safe. Killing Romulus was the best answer, but he could not do so with Meril and Gaspard by his side. The giant henchman showed him a glimpse of how strong he was the day Romulus drove his blade into Red Wolf's side.

Soon the deadly rogue would be upon them if he didn't do something to stop him. His mind made up, Red Wolf would leave and pray Tsura did not follow him.

"Why do you not celebrate the corn?" a soft voice asked from behind him.

He turned to see Raven. She was no taller than his shoulder. Her hair, parted down the middle, hugged her round cheeks. Beautiful Meadow's sister was enchanting, and he knew it wouldn't be long before she'd be married.

"You are not happy among the Ama?" she asked.

He did not know what to say to the girl. His emotions were for him alone and not to be shared.

"Why have you left your wife's side?"

"She is not my wife," he was quick to correct her, and he didn't miss the way her dark eyes fluttered.

"Who is the woman if she is not your wife?"

He stood and stepped away from her. He had no desire to be caught alone with Raven. The Ama took courting very seriously. Young maidens, although they chose their mates, were not to be alone with them until married. Red Wolf walked back toward the celebrations.

"She is a friend."

"Your friend holds hostility inside her heart."

It amazed him how the Ama could sense such truth within Tsura and himself. He held none of those traits and figured it was from growing up away from the tribe. Red Wolf was a merchant, a lover of the sea. He did not know how to sense the thoughts of others without using force. Which was what he'd done with Tsura. The two had argued back and forth since they'd been reacquainted, and he wasn't inclined to change it.

"She is special," Raven said.

Red Wolf did not change his features. He couldn't have the girl know she spoke the truth. Tsura was special, a Chuvani in her own right who held great powers. The Ama may accept this, or they may banish Tsura, believing her to be evil and filled with black magick. It was best he didn't say anything, even to Soaring Eagle, until he knew how his cousin would react.

"It is not right for you to be alone with me."

She shrugged.

"Soaring Eagle said you search to find a husband."

Raven smiled. "Yes, this is so."

"He will be very angry if he knows you have been in my company without a chaperone."

The girl continued to walk beside him.

"Go that way." He pointed to a path that led to the homes and gathering lodge of the tribe. "I will continue ahead and come around the other end."

She nodded, and without another word left in the direction he'd suggested.

Red Wolf took his time walking back to the celebrations for more than one reason. He wasn't prepared to see Tsura again. Her presence ignited too many emotions within him, and he was finding it difficult to control them. Besides he didn't really care for corn. Another difference he held from his people, a result of being gone too long.

The music from the celebration drifted into the forest, and a smile touched his lips. The Ama loved to dance, and he remembered the song they played from the times he spent with them when he was a child. He thought of his mother and father, gone now to be with the Great Spirit. Being a captive had stolen half of his childhood. He was thankful for the day Kade found him beaten and bloodied in a closet of a rundown tavern. He'd be forever grateful to the merchant who took him in as his own.

Even though he'd been given a second chance at life with Kade and Pril, he'd always felt as if something were missing. It wasn't until he fell in love with Tsura that the hole in his heart had mended. Whenever he'd return from being at sea with Kade, she'd be there to greet him with her beautiful smile and contagious laughter. Years went by before he realized he loved her more than the girl he'd sworn to protect above all things. He treaded lightly at first unsure if she felt the same way.

It wasn't until she was seventeen that he'd mustered up the courage to tell her under the rowan tree far from their home how he'd felt. He remembered her small hand reaching for his, before she leaned in and gave him a sweet kiss that tasted of the wild berries they'd just eaten. They shared a passionate love, and she promised to wait for him—to love only him. His chest ached and filled his throat with sadness.

All of it had changed the day Morgan Harris entered their lives. The Baron of Lithshire was all of the things Red Wolf could never be— handsome, wealthy, and titled. Morgan had greeted him on the docks the day he'd ported. Red Wolf had rushed down the plank in a hurry to see Tsura, only to be stopped by the Baron. "The lady wishes for you to have this."

The note was written in Tsura's hand. *I am in love with someone else and wish to marry. I am sorry.* He'd stared at the note in disbelief until he could no longer make out the words for the tears in his eyes. The words he'd read a thousand times since. Tsura had cut him in two, sliced away at his heart, and tore his soul to shreds. He'd planned on asking for her hand, to make her his forever. His lips could not form a word, his tongue swollen with emotion. He'd turned from Morgan, walked back to his ship, and never looked back.

Red Wolf blinked the wetness from his lashes. After all this time the memory still evoked those same painful feelings. Damn it. Why did he care after all these years? Why did the pain of losing her hurt him still? He slowed his steps, waited for the agony to fade to the recesses of his soul. He needed space from her, to not gaze upon her mesmerizing features and know she'd loved another—laid with another. He groaned. The sea would be his escape—the *Falcon* his only refuge and soon he'd be alone, leaving her behind...again.

# CHAPTER FIFTEEN

Tsura stood away from the gathering of men, women, and children. A large fire burned just outside the hut, where men danced around to music played by drums and a wooden instrument that resembled a flute. The tune flowing from the long stick was unlike anything she'd ever heard before. A soft melody played as Beautiful Meadow and five other women started to sing. Their voices blended to sound as one, and Tsura could not turn away from the display before her.

The Ama appeared to love life. They danced with enthusiasm, while the others smiled and laughed. It was clear to Tsura how much Soaring Eagle cared for his tribe, and they for him. She wondered if the Ama had ever been dealt a tragedy, and how they'd handle such an event. She knew what it felt like to lose a loved one, to have no control, to be helpless. She blocked the images before they entered her mind then pressed her shoulders back.

The young girl she'd watched follow Red Wolf earlier returned to the celebrations. Her dark eyes stopped on Tsura, and the corner of her mouth lifted. She may be unaccustomed to the practices of young maidens, but there was no mistaking what the girl wanted, and it was Red Wolf. An ache she wasn't familiar with resonated deep into her stomach. She bit down hard, grinding her teeth, and sent the girl a scathing glare. She could care less who pursued Red Wolf, but she'd not allow the maiden to think she'd play in her game.

She turned to escape the festivities and ran into Red Wolf's hard chest. She lost her footing and stumbled. He reached out, grabbed her shoulders, and held her still. The sun had begun to descend, leaving the land in simple grey shadows. She could make out his wide silhouette and long hair. There was no mistaking the strong arms that held here were his.

She stepped back away from him, and the fire behind her illuminated his high cheekbones and strong jaw. Black eyes stared down at her, and she inhaled. He was handsome. There was no denying it. She recalled how his hands had felt around her waist, how his cheek had fit perfectly into the crook of her neck. She closed her eyes, and heaven help her, she remembered the touch of his lips. She cleared her throat and clasped her hands together in an effort to compose herself. Images of what he'd done to her surfaced. She opened her eyes and met his. There had been a time he'd taken her breath away. Now when she stared at him all she felt was resentment.

"Are you not enjoying the celebrations?" he asked.

"I do not want to be here." She glared at him. He'd crushed her soul, and she'd never forgive him for it.

"Why must you be so difficult?"

"I am being no such thing. I've asked time and time again to go back to Jamestown where I will no longer be your burden, to which you have refused."

"You know damn well why you cannot return there."

"Bah! I am not afraid."

"I am aware of your ignorance to what awaits you there, but I cannot fathom why you'd place yourself in harm's way."

"My life is not your concern."

"Actually it is. You are Pril and Kade's daughter."

"I am my own person, and I answer to no one."

"Soon you will be on your way back to Bristol and the life you left there."

His mention of Bristol and the emptiness that awaited her there sent the blood from her head. She waited for the shock of the truth to pool from her body before she said in a deathly quiet tone, "I need not your protection."

"Yes, so you've said."

"I need nothing from you." She swung her arm out. "Be gone!"

He stepped toward her, and his wide chest touched her breasts. Without the corset she was accustomed to wearing, her breasts were free behind the deerskin dress, and she ignored the sensations his nearness caused.

She pressed her palms into him. No one had been this close to her since she'd found her home burned to nothing. Distraught and in shock, Mr. Willaby, her driver, had held her in his arms while she sobbed. She pushed the scene from her mind and heaved herself away from Red Wolf. The act only lasted for mere seconds before he pulled her into his tight embrace and brought his lips to hers.

The meeting was rough at first and before she could catch herself, before she could pull away, she inhaled him. His mouth moved against hers, and she was lost in his arms as she let his lips carry her to another world where her body hummed with pleasure. For a moment she was seventeen, under the rowan tree and in his protective embrace.

She stiffened. He never returned. He left her with broken promises and a broken heart. Tsura pulled her lips from his. For the first time in a long while her heart longed for what might have been. She wanted to weep, to lash out at him for what he'd done, what he'd caused. It had been because of him that her life had been destroyed. She pulled her features down into the scowl she'd perfected and glared at him. He was nothing to her.

She slapped him hard across the face.

"Do not touch me again," she said.

He smirked, but his eyes remained cold.

"It is as I thought," he growled. "Your taste is spoiled."

She raised her hand to smack him again, but refrained. The magick was there, in her fingers, ready to do him harm. The pendant hidden in her moccasins heated against her ankle. She'd removed the necklace when she changed into Beautiful Meadow's dress earlier. The lower neckline was unlike anything she'd ever worn and would have made the heirloom visible to all, so she wrapped it around her ankle tucking it safely inside her moccasin.

"You fight with it don't you?"

She frowned, using all her strength to expel the need from her body. Her brow perspired, and the sweat ran down her temples.

He held out his hand. "Touch my palm."

"I will not." She turned from him.

He grabbed her arm and swung her around.

"Son of a bitch." He held his hand tucked into his chest, the flesh burned. "You cannot withhold it forever."

She knew he was right, but she'd never stop trying. If she had to live alone in the hills to control the temptation, so be it. "I wish to leave here come morning."

"Do not think because we shared a kiss, I will let you do as you wish. You are staying."

"We shared nothing!"

"I have to say…it wasn't as I'd expected."

She raised an eyebrow.

"It was rather boring."

"You bastard."

"Yes, so you've said before."

She spat in his face.

His hand jutted out, and grabbing her arm, he slammed her into his chest. The magick was not as strong within her now, but still lingered in her blood. She forged against the rising heat commanding her body to reject the need.

"That was unkind. Surely, a Baroness does not behave in such a manner. Did Morgan not teach you anything during your marriage?"

She shook him from her and stepped back, placing distance between them. "Do not speak of my husband as if you knew him."

"Oh, I knew him. Upstanding, he was. I cannot seem to recall if it was his gambling or penchant for whore after whore that colored him respected."

How had he known Morgan was unfaithful to her?

He stared at her for a long while before he asked, "How could you love someone like him?"

She thought she saw a glimpse of remorse within his sable eyes, but when she looked again it was gone. She set her shoulders, determined to protect her heart and deny her past feelings for him.

"He offered, and I accepted."

"It is as I expected then."

"And what is that?"

"You were just another one of his whores."

She gasped.

"I despise you."

He bowed. "As I you."

She left him, walking into the crowd of Cherokee. She got herself as far from him as possible. Her lips burned with the reminder of his kiss, and she ran her forearm across them to wipe the sensation of his touch away.


Red Wolf turned and retreated back into the forest. What had he done? Tsura had felt so right in his arms, and everything had made sense for a little while. In the short time they'd been together he couldn't even look at her without disgust tainting his tongue. Then there were the moments that crept upon him, when he could not drag his eyes from her beauty, and the memory of holding her in his arms. He felt trapped. The weight constricted his chest, the breath within his lungs seized, and he was sure he'd suffocate from the memories.

She'd crushed him. Losing her had almost killed him. For months he'd considered any woman who held her features—the ebony hair, the green eyes. He buried himself within their folds, pretending they were Tsura. He'd fooled himself for a while, but soon none held the similarities. No one compared to what they had, and he'd been lost once again.

Now she was here, before him in the flesh, and he could not stop himself from wishing things were different. He battled back and forth with right and wrong with need and desire, with the loneliness and the want of something he could not have.

She had bewitched him yet again, and he could not go back from that kiss. The taste of her was as he'd remembered, fresh, alluring, and delicate. For those moments when their lips had met she'd brought his soul alive once more. His heart riddled with holes, had sung. The joy dissipated when she pulled her lips from his. Reality criticized him for being a fool. She'd made a mockery of him.

He knew she battled with something far deeper than he could comprehend and had made her change so drastically, but he did not care to know. He could not afford to get that close to her. As it was Tsura's nearness clouded his judgment and caused him to do things he did not want to do.

He'd kissed her, damn it!

He ran his hand through his hair in frustration. He'd taken her into his mouth, tasted her like he had before she'd cast him aside. And now what did he feel for her? *Nothing* his mind screamed. She threw you to the wolves without a care. She thought of wealth, of stature, of a title and she'd not found it with a merchant. He winced. The words—her words—bit into him still. Blast her to the farthest part of the earth. He did not want her.

# CHAPTER SIXTEEN

Tsura sat with her back against a tall elm tree. The first rays of sun streamed onto the ground before her, and she stretched her legs out to warm them. She fiddled with the hem of the dress, pulling it lower past her calves. She was not accustomed to wearing anything but corsets, long skirts, and a waist shirt. The dress Beautiful Meadow had made was loose and hung a few inches past her knees. Thank goodness the moccasins laced to the highest part of her shins otherwise she'd be violating all rules of proprietary. Not that it mattered way out here. She was dressed like most of the other maidens, except the few who wore long skirts traded from the white people.

Her plan had been to rise at dusk and leave the tribe without anyone knowing, but when she'd opened the door to Red Wolf's lodge she'd almost tripped over him. The bastard had known of her plans. He didn't trust her and proved so by sleeping on the ground. He'd stared up at her, and his eyes displayed no kindness. Instead, bitterness reflected in the dark pits, and she was sure he'd growled.

She stepped over him and proceeded to make her way among the first of the Ama rising for the day. The fire outside of the gathering lodge still burned, and two braves stood beside it adding logs. Mothers ordered their children to fetch water from the river and begin their daily chores. The Ama women were very strict in the upbringing of their children. They taught them respect for others as well as themselves and other daily lessons. She'd been shocked to see the men of the tribe go to their wives for council and other tasks. It was clear to Tsura the women were the leaders of their people.

"Good morning, Tsisquaya," Star Dancer said and plopped down next to her.

Tsura slid away from the girl, uncomfortable with the nearness of a child.

"What did you call me?" she asked.

Star Dancer's chubby cheeks lifted as she smiled. Her black hair hung straight past her waist, and she had two thin braids on either side of her face with yellow beads at the ends.

"Tsisquaya, Tiny Sparrow. This is what I have named you."

"I do not need a name. I am not Cherokee."

The child had to be no older than six and was identical to her mother, Beautiful Meadow. Her skin was the color of honey, soft and flawless. Tsura placed her hands under her legs to keep from touching the girl.

"Edutsi is one of us and you are with him."

"Edutsi?"

"Uncle...Red Wolf." The girl made a face.

It was clear Tsura's lack of Cherokee was annoying the child.

"I am not with Red Wolf," she said.

Star Dancer nodded. "It is so. You and he love each other."

Tsura had to keep from sticking her tongue out at the girl's absurd claim. There was no love between her and Red Wolf. At one time, yes, but now when she thought of him her stomach turned with bitterness.

"You see things that are not there."

Star Dancer shrugged and reached out her hand to her. Tsura pulled away, but the girl grabbed a strand of her hair and stared at it confused.

"I've not seen hair like this before."

She untangled her hair from the girl's fingers and moved away from her again.

"It winds around my finger and stays."

"They are called curls."

"I want them in my hair."

"These curls are always there. You cannot place them in your hair without the proper tools."

Her brown eyes lit up, and she moved to sit on her knees.

"I shall find these tools."

"Possibly in town, but you'd have to trade for them."

The girl's face fell, and Tsura felt a pinch inside her heart. She knew the child would never get the pipe-clay curlers her friends had worn back in Bristol.

"I will give you some of mine."

"I cannot ask you to cut your hair."

"You are not. I am doing this on my own."

She nodded.

"I need something sharp," Tsura said more to herself than Star Dancer.

The girl handed her a small knife, and she couldn't keep the shock from her face. The Ama did indeed rear their children in the ways of their life early on.

She took the knife and examined it. The blade was small and had an elk horn handle with a star carved into it.

"Where did you get this?"

"Edoda gave it to me when I killed my first elk."

Tsura understood this. Her mother had taught her how to use a bow and arrow when she was young. Pril was a remarkable shooter and wanted her daughter to know the same skill.

"The Cherokee women are taught all things a man is right from birth," Beautiful Meadow said, standing over them.

Tsura couldn't bring herself to smile a greeting to the woman's warm face, and nodded instead. She took a piece of hair from the nape of her neck, wound it around her finger, and sliced it with the knife.

"Here." She held out a clump of long thick curly strands to Star Dancer. "You will always have curls."

The girl shot up and flew into Tsura, wrapping her arms around her.

"Thank you, Tsisquaya!"

All her muscles tightened. She did not know what to do. Dread squeezed her ribs, and she gasped. Sweat formed on her forehead, her vision blurred, and she opened her mouth to tell the child to let go, but nothing came from her lips.

Unable to stand it any longer, she pressed herself out of Star Dancer's embrace, but the girl would not let go. Her skinny arms tightened about Tsura's neck. She tried to swallow, tried to calm her nerves, but she could not. The child smelled of innocence, of purity, and she remembered.

"No." She shoved the girl from her and scurried backward away from her. She allowed no one to touch her, no one to show her any form of kindness. It was undeserved—she was undeserved. Her body trembled, and her throat worked to keep the scream suppressed. Her hands shook as she brought them up to protect herself from the child in case she lunged again.

"Star Dancer, go fetch some water for Edutsi's woman," Beautiful Meadow said.

Tsura witnessed the forlorn expression cross the child's innocent face before she scurried to do what her mother had asked.

Beautiful Meadow knelt in front of her, concern etched in her brown eyes.

"I am sorry for your loss," she said.

Tsura bristled. She'd not spoken of it, not said a word. How had she known?

"Soaring Eagle told me of your husband."

"I do not speak of it." Her voice was harsher than she'd intended, but she didn't apologize.

"It must have been difficult for you."

Tsura brushed the dirt from her dress.

"How did he pass?"

She knew the woman spoke only out of sympathy, but Tsura wanted nothing to do with it. She did not discuss it. Why couldn't Beautiful Meadow leave it alone?

"I do not wish to speak of it," she snapped, her eyes slanted and mouth turned downward.

Beautiful Meadow nodded.

Star Dancer returned with the water and handed it to her mother. They spoke in Cherokee and Tsura had no idea what they were saying.

"Thank you, Tsisquaya, for the gift," Star Dancer said quietly.

She could see the girl had fastened a leather strip around the hair to keep it together and tied it with her own.

"You are welcome." She did not smile, but spoke plainly.

Star Dancer ran off to join the other children as they gathered baskets.

"What are they doing?" Tsura asked.

Beautiful Meadow handed her the cup of water before she said, "The children work the garden. Each morning they pick the vegetables for noon and evening meals."

"It is difficult for me to imagine Red Wolf living here." She took a sip of the cold water then placed the cup next to her.

"How so?"

"I've known him since I was a little girl, and he was a slave, but I've never seen him among his own people."

"He is missed by Soaring Eagle when he goes. They were like brothers before he was taken."

Tsura knew none of this. Red Wolf hadn't known his family and did not say much about them during their time in Bristol.

"It is amazing that he found the Ama at all."

"Yes, this is true. It had been so long Soaring Eagle was sure he'd been killed."

"He is content here."

"This is his home. Surely, you miss your home."

She straightened.

"I have no home."

Beautiful Meadow frowned.

"Red Wolf said you come from the other world."

"I came from this one."

"From this land…here?"

She nodded.

"Why did you leave?"

She did not want to tell of the magick, the Chuvani lineage, and the betrayal of her own family, and instead shrugged.

"Did you live in a town?"

"No, we traveled about living out of our wagons."

"Tsiguisi," Beautiful Meadow said.

"What does that mean?"

"Gypsy, you are a Tsiguisi."

"Yes, I am." It had been a long time since she'd acknowledged her heritage. Living in Bristol, Morgan insisted she hide her modest background, so she had been unable to speak of it to anyone. He had not known of her gifts either. She'd kept that part of her life a secret, not trusting him not to use them against her.

"We know of many Tsiguisi. They live among the hills and trees." Beautiful Meadow pointed to the mountains ahead of them.

Tsura knew this, and her mind trailed to the Peddlers, the clan she lived with until she was four. Were they still around? Had they become Renoldi? She wondered if they'd welcome her among them, the Branded One, who had placed them in danger for those years she'd lived with them.

"How are your feet?" Beautiful Meadow asked, nodding toward her legs.

The dandelion tea had helped, but it was the moccasins she wore that relieved the pressure and swelling her shoes had caused.

"They are fine."

"I must go and prepare the morning meal." Soaring Eagle's wife stood and without another word walked away.

Tsura watched Beautiful Meadow greet her children, Star Dancer and Fawn, with a wide embrace. The three laughed as they swung each other about in a game of affection. The bond was undeniable between Beautiful Meadow and her daughters, and Tsura yearned for her own mother. She hadn't seen Pril in months. She was sailing with Kade to the Africas where they would stay for an extended visit. Her mother had begged for Tsura to come, but she'd refused, incapable of detaching the anger and hate from herself.

She placed her hand inside of the moccasin and fingered the pendant. It was the only connection she had with her mother as she waited for the lump in her throat to pass.

# CHAPTER SEVENTEEN

"You are troubled, Cousin," Soaring Eagle said as he came toward him.

Tired and irritated at his cousin's cheerful disposition this morning, Red Wolf grunted. He'd let Tsura sleep on the bed of pelts inside his lodge while he laid his head on the hard ground outside of his door. He hadn't slept well, his mind going over the events of the night before and wondering if she'd try to escape in the middle of the night. He did not trust her, and rightfully so. She'd expressed numerous times she wanted to go back to Jamestown and be on her own. He was sure she'd try to leave in the night especially after their argument, but as the evening shadows turned into warm hues of morning Tsura had not left the cabin, and Red Wolf had hardly slept.

She'd risen an hour ago and without a word left the lodge to wander between the Ama and other tribes. The celebrations would remain for another seven days while the chiefs fasted to show their gratefulness for a bountiful crop. The Green Corn Ceremony was going well, and Red Wolf could see Soaring Eagle loved his people very much. He would be a wonderful chief.

"Your thoughts are full."

"I will be leaving at dawn tomorrow." He had to find Romulus and clear the threat lying over Tsura's head then he'd be free of her.

"You will not return."

"Micah will come for her."

"What makes you think she will want to stay with the Ama once you leave?"

He had thought of that, and knowing Tsura she'd run off the minute she knew he was gone.

"You cannot let her leave." He could not help the harsh tone of his voice. Tsura must stay safe.

"I will ask my braves to watch over her."

"Thank you."

"She will not like it."

Red Wolf chuckled. This was true.

"She is different—special in some way," Soaring Eagle said while watching his people prepare themselves for the day.

Red Wolf stiffened.

"She is a nuisance and difficult to please."

"No, she is lost. I see a deep sadness within her."

"Mourning her husband I suppose."

"This troubles you, why?"

"He was a bastard."

"And she married him instead of you."

Damn Soaring Eagle and his ability to know the truth.

"I don't want to talk about it."

"You love her still."

"You're wrong. I hold no love for her. I protect her for Pril and Kade."

"Cousin, you protect your heart." Soaring Eagle smiled and walked away, leaving Red Wolf to think about what he'd said.

He leaned against his lodge. The uneven wooden poles made it uncomfortable, but he was too tired to move. He cared not for Tsura. Soaring Eagle was dead wrong. His reasons were solely out of loyalty and nothing else. He brushed a piece of grass from his lap.

Red Wolf scanned the people for a glimpse of Tsura. With the celebrations still underway, and the fact she dressed as the Ama, it was difficult to pick her out. Then he remembered she'd not mingle within the crowd, but wished to be distanced from them instead. He stepped from his lodge and walked the outlining perimeter of the Ama land.

His side itched something awful. The sutures needed to be removed. The skin would soon cover them. He passed White Owl and his wife in front of their home preparing their morning meal. Both smiled and wished him a happy day. He wondered if he could stay here. If he remained with the Ama would he feel complete? Would he long for the sea and wish to go back? Their way of life seemed relaxed. They helped each other, their village secure with food, clothing. And not in danger of any attacks from other tribes, or the white man. Soaring Eagle had told him they traded with townspeople near and far and had formed a trusting relationship with the white man.

Red Wolf knew he'd always love the sea and the freedom that came with sailing across the blue waters, but he yearned for a family—children of his own. Had being away as a merchant changed his relationship with Tsura?

Was the distance the reason she'd found love with another? He'd questioned this several times throughout the years. If he'd been by her side would she have stayed? He flexed his hands.

The thought of marrying turned his stomach. His heart no longer possessed the ability to love as it once had, and he wasn't sure he could pretend. He wished for his own legacy, but at what cost?

"Edutsi, Edutsi!" Star Dancer and her sister Fawn ran toward him.

He bent, opened his arms, and hugged them.

The two girls were so small within his embrace, and his heart filled with joy. They were the remedy for an ailing soul.

"What are you doing this day?" he asked them.

"Look, look!" Star Dancer jumped up and down. Her long hair bounced about her shoulders. She held a piece of curly hair nestled within her own.

"What is this?"

"Tsisquaya gave it to me."

The only woman he knew with curls such as these was Tsura, and so he did not need to ask where the girl had gotten the strip of hair.

"That was very kind of her."

Star Dancer's round cheeks lifted, and she smiled.

"Tell me, little one, why have you named her Tiny Sparrow?" he asked.

"I named her this because she is similar to the bird itself."

"How so?"

"Sparrows are small like Tsisquaya, but they are also kind and nurturing."

Tsura was not either of those things, and he wondered if the girl had misplaced the meaning.

"You see Tsisquaya as such?"

Star Dancer leaned in and whispered, "I do, Edutsi, but Tsisquaya does not know this yet."

He smiled.

"I see."

The girl nodded.

"She is scared, but inside this is who she is."

"You are very wise, little one."

Star Dancer lifted her chin at his compliment.

"Tell Edutsi, where is Tsisquaya now?"

"She sits under the elm tree among her kind."

He chuckled and kissed her cheek.

"Will you go to her?"

"I will."

Star Dancer's brown eyes shone with happiness.

"Go, and see if Etsi needs your help," he said.

Star Dancer grabbed Fawn's hand and together they ran toward their lodge.

Red Wolf changed direction and headed toward the elm tree where Tsura sat. He spotted her leaning against the wide trunk of the tree. Her habitual scowl shadowed her lovely features, and he wondered again how she could mourn someone like Morgan. It irked him to know she'd loved the Baron, even when he was a cheat and a liar. Had she no morals? No sense?

Red Wolf had cherished her, loved her beyond his own control. He shook his head. He'd never understand.

A commotion among the tribes stole his gaze from her. A crowd had gathered, and from the conversation floating toward him, someone had been brought into the village. He pushed himself through the flock of people to where Soaring Eagle stood beside a white man with shoulder length blond hair and blue eyes. He immediately thought of Kade. It'd been years since he'd seen him, and he missed their long chats about the sea, life lessons, and competitive games of checkers.

The man's eyes were blackened and a deep cut split his bottom lip in two. Dried blood smeared his white shirt. Someone had roughed him up, and by the looks of him, he was lucky to be alive. Two braves, Swift Fox and Red Feather, stood off to the side, their horses behind them. The young warriors must've found the man while hunting and brought him here.

"Bring him some water and a blanket," Soaring Eagle commanded to two maidens.

Even though the morning air was warm, the man shook wildly.

"We will help you," Soaring Eagle said in a gentle voice.

"I...I seek someone," the man said.

The maidens returned with a blanket and a cup of water. Soaring Eagle took them and handed the blanket to the man. After he'd wrapped himself securely in the woven blanket, Soaring Eagle offered him the cup.

"Who is it you wish to find?"

The man took a slow sip of water—the cup vibrated in his hand.

"Tsura Harris," he whispered.

Red Wolf's heart stopped. He stepped forward prepared to protect her with his own life.

"Why do you seek this woman?" he asked.

Soaring Eagle turned toward him and motioned for him to come closer.

"He is my half brother, Miles," Tsura said, making her way through the crowd. "He is Hiram Monroe's son."

Miles rushed toward her but was stopped by Red Wolf and Soaring Eagle. They stood in front of him, blocking the path to Tsura.

"What do you wish from her?" Red Wolf asked.

Miles had been beaten and that did not sit well with him. Whoever had done the man harm would likely do the same to Tsura. He recalled the Monroes and knew they were wealthy plantation owners. If not for their money, why would someone wish to kill this man?

"A Corsair holds my brother James. He will kill him if I do not return with Tsura."

Red Wolf's blood ran cold. Romulus. The bastard merchant was going to trade one life for another. He'd known the Corsair would not stop his charge to find Tsura, and now he held her half brother captive.

"Where is he?" Red Wolf asked Miles.

"A full day's ride west, by the flat ground at the river."

He and Tsura had been there three days before. Romulus must've followed their tracks, but when Soaring Eagle and his warriors came upon them they'd erased all traces before heading toward the Ama tribe.

"Romulus did this to you?" he pointed to Miles face.

"Yes, but he will kill James if Tsura does not go."

"Tsura will not be going anywhere," Red Wolf said.

"But she must. My brother will die if she does not go."

"You are willing to have your sister killed to save your brother?"

Miles was quiet.

Red Wolf's skin heated. That is exactly what the snake wanted.

"Tell me, how were you going to go about this? Did you think Tsura would give her life for a brother she hardly knows?"

"Romulus said he'd do her no harm. He seeks not her life, but something she has instead."

"And what is that?"

"I do not know! Let me see my sister." Miles shoved Red Wolf, but he did not budge, and the fear on the Monroe's face did little to stop him from advancing on the man.

"I'd advise you to stand down," he growled, his voice ominous, a warning of what was to come if the plantation owner touched him again.

"We need to hurry. My brother's life awaits."

Red Wolf had to control himself from wrapping his hands around Miles' neck. The ingrate would not take Tsura.

"I will travel back with you."

"What good will that do?" Miles sneered.

"It will fix your problem without involving Tsura," he snarled.

"I want to discuss this with my sister."

Red Wolf turned to where Tsura had been standing moments before, but she was not there. He surveyed the faces among them. None held the pale skin and green eyes he'd been searching for. His stomach sunk.

"She's gone, damn it." He faced Soaring Eagle. "She's left to go to Romulus."

He knew his cousin understood the panic within him. The Corsair would kill her, and if Red Wolf did not catch up to her, he may not be able to stop it.

"Go check the horses, see if the woman is there," Soaring Eagle said to Swift Fox. The warrior raced toward the corral where the horses grazed. Time seemed to stretch as they waited for Swift Fox to return.

"He comes," someone shouted.

The Ama parted for the brave to make his way back to Soaring Eagle.

"The gate was open, one horse is gone," he panted.

Red Wolf was going to put her over his knee when he found her.

"What is going on?" Miles asked.

"You got your wish…Tsura has left to rescue your brother."

Miles' face dropped, and his bruised face lost all color. "She cannot go alone. I was to go with her. I had a plan."

"I'm sure you did." He walked away from the man, his mind racing. Tsura couldn't be more than fifteen minutes ahead of him. If he hurried he'd catch her within a half hour. She didn't know the land, and he'd use that to his advantage.

"I will go after her," he said to Soaring Eagle, and pointed to Miles. "He stays."

Red Wolf didn't wait for a response, desperate to get to Tsura before any harm came to her. He raced through the crowd. He was sure he'd be upon her before she met Romulus and his men, but it was the other creatures that lurked in the mountains that scared the hell out of him.

He saddled Caesar, mounted, and without another look back followed the tracks of the horse Tsura had stolen.

Tsura peeked through the wooden rods of Red Wolf's lodge. She watched him leave the Ama village in the direction she'd set the horse to canter in. Her plan had worked thus far. At first she hadn't known what to do when Miles appeared in the Ama village, but when he'd told her Romulus held her brother James, she did not remain to listen any longer. The Corsair wanted her, or James would die. Determined to not allow that to happen, she'd snuck away while Red Wolf spoke with Miles. She led one of the horses from the corral, faced it in the opposite direction Miles had said, and slapped it on the bottom. Red Wolf would be too distracted with finding her to notice which path the horse had gone off in.

She'd find Miles, and together they'd rescue James. Tsura's desire to live had been dampened by her horrific past, and she'd sacrifice herself for James.


Tsura lay beneath the heavy pelts for the better part of a half hour while Miles paced the lodge. Soaring Eagle had placed him here with two braves to guard the door. She'd wanted to burst from the furs the minute the door had closed and Miles had been escorted inside, but knew the braves were listening outside.

Enough time had passed, and she sat up tossing the pelts from her body.

"Tsura." Miles ran toward her.

She held up her hand to stop him from embracing her. "You must keep your voice down," she whispered.

He nodded.

"We cannot dally. We need to escape and get a move on. Red Wolf will be heading back soon and angry as a hornet when he finds the steed without a rider.

Miles nodded.

"Are you well enough to travel?" she asked.

"Yes, yes."

"Good. We will need to steal two more horses." She turned toward him. "You know the way to where Romulus holds James?"

"I do. It is where I said earlier."

"We need to go now." Red Wolf knew where Romulus was too, and he'd be hot on their trail.

She stepped toward the door, and the silhouette of two men shone through the wooden sticks. Blast it all. There had to be another way out. She scanned the room. Thick and skinny logs held together with mud and grass surrounded them.

"Here," Miles whispered. He stood next to a basket, and when he moved it she saw the hole, a half moon shape by the floor.

"Yes, this will work." She went to the opening and knelt. It was no bigger than the width of Tsura's forearm. She pulled at the wood around it, snapping the twigs in two. Damn it. She paused and waited for the door to burst open. She held her breath. No one came, and so she pulled one more piece, breaking the wood.

"This should be wide enough. Do you think you can fit through there?"

Miles nodded.

She removed the moccasin from her left foot and unwound the pendant. Tsura searched the lodge for a place to put it so that Red Wolf would find it. He'd know to take it to her mother should she not return. The quiver he used lay against the wall, three arrows protruded from the opening. She went to it and gently placed the pendant inside.

Miles watched her intently, and she offered him no explanation.

"I will go first," she said.

Tsura popped her head out the other side of the lodge and was relieved to see a field of tall grass. Red Wolf's home had been built on the edge of the tribe's land. She crawled the rest of the way, freeing herself from the lodge and the men who guarded the door. Her knees scraped against the tiny rocks in the ground, but she dare not utter a word of discomfort lest someone hear her.

She was thankful the deerskin dress covered her to the calves, and the moccasins laced to above her shins. She wasn't comfortable showing Miles any skin. Brother or not, it was improper, and damn it she was a lady even if she didn't look it. She leaned against the back of Red Wolf's lodge and waited for Miles to follow.

A horse neighed to her left. Tsura jumped, startled. She reached for a rock ready to strike whoever had found them. Raven came around the corner. Her dark eyes met Tsura's and without saying a word, the girl dropped the reins of the grey steed, turned, and left.

"Unbelievable," Miles said in awe. "Why would she help us?"

Tsura knew why. The young Raven wanted Red Wolf and eliminating Tsura from the Ama was her best chance. She shrugged off the notion to stay and stood.

"One steed it is," she said, mounting. She waited for Miles to climb up behind her.

Accustomed to horses, she knew how to ride sidesaddle as a lady should and thanks to her mother, astride with her legs wrapped around the animal's back. She preferred the latter. She shimmied the dress up to her thighs, biting back the urge to toss her legs together and ride with the dignity a lady should, and clicked her tongue.

The horse took off into the field. Tsura urged the animal to go faster for fear Soaring Eagle and his men would be behind them. She glanced back, and her shoulders sagged. No one was there. Raven must've distracted them. The wind whipped Tsura's long locks from her face. She closed her eyes and let herself feel free for only a moment. She released the small amount of tension she carried with her at all times, relaxed the scowl that masked her face, and took in a gulp of air. The moment was brief, a sliver of what she could allow to pass, lest she give in to the memories, the sorrow, the heartache and crumple to the ground never to get up.

She opened her eyes on the verge of tears, and blinked them away. She would not cry. She would not give in. Placing her lips into a hard line, she leaned forward, and urged the horse onward.

# Chapter Eighteen

Red Wolf grazed his fingers over the hoof prints on the ground. The deep indentation and the way the back hooves had pressed into the soil told him it held two riders. He sighed. Relief flooded him, and he waited for his heart to resume its natural beat.

He'd come back to the Ama without Tsura. It wasn't until after he'd trailed the beast for two hours did he realize it was what she'd intended. He hadn't been thinking when he left, hadn't taken notice of the direction the animal went until he'd found the horse with no rider. He cursed himself for being hotheaded and not thinking before he raced after her. He clenched his hands into tight fists. When he found her she'd be lucky if he didn't kill her himself.

"They ride together." Soaring Eagle confirmed what he already knew. His cousin insisted on traveling with him to rescue Tsura and her stepbrothers from Romulus. Red Wolf didn't see the need for the Chief to leave his tribe during the Green Corn Ceremonies, but Soaring Eagle refused to listen.

In truth he was relieved to have the company of his cousin. The conversation took his mind off of the things Tsura could be going through at the hands of the evil Corsair and his men.

"You worry for her." Soaring Eagle walked his horse alongside Red Wolf's.

He didn't answer. He couldn't. Worry did not touch on the enormity of what he felt and what he'd do if something happened to Tsura.

"We will make it there in time."

"We better," he said and kicked his heels into Caesar's sides. The air was warm, and his skin glistened from the heat. He relished in the wind as his horse cantered through the valley.

Tsura was still an hour ahead of him, and he pushed Caesar further than he ever had before. He knew he couldn't run the horses continuously and would need to let them rest soon. He glanced up at the sun. It was lower than before. Dusk was setting and soon they'd be covered in darkness.

They crested a large hill and overlooked the meadow below. Red Wolf remembered traveling through it with Tsura days before. It was here she'd tried to sacrifice herself to the cougar. He rubbed his chest. The gnawing ache resonated around his back, and he straightened to shake off the pain.

"You cannot free yourself of emotion," Soaring Eagle said, coming up beside him.

He glared at his cousin.

"It is love you feel."

"It is no such thing."

Soaring Eagle's brown eyes softened, and Red Wolf watched the sympathy roll from them.

"Why do you deny yourself?"

He remained quiet as they walked their horses side by side.

"You cannot change what you feel."

Red Wolf glared at him, anger merged with fear, and he growled, "I feel nothing."

"You feel plenty. I see it upon your face, Cousin. You are afraid something will happen to her,"

"That is duty…not love, you fool."

"You are wrong. This duty you spout of comes from where?"

"From my love of Pril and Kade, you know of this."

He was getting irritated at his cousin's constant accusations. The White chief may be wise among his people, but when it came to Red Wolf's emotions, he was as daft as a headless chicken.

"Yes, but what if Pril and Kade were no longer among the living?"

"What are you getting at?"

"Would you protect her then?"

Red Wolf scowled at Soaring Eagle. Damn him and his questions.

"No," he said quietly.

"You wish to deceive me?"

"I wish for you to bloody well be quiet."


Tsura's back ached from turning to see if Red Wolf was behind them. She was sure each time she turned she'd see his silhouette on the horizon against the falling sun.

Miles leaned into her. The way his body slumped against her back in a lethargic stupor told her he was asleep. She'd been surprised he'd held on for so long. Injured and sore, she knew he needed rest.

She scanned the valley around them, the trees familiar. She'd been here with Red Wolf before coming to the Ama. Soon they'd be upon the evil Romulus. She shuddered. When she thought of the horrible merchant, her blood ran cold. He should've died that night a year ago. It had been him she'd wanted to kill, not the men who worked his ship. She sucked in a deep breath. She'd accepted her actions long ago, and she was not sorry for them. They were the very reason she'd killed so many. The shock of what she'd found had sent her into a downward spiral and blurred all she'd been taught. The earth started to spin. She blinked and held on tighter to the reins.

Romulus had stolen her life. He'd taken from her the one person she loved more than anything. The one being she'd die for. Tsura's eyes watered. Now with him gone…there was nothing left of her.

The Corsair would want her dead for the things she did, and he could have her, but he'd release James first. No power would eject from her fingers, no spells would pass her lips, and there would be no magick. She'd remain the same as she'd been for the past year, empty, desolate, and void of all things she once was.

She walked the horse over a small hill. A forest of black trees stood before her, and she saw the orange glow of the fire.

"Miles," she nudged him, "we are here."

He grumbled, and she felt him pull upward away from her.

"It is through the trees," he said.

She nodded and led the horse toward the aura of the fire. They had barely broached the first stand of trees when Miles was torn from the horse. Tsura snapped her head to the side to see what had happened, when large hands gripped her arms and ripped her off to land on the ground.

The air flew from her lungs, and she curled forward to ease the strain within her ribs. She tossed the hair from her face and stared up at the largest man she'd ever seen. Before she could utter a word, he yanked her up onto her feet. Keeping his hand around her upper arm, he ushered her into the forest behind Miles and another shorter, stouter man.

"Release me at once." She tried to pull herself free, but the man's hand remained tight. "I can walk on my own. I came here willingly."

The monster didn't look at her, instead he tugged on her arm to make her move faster. They came into a small clearing with a large fire burning to the left. Three horses were tethered to the trees. She scanned the area for James. Her chest seized when she saw him. He sat atop a brown gelding, a noose around his neck. The rope was swung over a large deformed branch and the other end tied to the horse. Romulus was going to hang him.

Her stepbrother had been badly beaten. His handsome face showed the shadow of bruises. Deep gashes cut up his cheeks, chin, and forehead. His once blond hair was tainted crimson, a sign his head was split as well.

He sat on top of the horse, his head tipped to the side, and for a moment she worried he was dead. When he shifted slightly, she exhaled and searched for the vile man who'd done this.

Romulus walked out of the bushes, a dagger gripped in his hand. She had never seen his face, only knowing of his horrid reputation and what he'd done to her home.

Her face heated as the need for revenge overcame her, but just as it reared inside of her soul it faded away to nothing. If she allowed the vengeance to take over, she'd have to deal with the past, and she did not want to relive it, refused to think of it—see it in her mind's eye. Tsura knew that with one swipe of her hand, with the right words spoken, she could kill Romulus and his men. Her fingers twitched, the need arose again, and she fought it. She was terrified to release the well of emotions she so carefully kept hidden, trapped inside her soul. For surely if she used the magick, she'd drown in a flood of despair unable to ever recover. No, there would be no magick this night.

"Good evening, Baroness," Romulus said as he walked toward her. He wore his hair long upon his head and face too. The beard touched his chest, and she spied gold and gems woven into the coarse curls. His mouth was wide and full of crooked, stained teeth, and he stood a foot taller than her. His stature was thin, but he held himself much larger than what he was. His demeanor screamed of his wicked nature and lust for blood.

She tipped her chin. "Release my brother at once."

The Corsair turned toward James before he swung back to face her, arms open, the dagger glistening in the firelight. He gave her a wide grin.

"This can be done." His smile disappeared, and she watched as his features grew dark. Jagged edges formed along his cheekbones, and his eyes glazed to reveal hollow depths. "But first I want something in exchange."

He sought her life she was sure of it. "You may have me."

Romulus laughed. He paced in front of her with much drama as he swung his arms up and down in slow movements. He suddenly stopped and pointed his dagger at her. "I seek something far more valuable than your life, Baroness."

What could he want other than her blood for what she'd done to him?

"Speak what it is you wish for."

He placed the tip of the knife to her chest and traced a half circle from one end of her neck to the other.

"I should seek your life for what you've done to my ship, and that may come afterward, but I am in need of what it is you hold."

She grew stiff, the air in her throat thick and heavy.

"It is worth more than all the riches in the world."

Tired of his antics, she glared at him. "Speak it!"

His eyes lit. "The ruby."

"What do you ramble of?"

"Do not toy with me. I have seen it." He ran the knife up toward her cheek and pressed the blade into the bare skin.

"You've seen nothing. This ruby you chirp of does not exist."

He grabbed her hair and turned her head toward James. The knife he held dashed out and slit her dress down the middle to expose the tops of her breasts.

"Where is it?"

She knew he was looking for the pendant. She was relieved she did not wear the necklace, but instead had left it tucked away in Red Wolf's quiver. She'd never release the talisman to him. It was the Chuvani lineage. She promised her mother she'd keep it safe and protect it with her life. If she died this night, Red Wolf would return it to her mother where it belonged.

She refused to answer him.

"Damn it, tell of it or he will die!"

"I have no pendant."

"She does hold magick," Miles cried out. "She is very powerful."

What was he thinking? She'd sworn never to use the gifts again. He knew this, and yet he was spouting of it to their enemy.

Romulus released her and walked to stand in front of Miles.

"Powers without the ruby?"

"Yes, she is a gypsy, a Chuvani. I have seen this. I have watched her count a spell."

"Excuse my brother, he is not of right mind." She had to distract him from the pendant, and playing Miles for a fool was her only chance.

Romulus stepped back to her side. "Powers without the magickal pendant? Are you a witch?"

"Not a witch you fool, a gypsy," Miles spat.

Romulus turned quickly, backhanding her brother so hard he fell to the side, and the Corsair's guard pulled him back up.

"Do not speak unless I have asked it of you," Romulus said in deadly tones.

Miles nodded and remained mute.

"A gypsy, you say," Romulus said. "Is it not from the pendant you draw your powers?"

She remained silent.

He stepped to her side and yanked her backward by the hair.

"Answer me!"

"You are delusional. I hold no magick, nor is there a pendant. My brother has taken too many cuffs to the head to be considered sane. Release us at once."

"You think me a fool, but I've seen what you can do. I was there the night on the docks."

She refused to change her demeanor. He'd not know of the truth, he'd not see the magick. It did not exist inside of her anymore. It was a curse. She rebuked it, despised it for what it had brought into her life...but more importantly for what it could not do.

"Let us play a game shall we?"

"I will not be goaded into anything you try."

"Does your brother spout the truth?"

"You will fail," she growled.

He leaned in and whispered, "I never fail."

"How do you propose to show something that does not exist?"

"Ahhh, Baroness, I will simply give you no choice but to act. If the power lies within you as your brother states, you will have to use it."

The night one year before, she'd gone to the docks covered in ashes and charcoal, empty and filled with rage. She was desperate for vengeance. There had been no thought to who would see, and she'd not cared what happened to her afterward.

The harbor was cloaked in darkness, the gaming halls and taverns full of drunkards. She walked along the wharf, the hood on her black cape pulled up, the fury so powerful her hands pulsed with pain. She spotted the ship, and her mind shrouded with revenge. Venom shot from her eyes as power she did not know she had expelled from her hands to cast the mast down upon the men on the ship. Words shrieked from her lips, and the boat was consumed in flames. She heard the shouts, the cries for help as men leapt into the waters. The smell of charred wood, the screams for death to come filled the air...and she walked away.

Tsura shook her head. The memory so vivid in her mind, the reasons so fresh in her soul, she felt the sorrow creep up her throat to choke her, and instead of succumbing to it, she smashed it back down.

"Enough of your games," she hissed. "Release my brother."

"Let us see what you can do." Romulus walked to the horse James sat upon, and without another word picked up a branch and slapped it across the animal's rear.

"No!" Miles shouted.

Tsura gasped.

The horse shot out from under James, and he dropped to dangle by the rope around his neck. His legs kicked the air, and his hands bound behind him shook violently.

"Help him!" Miles screamed at her. He struggled against the man who held him.

Tsura watched as James's body twitched, spittle dribbled from his chin, and his blue eyes began to fade. Her arms throbbed, the need filled her fingers, and she clenched her hands into balls. She could not use the magick. It hadn't saved him, and it wouldn't save James. Romulus would know, he'd want the pendant, and she would not give it up. Her body heated, and sweat trickled down the sides of her face. The guard holding her yelped as her skin burned his flesh, and he released her to clutch his palms to his chest.

She took off toward James, grabbing the reins of the horse closest to her. She reached him and pressed his feet into her chest. On her tiptoes, she wrapped her arm around his legs and pushed his body upward to loosen the rope. He moaned, and she sighed relieved he still lived. He was heavy, his weight almost too much for her thin frame. She used all her strength to keep him steady while she tried desperately to pull the horse beneath him.

"Release him," Romulus shouted.

She staggered to the side, holding James upright while she urged the horse closer.

She heard the whistle of the blade as it flew through the air. Blood dripped onto the top of her hand. She glanced up, and all hope seeped from her. Romulus' dagger struck James in the throat. His eyes stared down at her…the life within them gone.

She let go of his legs, her arms listless, mind clouded.

"Damn you, Tsura. Do something!"

She heard the desperation in Miles' shouts, the fear—the horror that laced his words. Unable to take any more, she hung her head. Shame swallowed her, and she closed her eyes against the sudden rush of tears. Her chest tightened, causing her back to curve and her soul to ache.

She wheezed and panic wedged inside her throat. The truth of it all was too much, the agony of what she could not control beat against her breast, and she released two tears. The sob lingered upon her lips, but she held them closed afraid to let go.

Miles wept, the sound broken, desolate. It resonated around the small clearing to pierce her heart. Tsura knew he'd not want comfort from her and remained still.

Romulus stalked toward her—his hand jutted out and clutched her neck. She didn't fight him, praying he'd kill her instead. He walked her backward into the waiting arms of the monstrous guard who held her earlier.

"Give me the damn ruby!"

He squeezed, and she brought her eyes to his in a silent challenge. The bastard shouted for the necklace again and again and again. The sound muffled, her vision blurred, her breath gone.


Red Wolf jumped from Caesar's back and grabbed his bow. They'd heard the commotion from the small hill outside of the forest, and without waiting for Soaring Eagle he'd kicked his heels into Caesar's sides and raced toward the trees.

He knew Tsura was in trouble. Miles' screams were heart wrenching, and he'd guessed James was dead. He pushed through the branches careful of his steps so as not to alert them of his presence.

The large fire brightened the area, and Red Wolf could see everything. Meril held Miles, who was slumped forward, and broken sobs wracked his body. The giant Gaspard detained Tsura, and Romulus seized her throat. He needed to act now, or the bastard would kill her. Without another thought, he reached inside the quiver on his back and pulled an arrow. Aiming the weapon, he released the string. He did not wait for the arrow to hit Romulus before he pulled another one from his back and aimed toward Gaspard.

Romulus screamed and pulled back his arm, freeing Tsura.

Another arrow flew past Red Wolf to lodge into Meril. Two more came quickly afterward, each penetrating into the guard. Soaring Eagle had arrived. He raced through the trees. He had to get to Tsura, to protect her. Red Wolf jumped over a fallen log and burst through the bushes. All he saw was Tsura. She stood staring straight ahead, no expression upon her face.

"Run!" he shouted toward her.

She didn't move, didn't turn toward him.

He hadn't seen Gaspard until it was too late. The brute came out of nowhere, tackling him to the ground. He laid his fists into Red Wolf's sides, knocking the air from him. Gaspard pounded his ribs until Red Wolf was sure each one was broken.

He was able to get his arm free and brought his elbow up to ram into Gaspard's throat, choking him with the blow. Red Wolf took the opportunity to throw another punch, but it did nothing. The man's face was made of stone. The quiver on his back pressed into his spine, and he ripped the flesh from his body.

Gaspard laid another meaty fist into his side, and the air whooshed from his lungs. Damn it, the bastard was relentless. Tsura. Was she safe? He tried to look, but could see nothing with the bloody oaf on top of him.

He had decided to bring his legs up and try to kick the giant in the back when Soaring Eagle's face floated above him. His cousin had jumped on Gaspard's back. With a warrior's skill he took his knife and sliced the man's throat. Blood sprayed all over Red Wolf before Romulus' guard fell forward dead.

Soaring Eagle pushed the man to the side, freeing him.

"You couldn't have pierced his heart?" Red Wolf asked annoyed.

Soaring Eagle shrugged and placed his hand out to help him up.

"Romulus?"

"He got away while we were battling the others."

Red Wolf ran his forearm along his forehead to wipe the gore from his face, and then searched for Tsura. She no longer stood where he'd last seen her. He scanned the small area. His heart stopped when he saw the knife glisten against the firelight.

He pushed Soaring Eagle out of the way, reached for his dagger tied to his leg, and threw it. Miles' back arched as the blade dug into the middle of his spine. The bastard was going to kill his own sister. He ignored the pain in his sides and stalked toward the coward. He glanced at Tsura. She lay on the ground, her hair disheveled, the deerskin dress torn down the middle smeared with dirt, and blood. Her right cheek swollen and red, a small cut on her throat.

Violent rage pulsed in his veins. Miles would die this night.

Red Wolf picked the man up by the collar of his shirt and drove his fist into the already beaten face. Miles crumpled to the ground. Soaring Eagle sat beside Tsura as he continued his onslaught on the stepbrother she'd have sacrificed herself for.

He yanked him up, choking him with the tight grip on his collar.

"Slow and painful...that is how you are going to die," he growled.

Blue eyes stared into his, no hint of remorse, no shadow of regret. Rage smothered him, and he drove his fist into Miles' stomach, pummeling the body until he couldn't hold him any longer. He went to retrieve him one more time, to continue feeding his rage, when Soaring Eagle laid his hand upon his shoulder.

"He is dead, Cousin."

He could hear nothing but the beating of his own heart and the rush of blood as it ran through his veins. He panted and his chest expanded. He wasn't done. He desired retribution—justice for what Miles had done to Tsura. He shoved Soaring Eagle's hand from him and stepped toward Miles.

"She is hurt."

The statement stopped him. He'd known she was injured, but was unaware of how bad. He went to Tsura and knelt in the dirt beside her.

"Did he stab her?" he asked, running his hands along her body to check for any blood.

"It is far worse," Soaring Eagle said.

"What do you mean?"

He knelt beside him. "She suffers greatly in here." He pointed to her heart.

Understanding pressed on his forehead, and he assessed her again, concentrating on her face this time.

She stared past him, her green eyes dull and muted. No vigor shone within the emerald depths. Two shades paler than her already whitish skin, she held no color anywhere. Red Wolf's heart ached for her, for what she'd seen, for the circumstances afterward. Her injuries were mild, a few scrapes and bruises. He'd fix them in no time.

He ran his hand along the side of her face. Her expression remained the same, lifeless and unchanging. How did he heal her mind, her heart, and her soul? He placed his forehead to hers.

"I will not leave you," he whispered before he slid his arms underneath her and lifted her from the ground.

"Take her to the valley. I will bury the dead and meet you when I am done," Soaring Eagle said.

Red Wolf nodded, afraid if he spoke his voice would give way to the tears he held back. He walked with her cradled against his chest, her eyes still open and the same stillness present upon her face. Romulus must've killed James before Tsura and Miles had arrived. The loss was crippling her. She could've saved him—used her magick to break the noose or untie his hands. The powers she held were far greater than Romulus and his men and yet she hadn't used them to help herself...again.

He'd seen this behavior from her throughout their time together. The cougar, her desire to return to Jamestown no matter what the threat, and now, sacrificing herself for her brother. He was still baffled as to why she wished to hold her powers within. Why hadn't she killed Romulus for what he'd done? Instead, she became subservient to the evil Corsair, and it had almost cost Tsura her life.

He stopped to stare down at her. The refusal to use the gifts bestowed upon her had Red Wolf wondering—had she watched James die? Would she do such a thing, reject the gift when there was such a dire need of it...all because of one man, all for her love of Morgan? It was absurd to think she cared for him that much, but her previous actions, the arrogance, harshness, and visible hatred he'd seen slash from her eyes told him it was possible.

He shook his head. No, she'd not watch James die...or would she? Red Wolf wasn't sure, and he'd begun to realize he knew nothing of the girl he once loved more than life itself.

# Chapter Nineteen

Tsura lay on her side. The flames from the fire leapt out to lick the air. She moved her tongue. The muscle, heavy and coated with misery, had made it impossible for her to utter a word since Red Wolf had rescued her. Both of her brothers were dead, and she didn't know how to process the event within her mind. Instead of bringing it forth she placed a blanket over her emotions. Avoidance was her only weapon against the images that plagued her.

Seeing the Corsair for the first time had brought a surge of sensations she'd fought hard to bury. He'd changed her life forever, and she despised him for it. She sucked in a breath as she was thrown back in time.

Mr. Willaby pulled the carriage up the long driveway. The afternoon was bright, the sun high within a blue sky. Tsura had gone into town to be fitted for a new gown. It had been a lovely morning with a bright blue sky and warm sun. The time away from the home, from her problems with Morgan, had been welcomed. She returned refreshed, ready to face whatever he threw at her today with a new perspective.

As the carriage climbed the driveway to her home, smoke filled the compartment where she sat. She popped her head out of the small window, and her stomach pitched. The right side of the large two storied home was swept up in bright orange and red flames. Tsura's heart stopped. Without waiting for the carriage to halt, she jumped from the platform and raced toward the house. Panic clawed the back of her throat, muffling her screams as her legs bounded across the lawn. She remembered the weight of her skirt, the pull from the fabric as she tried to get to him as quickly as possible. She passed the servants as they exited the home.

Smoke assaulted her face when she tore open the door, and she climbed the stairs to his room. The higher she went the thicker the smoke became.

The haze blinded her when she reached the second floor, and her eyes watered. Her lungs burned while she hacked into her palm. She tasted ash, soot—the residue clung to her teeth.

She picked up a heavy porcelain vase and threw it against one of the large windows overlooking the yard. The glass broke permitting some of the smoke to billow from the hall. She was desperate to find him, to hold him, to make sure he was all right. She came to the door of his room pushed it open—

Tsura sat up, her throat constricted, her chest heavy and compressed. She could not inhale. She could not breathe! Oh dear God she saw him…she saw him. Loud gasps escaped past her lips as she scratched at the air around her.

Red Wolf was beside her in seconds, his strong arm wrapped around her back.

"You're safe, Tsura."

No she wasn't. She'd never be safe again. Her dreams, memories, and own wickedness would haunt her for the rest of her life. She'd been useless to help him, to breathe life back within his charred lungs—to mend his burned flesh. All she could do was hold him…and weep.

One tear slipped through her lashes to dance down her cheek. She'd not give in. She wrung her hands and concentrated on the anger—the rage. She'd not become weak. Not now, not ever! Damn it there was no resolution when it came to opening the wounds, for she'd never recover. The sob pressed against her closed lips. She fought with herself, refused to give in as her body shook.

Tsura closed her eyes as Red Wolf's thumb wiped a tear from her cheek. She turned from him. Afraid of what might happen if she permitted herself to trust him, if she let him hold her—protect her. He did not release his grip on her. Feelings of suffocation arose. She pressed herself away from him and out of his embrace.

He let her go, and she inched back to where she'd lain before. She felt his dark eyes upon her and shivered. How had she gotten here, in this place where she had nothing left within her heart, where she questioned why she lived? She had no answers, and she shook her head slowly from side to side.

She let James die today, hang before her, and no matter what she told herself or the excuses she'd used…she'd been wrong. He was her brother, placed into a horrible circumstance because of her, and she should've done more. She fidgeted with the hem of her dress, twisting the leather within her fingers. Miles had attacked her once he'd been freed from Romulus' guard. She didn't fight back, deserving his assault. When she'd fallen to the ground after he'd punched her, she knew he intended to kill her. Tsura welcomed the dagger as he held it over her heart. She waited for the stab of the blade to pierce her flesh, the life to fade from her existence.

It was not to be. Red Wolf had stopped him, and she didn't know if she was relieved or angry with him for doing so. Relieved for it had been him who fought for her, angry because had he not deserted her three years before. Perhaps she'd not feel so alone now. Tsura reminded herself it had been duty that placed him within her life, honor toward her mother and Kade and nothing more.

Red Wolf stirred the embers with a long branch. He needed some warmth from the brisk morning air. He'd woken early to the singing of cardinals flying above, and before he opened his eyes he relished in a moment of calm. The quiet brought him back to the sea. To the morning hours when his men were still asleep, and he'd stand at the mast, the salt water misting his face and contentment resting upon his shoulders.

He'd formed a relationship with the waters and the *Falcon*. They were a part of him. His men, his ship, and the sea were in his blood. His life had been full of joy. It wasn't until Tsura had rejected him, that he'd no longer felt this. When he stared at his crew he experienced a bleak yearning for what he had lost and could no longer find.

Soaring Eagle returned from the river, four fish stabbed onto an arrow. "She has not woken?" he asked.

Red Wolf glanced up from the fire to stare at Tsura sleeping on the hard ground by a pine tree twelve feet away.

"No."

"You do not wish to wake her?" Soaring Eagle placed the four perch onto the steaming rock beside the fire.

"I do not know what will greet us when I do."

He didn't miss his cousin's smirk or the low chuckle he tried to hide.

"You are afraid of your woman?"

Red Wolf glared.

"She is not my woman, damn it, and I am not afraid."

Soaring Eagle shrugged and flipped the sizzling fish.

"I do not know how to speak to her," he confided.

"With your heart."

Red Wolf thought of what his cousin said. He'd closed off all feelings he'd had for Tsura long ago. She'd rejected him, and he'd never forget the pain her words had caused. He did not want to go back. He did not want to open his heart to the agony ever again. It was easier to despise her, to fight with her, to ignore her.

When she lay at the mercy of Miles last night he'd forgotten of the past, of her denial of him, and thought only of saving her life.

His stomach tightened when he'd seen her face, bruised and cut, her hair pulled from the braid, and her dress smeared with blood. He'd watched her sleep, and waking from a nightmare, he'd gone to her. The short time he'd held her in his arms his soul soared with desire. When she pushed him away, he did not know what to do. Left empty, his heart cried out for her. Tormented by the past and the present together, he wondered how it would ever be possible for his broken heart to heal.

"It is not such a difficult task, Cousin," Soaring Eagle said.

"You know nothing," he snapped, recalling her rejection.

Soaring Eagle placed a hand upon his shoulder. "Do not allow your pride to rule your behavior."

"Pride?" His lip curled in disgust.

"Yes, pride. Release it, and you will see your future clearly."

"And how do you propose I do this, oh White Chief?"

Soaring Eagle ignored him and said, "You must let go of your anger toward her, and yourself."

Red Wolf shook his head.

"I hold no anger toward myself. She is the one who rejected me," he whispered so Tsura didn't wake.

"I think you do."

"How say?"

"You gave up—accepted what was to be and left."

Soaring Eagle's last statement sent his blood to boil, and he stepped closer to him, his muscles clenched. "Tell me this, Cousin, have you ever had your soul ripped from your body, felt a pain so immense you thought you'd surly die from it?"

Soaring Eagle remained quiet.

"I thought not. So do not speak to me of this pride."

"But I have."

"You speak lies." Anger spewed from his lips. He was unwilling to control it and did not give a damn if Tsura woke or not. "When has this happened to you?"

"You forget this because you are too involved in your own feelings to remember."

"Is that so?"

"Yes, you relive the past. You savor the anger, the hurt, letting it control who you are."

"Enough with your lessons in how I should bloody well behave. Tell of it." He tossed the stick he'd been using to stir the hot coals. "When have you loved someone and they left without any choice of yours?"

"When I was twelve winters…and my best friend vanished without a trace." Soaring Eagle turned and walked away.

All the anger bled from him. He felt terrible. He'd never thought of how Soaring Eagle must've felt when he hadn't returned that day. They'd been inseparable up until that point, and he'd been too caught up in his own emotions to consider Soaring Eagle's. He shook his head. He was an ass.

"The fish is burning."

He turned. Tsura stood with the blanket he'd placed on her last night wrapped around her shoulders.

"Damn it."

He pushed the perch from the rock into the grass.

"I will find something else to eat," he said to her.

"It is fine. I am not hungry."

"How are you feeling?"

"I wish to return to Jamestown."

"Romulus escaped last night. He will continue to hunt you."

She shrugged, and he wondered again how she ceased all care toward herself.

"I cannot permit it."

Her green eyes flashed.

"And when will you allow this? Surely you see that I am in less danger with Romulus' men dead. I will go back to Jamestown whether you permit it or not."

"You will do no such thing."

"I fail to see why I am your concern."

"Pril and Kade—"

"Oh, yes, your duty, correct?"

"I cannot release you to the wolf when I am capable of protecting you."

"I needn't say this any clearer. I am in no need of your damn duty."

He flexed his jaw. Her insistence to battle him on returning to Jamestown irritated him, and his anger flooded back ten fold.

"Was James dead when you and Miles reached Romulus?" The question flew from his lips before he could stop it, and he bit back the apology he knew he owed her.

Tsura fiddled with the edge of the blanket, her eyes narrowed, her lips pursed.

He stepped closer.

"Was he?"

"No," she whispered.

Red Wolf stared at her in disbelief.

"Was there a reason you did not save him?"

"I tried to…but it was not enough."

"The magick was not successful?"

"I used no magick."

A part of him was not surprised at her answer, but it did not mean he understood her actions.

"Why not?" He waited for her to continue, to tell of why she'd do such a horrible thing, but she remained silent. "Speak of it," he shouted.


Tsura watched the display of anger change to rage on Red Wolf's handsome face and did nothing to stop it. He asked her about James, and she'd told him the truth. She would not lie, even though she wanted to. She wished to forget the incident ever happened, to think of James back at Monroe mansion living a happy life. She squeezed her eyes closed to stop the tears.

"Damn it, tell me why." Red Wolf advanced toward her, and she remained where she stood.

"No."

"No?"

She spun from him and marched toward the three horses grazing on the grass by the trees.

"Where do you think you're going?"

He grabbed her arm and swung her toward him.

"Leave me," she hissed.

"Answer the question." He still held her arm and applied pressure to the bone.

She did not shove him from her. Instead, she fought with the need to blast him across the field. Her temperature rose, and she clenched her teeth.

"He was your brother," Red Wolf whispered, and the words tore a hole in her determination to keep quiet.

"I do not use the magick any longer."

He didn't need to know the gift she held was useless, that she did not believe in herself enough to have rescued her brother. She refused to tell him Romulus wanted the pendant, and if she allowed the gift to pulse through her fingers, the spell to pass by her lips, he'd have known the ruby existed.

"Why would you not help him?"

"I could do nothing."

"I know the gift lies within you, I've felt it. Do not mislead me any longer."

She wanted him to think she was a horrible, ruined, vile person. Tsura realized she was all of those things the morning one year before when she sat upon the floor cradling him in her arms. She'd tried to put life back within him…but her efforts were useless. She shook her head. She'd did not think of it then she'd see it, and worse yet, she'd feel the shame, followed by the agony.

Tsura turned from Red Wolf, her control weakening, and concentrated on blocking all memories of the past.

He hadn't released her arm and swung her back around to face him. Not prepared for his abrupt behavior, she hadn't the time to wipe the one tear that lay upon her cheek.

"How could you watch your own brother die and not do anything to help him?"

She bent her head. His questions pierced her heart, and she could not remain indifferent any longer.

He placed his thumb under her chin and nudged.

"Tsura, why can you not tell of this?"

She lifted her eyes to his and let him see a glimpse of the remorse that lay within the green depths.

"I wish to be alone."

He gripped both of her arms and shook her.

"Answer me, damn it. Why did you let him die?"

"I did not wish it," she screamed. "I tried to save him. I held his legs. I used all of my strength to help him…but it was not enough."

"But you did not use the magick."

"No, I did not," she whispered, her voice broken.

"It is who you are. Why do you continue to deny this?"

She glared at him.

"It is not who I am. The power is a curse. It has been such since the day I was born. I see no gain from the gifts I've been given."

"How can you say this? You can do wonderful, amazing things with your gift. I have witnessed this."

"You have not lived it as I have. You have not sat beside a loved one desperate to save them only to fail." She shoved him from her and walked away.

"How did Morgan die?" he asked, his voice quiet and calm.

She stopped mid stride, unprepared for his question.

"Please, confess it to me."

She faced him and was taken aback at the softening of his features. The hard lines and heated eyes no longer bore into her. Instead she saw remorse and sympathy, and she gnashed her back teeth together.

"I need not your pity."

He reached for her hand, and she swung it away.

"I ask you not out of pity, but curiosity and a need to understand."

"He was stabbed and burned to death," she growled.

"Who killed him?"

"Romulus."

"Why?"

She sighed. "For money."

"A gambling debt." He didn't ask it, but instead stated that he knew.

She nodded.

"How is it you could not save him?"

She shivered and pulled the blanket tighter around her.

"He held too many mortal wounds."

"What do you mean?"

"When a Chuvani heals someone she takes upon herself the ailment of the wounded."

"Yes, I know of this."

"If there are too many mortal lesions, a Chuvani will die without ever healing them."

"But what of the pendant. It is powerful all on its own."

"The talisman…" She paused, remembering. "It is the reason I am here."

"You almost died saving him? You were willing to sacrifice your life for Morgan's?"

She closed her eyes and nodded. There was so much more to the fateful day she did not want to discuss. Telling him this part made it easier to avoid the rest.

He pulled her into his embrace. Her cheek pressed against his hard chest.

"I cannot know how you must've felt," he whispered into her hair. "I am sorry."

Tsura felt the anguish creep up her spine, the bleakness chased it, and she stiffened. She struggled with the realities of the day a year past—of what had really happened, of how she lost so much more than her husband. She bit the inside of her lip to keep from crying out. The regret of leaving, the anger at herself for not being able to do more—the impossibility of what her life meant now. She groaned low in her throat, the pain welling up from deep within her soul. She clenched her palms, squeezed her eyes closed, and willed the day to disappear from her mind.

She was too afraid of the emotions—of letting them see a sliver of her grief—to open the door to her soul. Her weakness would be her undoing, and she'd fall to her knees and sob. She hadn't cried. She hadn't thought of him, and she would not submit to it now. She stepped from Red Wolf's embrace, the hard lines, cold eyes, and stone features placed upon her face once more.

"I am not in need of your affection," she said and walked away.

# CHAPTER TWENTY

Red Wolf slid the blade down the length of the arrow he held. Thin shards of wood floated to the ground and landed in the small pile at his feet. He'd woken early, grabbed his bow and quiver, and left the village. The distance away from the Ama and Tsura was what he needed. While he hunted for game, his thoughts raced, trying to make some sense of the last few days.

His mind became relentless in its mission to understand why Tsura had not rescued her own brother. Why she'd been so adamant to reject the gift she held. He'd not spoken to her since their conversation about Morgan, but he could not help but think something was missing within the words she'd said. He stretched his arms outward to ease the discomfort in his chest. He could not fathom all she'd told him. His throat filled with misery at the thought of her loving someone so much she'd give her life for them. How had he been so blind not to see it? He'd been shocked to learn she'd tried to rescue him, and almost killed herself in the process.

He replayed their last moments together under the rowan tree, and he still could not see the betrayal she'd planned. Tsura had professed her love, said she'd wait for him. When she handed him the immortal flower, a token of her affection, his heart had swelled with joy for he had treasured her. Overcome with a profound desire to be with her, he'd taken Tsura in his arms and made love to her. The night was forever etched inside of his soul.

He inhaled as the knife he'd been using to carve his arrows sliced a piece of his skin from the thumb. Blood dripped from his hand onto the shavings below. He made no motion to wipe it, but instead stared at the wound lost in his memories.

"Do you remember when we slit our palms and became one?" Soaring Eagle asked, standing over him.

Red Wolf glanced up. He squinted against the bright sun.

"I do."

Soaring Eagle sat down beside him.

"The Itse Selu has ended. The other tribes prepare to leave."

"It was a success then?" Red Wolf welcomed the conversation taking him from his thoughts of Tsura.

"Yes, we are pleased. I see you were successful in your hunt this morning." He motioned toward the two prairie chickens, skinned and hanging upside down from the three poles Red Wolf had tied together.

"I was."

Soaring Eagle picked up one of Red Wolf's arrows. "Cousin, you cannot tell me you've forgotten how to skin these?"

He took the arrow from him and studied it. The stick looked like all of the others.

"What is wrong with it?"

"You are whittling them too thin." He pointed to the end where the arrowhead goes. "The top needs to be stronger. It is what strikes first."

Soaring Eagle was correct in his appraisal. Red Wolf had been thinking of Tsura and had not given his full attention to the task.

"We will use these for the young ones while they learn." He took the four arrows Red Wolf had carved and placed them to the side. "Do you wish to tell me what it is that bothers you?"

His cousin knew him well, and Red Wolf could no longer hide his feelings.

"I am sorry for my words earlier." He'd not spoken to Soaring Eagle since their argument, and the guilt of what he'd said turned his stomach. He needed to make it right.

"They have already been forgotten."

Red Wolf sighed. It was the way of the Cherokee. Family meant everything, and Soaring Eagle was all he had left.

"It is not from our argument earlier that you seem so forlorn. What burdens do you carry within your heart?"

He remained quiet. How could he confess all that consumed him when he did not even know what it was?

"What will you do when she returns home?"

"Go back to the *Falcon* and continue my life as a merchant."

"You do not sound so convincing." Soaring Eagle smiled. "Have you spoken to her since our return?"

He shook his head. He'd not even tried to confront Tsura. He didn't know what to say, and so he stayed away.

"She sits under the elm tree all day until nightfall. Beautiful Meadow tells me she speaks not one word."

"She is upset because she did not save her brother."

"How could she, but one woman against three men?"

Soaring Eagle did not know of Tsura's powers, and Red Wolf wasn't sure how he'd react when he told him. The Cherokee did not believe in magick. They saw it as a form of evil and stayed away from it, but he wanted his cousin to know the truth.

"She is different."

"Yes, I see this when I look at her."

"Not different in the way you see her, but…gifted if you will."

His cousin leaned in to listen.

"They call her a Chuvani…the highest of her people. She was born with unique abilities."

"What abilities do you speak of?"

"She has the gift to count a spell, move objects with just her mind, and heal a wound by laying her hands upon it."

"These gifts you speak of are from evil."

Red Wolf opened his mouth to defend Tsura, but Soaring Eagle held up his hand to stop him.

"I do not see such evil within her. I cannot say I believe the words you have told me, but I will promise to keep them between us."

"Thank you."

"If she can do all of these things why did she not aid in the rescue of her own brother?"

"She does not use the magick any more."

"Why not?"

"She could not restore life within her husband after Romulus stabbed him."

"It was as you thought…the Corsair killed her husband."

Red Wolf nodded.

"How is it she could not heal him?"

"He possessed too many mortal wounds." He went on to explain what Tsura had told him days before.

"She holds guilt within her heart," Soaring Eagle said, "but when I look at her I see more than a woman mourning the death of a husband she could not save."

"I see no such thing. It is clear how much she loved Morgan."

"How have you seen this? Did you live among them when they were together?"

"No, but the words she's spoken, the anger and sadness she portrays speak volumes to how much she cared for him."

"You do not see her as I do."

"What does that mean?"

"You look at her with resentment for choosing another, but did you ever wonder why she did?"

"Yes, she is a witch." Red Wolf couldn't keep the bitterness from his voice.

"You are both one in the same…despising the other for what you could not have."

"And what is that?"

Soaring Eagle picked up the arrows beside him and stood. He stared at Red Wolf. "Each other."

His cousin had lost his mind. Tsura held no affection for him. He didn't think she'd ever had. Their past together had been built on her lies and him believing every bloody word she said.

He leaned forward to grab another piece of wood. The skin on his side pulled, and he remembered the stitches there. Laying his knife on the ground he removed his shirt, and examined the flesh. The wound had healed days before, and the skin had begun to cover the thread. Damn it, this was going to hurt.

He picked up his knife, swiveled so that his body sat at an awkward angle, and brought the blade to the thread.

"Do you seek to impale yourself?" Raven asked.

The girl's beauty was striking, and Red Wolf had to remember she was Soaring Eagle's sister in-law.

"I attempt to remove the sutures from my side."

"Here, let me help you." She went to him, laid her hand over his, and took the knife.

Red Wolf didn't argue with her. He'd already left them in far too long. He gritted his teeth in anticipation. The pain of having them removed would surpass the lesion itself.

"How did you get this wound?"

The edge of the cold blade pressed into his side, and the skin pinched as the thread was pulled through.

"I was stabbed."

"By whom? The cut is very long." Her concern softened his stature, and he relaxed under her hand.

"A Corsair."

"The same one who hunts your friend?"

He inhaled sharply. The blade caught on a piece of thread that was attached to his skin. There had been nothing wrong with her questions, but Red Wolf did not want to discuss Tsura or Romulus with the girl.

"Have you chosen your mate?" he asked, moving their conversation in another direction and away from Tsura.

"I have."

"In which tribe does he reside?"

Another pinch from the knife sent a jolt of pain up his side, and he leaned away from her.

"You are bleeding," she said and used the hem of her dress to wipe his ribs.

"There is no need to—"

She laid her hand upon his shoulder, sliding it down his back in a zigzag motion.

"It is my pleasure."

He sensed the change in her, and his body tensed.

"How many are left?" he asked.

"Two."

He nodded and waited as the two were pulled from his flesh. He was about to move away from her when she began lathering something over his skin.

"What is it you are doing?"

"It is the wax from a bee. I will place it over your wound to heal."

Raven's hands moved along the scar in an up and down motion. It wasn't until she pushed outward to run her palms along the front of his chest that he knew she desired more from him. He shifted to pull away from her, but her fingers dug into his flesh, and she tugged him back toward her.

He turned abruptly to tell her to cease and was met with her lips upon his. For a moment he did not know what to do as Raven's mouth devoured his. He was wanted and hadn't felt that way in a very long time. He allowed himself to linger, to taste her, to be needed, before thoughts of Soaring Eagle, of Tsura entered his mind, and he pulled away from her.

She gazed up at him with stars in her eyes, and he felt terrible. He'd not shared those feelings for her, and he'd used the opportunity to nourish his tattered soul. The girl hadn't deserved to be treated with such disregard, and he didn't know how to convey that he'd used her.

He'd been ruined by love, and the very thought of caring for another sent his stomach into a roll. He opened his mouth to tell the girl to set her sights on someone else, but before he could speak it, she smiled and walked away.

He watched as Raven passed Tsura, motionless by the woodpile in front of his lodge. She turned away, and he glimpsed sorrow upon her face. When her eyes finally met his, she'd hardened her features and stared right through him.

Should he explain? Tell her it meant nothing? Did he offer her an apology? The longer he stared at Tsura the more he detested her. He owed her nothing. No explanation, no apology. She loathed him, and he wasn't overly fond of her either. They were both repelled from the other, and he could do whatever he damned well pleased. She had no claim to him...but why did it feel like she did?

He stood taller, moved his chest outward, and smirked at her. He'd not feel guilt.

"What is it you need?" he barked.


Tsura thought Red Wolf appeared sorry for what he'd done, but soon the remorse vanished to be replaced with a sly smile and devious eyes. When she'd left her spot by the elm tree, she'd made her way through the Ama deep in thought. She wanted to ask Red Wolf to take her to the place where her birth mother, Vadoma, was buried.

She'd never felt any sort of connection with the woman, never meeting her, only being told of the awful things she'd done and why. Her mother, Pril, confided Vadoma had been in love with Hiram Monroe, and when he did not return, her heart grew black. The Chuvani despised anyone of happiness and of love. Tsura recognized the sadness, the hurt, and the betrayal Vadoma must've felt. She'd experienced the very same when Red Wolf had not returned.

She noticed him now, shirtless, arms crossed over his chest, the look of indignation upon his dark features. She did not retreat, but instead lifted her skirt and stepped toward him. She'd been thankful Beautiful Meadow had brought her washed clothes the night she'd returned to the Ama. She felt more like herself within the heavy skirt and buttoned to the neck blouse. The pendant lay against her chest, a reminder of what she wished to be left behind.

"You disgust me," she said in low even tones.

"Your feelings are not of my concern."

"Do you not take into consideration the young maiden's thoughts?"

"What of them?"

"It is clear she holds affection for you."

"What I do with Raven is none of your concern. Now take your envy somewhere else."

"Envy! You think me jealous?"

He shrugged.

"I can assure you I am not."

"Your actions belie you."

"There is nothing between us."

"And there never will be."

His words stabbed into the only part of her heart she'd left intact to hold the memories. Damn him and his arrogance.

"You're a bloody fool," she spat. "I have more pride than to be with the likes of you."

"Oh yes, your pride." He leaned closer. "The very reason you did not marry me. Your blasted damn vanity."

She'd not tell him the truth. He'd assumed so much already, thought the worst of her. She added a brisket to the already burning flame that raged between them.

"That was not pride, you ass. It was wits."

"Wits you say!" He laughed. "A bloody whoremonger seeking what the title could offer you." He stepped into her space, close enough she could taste the hatred as it dripped from every word he spewed at her. "You sought to ruin me. You craved the title, the riches—the luxury of it all."

"I owe you no explanation. Get out of my way."

"Yes, damn it, you do."

She moved to step around him, unable to take his assault on her any longer.

He refused to let her pass.

"Move at once."

"I am not one of your servants. I will not bow to your commands." He pressed his face closer. "Tell me, was it your plan all along to deceive me?"

She brought forth the past, and the visions knocked the wind from her lungs. He'd not returned, left her alone without word, without care, her soul torn. She narrowed her eyes, and bitterness lay upon her tongue.

"You were not worthy." She growled the words wanting to hurt him, to cut his heart in two like he'd done to her.

He stepped away from her, his lip curled, and then spat into her face.

Rage pulsed through her veins and beat into her fingertips, the need there, wanting to strike out at him. She clenched her jaw, sweat beaded on her forehead, and she turned from him.

"You filthy witch. I pray no mercy is ever bestowed upon your blackened soul," Red Wolf called after her.

She shut him out, quieted her mind to his taunts as he continued to yell at her while she walked away. She'd given him what he thought he knew, told him she cared for Morgan. When in truth Red Wolf had been the only man she'd ever loved.

He had no knowledge of the life she'd led with her husband. He was not aware of the hurtful words he'd spewed, the women he'd bring into their home to parade in front of her, the gambling, the drinking, the fits of rage. Morgan cared for her no more than he'd cared for a dog.

She shivered. What had happened those years ago? Why had Red Wolf not returned? For a time she thought a terrible storm had struck the *Falcon*, but when she'd been told he'd docked and did not come to see her, did not come home, she was left wondering what she'd done wrong to make him not love her any longer.

She married Morgan out of desperation and a yearning to fill the emptiness Red Wolf had left inside of her soul. She thought of what she'd received instead, and her heart grew cold once more. Blast Red Wolf for the bastard he was, but more importantly for not being by her side when she needed him the most. She held her hands into tight fists. The tears hovered within her dark lashes. She'd not submit to the heartache. With the swipe of her hand, she wiped the wetness from her eyes.

Anger was her only defense against the things she could not change. It was simpler to place her features into hard lines, draw her mouth down into a permanent frown, and let resentment cast from her eyes.

She needed distance from him, and all of the emotions he stirred within her. She spotted the elm tree—it'd been her refuge away from the Ama, and Red Wolf. She would go there. She kicked her legs out, quickening her pace. The air flew from her lungs, and she stammered to right her footing. Star Dancer's arms wrapped around Tsura's legs. She tried to keep her balance, lest falling over at the girl's affectionate attack.

"Tsisquaya, look," the girl squealed. She pulled on the piece of curly hair Tsura had given to her, tied with leather twine and placed into her own hair. "I have curls just like you."

"Yes, I see that you do," she said slowly, trying to remain indifferent to the child and not show her previous anger at Red Wolf.

"Etsi says I can keep it as long as I like."

Tsura glanced at Beautiful Meadow who walked toward them. Soaring Eagle's wife smiled down at her daughter and a pang entered Tsura's heart.

She rubbed her palms together.

"Come, we are going to the garden to pick vegetables," Beautiful Meadow said.

She hesitated, but Star Dancer placed her small hand into Tsura's and pulled her along. With no more fight left within her, she followed the child.

The Ama garden was not the small patch in the ground she'd had back in Bristol. It spanned the length of the tribe's land. Tall stalks waved in the warm breeze, and the sweet smell of corn filled her nostrils.

"Is this all corn?" she asked.

"It is the home of the three sisters," Beautiful Meadow answered. "Corn, squash, and beans."

"There is nothing else, just the three?"

"There is no need for more. The Ama will not go hungry when the sisters are among them."

"I do not understand."

"The three—corn, squash, and beans—thrive when grown together. One cannot be without the other. We have never strayed from this knowledge and in turn the sisters have never failed us."

"What sort of things do you make with only the three vegetables?"

"The Ama women have learned to use all three within their cooking."

"I cannot fathom how."

"There is much for you to learn." Beautiful Meadow picked up two woven baskets and handed one to Tsura. "Fill yours with the beans," she said and pointed to the heavy beanstalks to their left.

The Ama children played in the distance throwing long sticks into the ground. Their laughter carried across the field, and soon Star Dancer was off running toward them.

"What is it they play?" Tsura asked.

"It is chunkee. The children roll a round rock, and when it stops they throw their spear trying to place it as near to the stone as possible."

She nodded.

"This is great fun for them and helps with their skills as they become warriors."

"Yes, but the girls participate too?"

Beautiful Meadow laughed, the sound light and airy.

"The Cherokee women are taught all ways."

Tsura moved her basket to the right side resting it upon her hip. She had seen many examples of what Beautiful Meadow had said. The women knew how to do most anything the men did along with cooking, cleaning, and sewing. She pulled a bean and dropped it into the basket.

The air was warm, and she unbuttoned the top of her blouse. She watched the other women talk happily with each other while working, and for the first time Tsura missed the friendships she'd left behind in Bristol. She'd been inconsolable after the fire and turned away everyone who came to call. Soon the doorknocker ceased, as did all the visitors, and she was left alone.

She couldn't stop her eyes from straying to Red Wolf's lodge. Why did he hate her so? He'd treated her as if she'd done something terrible to him. She searched her mind, going back to the day he did not return. Sitting on the settee she anxiously waited for Red Wolf to walk through the door. She had missed him terribly the two months he'd been away at sea and had counted the days until his return.

Morgan Harris had come to call several times while Red Wolf was gone. She'd asked Monty the groundskeeper to deliver a note to him of her refusal and love for another. Tsura inhaled. She hadn't known then how her life would turn out. Now she remained alone, and worse yet, alive. She pulled her spine straight, tipped her chin, and resumed her stature.

# Chapter Twenty-One

Tsura crushed the corn into the stone and mortar until the dried kernels had turned to powder. She watched as Beautiful Meadow took a bowl of ground cornmeal, added water, and worked it into dough. She then went to the skillet sitting next to the hearth and dribbled the fat from the deer meat she'd fried earlier into the dough.

"This adds flavor to the bread," the woman said as she kneaded the dough then placed it back into the skillet to rise.

Beautiful Meadow had called upon her early this morning before she'd had a chance to take up her usual spot at the elm tree. The other woman gave Tsura no choice, insisting she come and learn the ways of the Ama. She'd been planning her escape since her argument with Red Wolf days before. There had been no reason for her to remain among the tribe, now that Romulus' men had been killed. She was desperate to flee the memories Red Wolf's presence caused and be rid of anything related to the past.

The hot afternoon sun beat down upon them while they worked at a table in the yard. She was thankful for the leather twine Beautiful Meadow had given to her so she could tie her hair back. The long locks were thick and heavy. They held the heat from the sun and caused her neck and back to perspire.

"Have you made selu tuya, corn, and beans before?" Beautiful Meadow asked, placing a large bowl onto the counter.

She shook her head and moved the bowl of ground corn to the side.

"You will skin the cobs of four corns, and I will do the beans. Place your corn into there." She pointed to a black metal pot in front of them.

Tsura reached into the basket below the table to pull out four cobs. She removed the husks, placing them to the side to be dried and used for the making of mats, baskets, and dolls. She took the knife Beautiful Meadow had given to her and skinned the corn into the pot.

She scanned the village as she worked alongside Beautiful Meadow. She was beginning to feel at ease here among the Ama. Red Wolf had kept a close eye on her and when he was not around, two young braves seemed to always be within close distance. She still desired to leave, to live a life alone far away from anyone, but she did not wish to do so today.

A group of men entered the village and the Ama greeted them with wide smiles. The three men appeared different, yet the same. White shirts, adorned with beaded necklaces, and black pants. The man standing in the middle wore his dark hair long tied at the nape of his neck. His wrists were covered in bracelets of all kinds, some beaded leather, and some metal. The men stood beside their wagon while the Ama brought forth mats, baskets, corn, and other vegetables from their gardens.

"Tsiguisi," Beautiful Meadow said.

Tsura peered at her.

"Gypsies."

She looked back at the men.

"From where?"

"From the hills."

"What do they come here for?"

"They bring honey, bees wax, and other herbs we do not have here. We trade."

Tsura wondered if these were the very gypsies that wished her dead. She stopped skinning the corn to stare at them.

"What clan do these gypsies come from?"

"The Renoldi."

Tsura dropped the knife she'd been holding and picked it up quickly so Beautiful Meadow didn't notice. The Renoldi had been the very clan that betrayed her mother, Pril, and sought to hand her over to the Monroes to be killed. She chewed on her bottom lip and ran the blade slowly along the corn. She was curious if they sought her still. Had the time passed lessened the anger within the clan? Was her aunt Magda still alive? She peeked at the gypsies again. A part of her wanted to know where she came from while the other warned her of the dangers such knowledge could bring.

"You know of this clan?" Beautiful Meadow asked.

She shook her head, wanting to keep knowledge of the Renoldi to herself.

"It is not the one you came from?"

"No. I do not think the clan I came from exists any longer."

"How do you know of such a thing?"

She shrugged. Beautiful Meadow did not need to know Tsura had been the reason her clan was ripped apart. Her uncle Galius deceived the Peddlers while hiding the Branded One among them. He'd killed his own brother and niece for the power of the pendant.

"Come, let us go and see what they've brought." Beautiful Meadow put the bean she'd been holding back into the bowl and grabbed Tsura's hand.

She dug her heels into the ground reluctant to go, but it didn't seem to stop Beautiful Meadow from pulling her along behind her.

Tsura spotted Raven. The girl rested a basket upon her hip and chatted with one of the Renoldi. She pulled a rolled mat from the basket and handed it to the man, who gave her two jars in return.

She did not wish to see the other woman, knowing she shared a kiss with Red Wolf and goodness knows what else since then. Tsura pulled on Beautiful Meadow's arm and the woman turned toward her. She opened her mouth to tell her a lie, a reason she could not go, but no words would form.

Beautiful Meadow gave her a knowing smile, and Tsura knew the other woman thought it was from her reluctance to be around anyone. Soaring Eagle's wife smiled and gave her hand a light squeeze before releasing it to walk away.

Tsura headed in the direction of the elm tree passing by Star Dancer and Fawn as they played in the yard. She watched the girls as they danced around, holding their corn dolls to their chests while singing in Cherokee.

"They sing about love."

Red Wolf stood beside her. There was a hint of malice in his words, and she braced herself for whatever it was he wanted.

"Do you still believe in such things?" he asked.

"I believe in nothing." What she said was the truth. She'd never find love. Her heart was closed off to it.

"You were not at the elm tree."

"I was helping Beautiful Meadow with her chores." She clasped her hands tightly together.

"Do you still wish to leave?"

She brought her eyes to his, and her breath caught in her throat. He'd changed from his white shirt and pants into a deerskin breechcloth and nothing else. His bronzed chest glistened in the sunlight. His long hair fell down to the middle of his chest, the red feather still tied to the side.

"I do."

"I will return you to Jamestown and await with you until Micah's ship ports."

"What of Romulus?"

His dark eyes flashed, and she braced herself for his next words, knowing they would be harsh.

"I thought you feared not the Corsair?"

"I do not, but I have asked this of you several times and you've resisted. Why have you changed your mind now?"

"I will find Romulus after you've left."

"I see."

His face was rigid—unmoving.

"Have your things ready by morning. We leave at dawn."

He did not wait for her to answer before he walked away.

She watched him go, unsure of what to do. The news was welcome, but why was she not pleased? Tsura searched the village, embracing the Ama for the first time. She let her shoulders fall. Soon she'd be back in Bristol...alone, no one to bother her. Is that not what she'd wanted all along?


Red Wolf ignored the pain in his chest. He'd been desperate to put Tsura out of his mind. The words she'd said had kept him awake, and he'd not slept in days. His body ached from the lashing of her admission. His mind spun from the realization of what he meant to her. He'd finally known the truth. It was as he'd imagined. She'd desired the name, the money...the extravagant home.

He flexed his jaw. He could give her none of those things. All he'd ever had to offer had been his love, but that was not enough. She'd wanted more—needed more—and he could not change it.

He had to be rid of her, to erase the memory of her lips upon his, the way her hand fit within his own. Distance would allow his heart to mend. As it was before, the time away from her would become easier.

Red Wolf stopped at his lodge to grab his bow and arrows. He eyed the tomahawk Soaring Eagle had given to him laying next to the door. He stalked toward it and gripped the leather handle. The urge to throw it overcame him. He squeezed the weapon until his knuckles turned white. Humiliation poured over him, soaking his soul...he was not worthy.

# CHAPTER TWENTY-TWO

Tsura left Red Wolf's lodge and headed toward the river. She'd not eaten the evening meal with the others, instead deciding to take some time to wash up before she left for the long trek to Jamestown in the morning.

She saw no use in telling Red Wolf where she'd gone. The river could be seen from his lodge. All he'd need to do was look out across the grass and see her. She'd taken her small reticule. Tucked inside was her rose soap and a brush. Tsura anticipated the cool water as it ran through her dull and dirty hair, cleansing her of the grime she'd worn for the past week. She'd traveled to the river once before during her time with the Ama for a quick scrub down, but under Red Wolf's scrutiny she'd not been able to linger.

"Where do you go?" Star Dancer asked, skipping alongside her.

"To the river." She glanced down at the girl and the doll clutched within her arms. The long piece of curly hair fastened within her own swayed back and forth as she pranced beside her.

There was no sense in telling the child to go home. Star Dancer was a determined soul, and she'd follow whether Tsura wanted her to or not.

They reached the bank of the river. The water rushed by in white-capped waves and swirls. Trees grew along the edges in patchy clumps to offer shade from the sun. The river ran down from the mountains across the Ama land to twist around the hills and disappear. Tsura placed her bag down to rest against the trunk of a Chestnut tree. She sat down to unlace her moccasins and slid them from her feet. Star Dancer did the same, mimicking everything Tsura did.

She removed her skirt and blouse, leaving only her petticoat. The pendant lay upon her chest, a reminder of who she was, and why Tsura's life had not been like that of her peers. The suns rays reflected off of the ruby and cast translucent colors to dance before them.

"Your necklace is pretty. Where did you get it?" Star Dancer asked.

"From my mother." Tsura removed the pendant, holding it within her hand.

"Can I see it?"

"No." She didn't want to explain the power Star Dancer would feel when she held the ruby in her hand. The girl would know it was special.

"I am going to place it in here for safe keeping while we wash up." She dropped the necklace into the foot of her moccasin.

"Will you let me see it when we are done?"

She didn't answer and hoped the child would forget the necklace after they washed in the river.

Tsura reached for her rose soap and waded into the water. The cool river eased her heat-exhausted muscles. Careful not to go too far from the water's edge, with Star Dancer right beside her, Tsura knelt and immersed her whole body. Her skin became covered in tiny bumps, and she shivered.

Soap in hand, she dunked her head. A splash beside her told Tsura Star Dancer did the same. She emerged from the water and rubbed the soap into her hair. She inhaled the scent of the rose perfume and released the tension in her shoulders and neck. Eyes closed, she concentrated on the sounds around her. The river splashed and gurgled, and birds chirped somewhere behind her.

She no longer heard the girl.

She opened her eyes and looked to the left, then right. The water splashed around her as she spun. Star Dancer was not there. The soap from Tsura's hair ran down her forehead and into her eyes. The lather stung, and she rubbed it away with water.

"Star Dancer?" she called.

There was no answer.

Tsura scanned the land. She gasped when she saw the girl's moccasins still on the ground beside her own.

"Oh, dear God."

She spun around and water sprayed her face, but she ignored it and searched the river. There! Something bobbed in the middle of the stream. She took a step, and as the water hurried past her legs, she fought to keep her balance. A black head went under the water and came back up again. It was Star Dancer, and she was being swept away! Panic set her heart to racing, and fear coated her throat. Tsura dived into the river, swimming toward the girl.

The waves smashed into her, and she let the current push her toward Star Dancer. Her mouth filled with water and she coughed, gasping for air. She was desperate to reach the child. Her arms sliced through the rapids frantically. Star Dancer was within a foot of her now. She reached out her hand, grabbing the girl's arm and pulled, but Star Dancer slipped from her grasp. Tsura pressed harder, kicked stronger, and this time when her hand reached out to grip the girl, she did not let go.

She yanked the girl to rest her head on Tsura's shoulder. The current was strong. Her strength rapidly dissolved as the river pushed against her. She struggled against the rapids while trying to keep the girl's face above the water.

Thank goodness she didn't have her skirt on—the heavy material would pull them both under. Tsura kicked her legs wildly while swimming to the water's edge. Her body was tired and her muscles throbbed. She was sure her lungs would burst. She set her jaw. Star Dancer would not die. She'd get her to shore.

Determined to rescue the child, Tsura concentrated on the trees in the distance and swam toward them. She sighed when her feet touched the rocky bottom of the river and she was able to walk with the child in her arms to land. Her legs felt weighted. She stumbled as she dragged her tired body to the grass. She tripped on the edge and fell forward into the sand and onto her knees. The child still in her arms, she gently laid Star Dancer down. The girl's small lips had turned blue, and Tsura realized she was not breathing.

"No. No. No." She scurried closer to sit beside the girl, and gripping the child's shoulders she shook her. Tsura positioned Star Dancer between her legs and using the palm of her hand pounded on the girl's back. Water sputtered out of Star Dancer's mouth and the girl took a shallow breath, but did not open her eyes or move.

Tsura continued her onslaught on the girl's back. Each time small amounts of water exited her mouth, but Star Dancer did not improve. Sweat trickled down Tsura's temples as she fought the need to lay her hands upon the little girl and heal her.

She shook her head. The gift had not revived him, the magick had not worked, the power within her was useless, a waste. Tsura reached for the child again, intent on saving her another way, when she was yanked backward. Rough hands wrenched her up, and cold metal dug into her throat.

She froze, her eyes never leaving Star Dancer as she lay on the ground before her.

"I have found you at last," Romulus whispered into her hair. The Corsair reeked of sweat, his clothes stale and soiled.

She spotted his bandaged hand, wrapped in fabric he'd torn from his shirt. Red Wolf's arrow had punctured him there. Judging by the way the bandage smelled the wound was infected. She wriggled against his hold. The child's breaths were still slow, and her lips remained tinged a light blue.

"Release me. The girl needs my help."

Romulus peered over Tsura to look at the child.

"The girl is none of my concern. I've come for the pendant."

She was thankful they'd not come ashore where her clothes were for surely he'd have found the pendant tucked in her moccasins. She tried to push him from her, but his hold on her tightened.

"There is no pendant, you fool. Now let me go so I can aid the child."

He yanked her closer toward him, and growled, "I know the ruby exists, and Red Wolf will trade it for your life."

"Red Wolf cares not for me. He will not trade a saucer for my safety."

"You speak lies." He shook her again. "I have seen the ruby, and I will get it."

Tsura's fingers ached as the need arose within her. She had to help Star Dancer. If Romulus took her, she'd not be able to do so. She searched the area. They'd gone further down the river than she'd thought. The Ama village could not be seen from where they stood.

"You will have to kill me. I will not leave the child."

He shrugged.

"I will kill the child first."

Her breath caught in her throat. He wouldn't. She was innocent, had done nothing wrong.

Romulus moved the gun he held from her throat and aimed it at Star Dancer. She saw the spark from the pistol as he cocked it. Tsura drove her elbow into the Corsair's stomach, his hold on her loosened, and she lunged for the girl. The gun went off. She cried out. A searing pain erupted in her leg. She lay over the child—the lead ball had missed Star Dancer and struck Tsura instead.

Romulus heaved her up. The pain in her ankle surged upward to her thigh, and she crumpled to the ground.

"Get up," he screamed.

Tsura refused to do as he said. She'd die before he'd take her anywhere. This had been what she'd wanted for the past year, someone to end her miserable existence. But as she sat upon the ground, Star Dancer beside her, she realized today could not be the day. The girl needed her help. She had to get the child to the Ama—to Beautiful Meadow and Soaring Eagle.

Blast Romulus. He could go to hell. She'd not leave Star Dancer. The Corsair pulled on her again, and she threw her arm into him, slapping the side of his head. Rage pulsed in his dark eyes, and he scowled at her.

She brought her arm up to block the pistol as it came down upon her, but he was stronger and the metal crushed against her cheek to jar her vision. Tsura's face throbbed, she felt the skin swell. She fought back, digging her nails into his flesh. Two more blows to the face had her seeing double, and she reached for something to anchor herself on. Romulus grabbed her hair, tipped her head back, and cuffed her with the back of his hand.

Tsura blinked and stretched her arms toward Star Dancer before she fell forward.

Red Wolf heard the sound of a pistol in the distance. He stood, letting the deer hide slide from his legs. After their evening meal, White Owl had asked him to sit at his lodge and help him skin the two deer he'd killed that morning. Red Wolf obliged, knowing Tsura was at the river with Star Dancer.

"The shot comes from the east," White Owl said.

"The river." Red Wolf hurried to the edge of the Ama village to where he'd last seen Tsura and Star Dancer. They were not there. He searched the surrounding land but it was barren of the two. He raced toward the river desperate to know they were not harmed. The breechcloth flapped against his thighs, while his moccasin covered feet pelted the ground as he sprinted toward the walnut tree.

Their moccasins sat beside each other, Tsura's bag and clothes lay neatly folded on the ground, but neither woman nor child was there.

"Cousin, where is my daughter?" Soaring Eagle asked as he came to stand beside him.

Red Wolf sensed something was wrong, but did not want to alarm his cousin until he knew for sure.

"The pistol fired from this direction, but I do not see Tsura or Star Dancer," he said.

A small crowd of Ama had gathered. He saw the worry within Beautiful Meadow's brown eyes. Raven stood beside her and offered support.

"Their tracks lead into the water," White Owl said, pointing to the footprints in the grass.

"I will carry the woman's belongings," Raven said.

He didn't object, his concern for Tsura and Star Dancer more important.

"Let us go further upstream to see if they are there," Soaring Eagle said. Not waiting for them to follow, he took his wife's hand and together they walked along the water's edge.

The hairs on his neck stood. Tsura had no need to stray. She knew they were leaving tomorrow. He sensed danger. The water rolled, crashing into waves as the river ran further east. He searched the ground for signs they'd walked onto shore, but there was nothing. They strode in a line of ten Ama, Raven beside him as she carried Tsura's moccasins and clothes.

"I do hope they are not hurt," she said to him.

He wondered if the girl really meant the words she'd spoken. It'd been clear she did not care for Tsura in the way she'd dismissed her whenever they were near one another. When Raven cornered him at his lodge yesterday, he'd had to explain to her that he did not hold any feelings for her. With no desire to hurt the young maiden, he'd tried his best to say the words as sincerely as he could. She'd insisted that he must feel something for her...after all they'd shared a kiss. He winced remembering the moment, a lack of judgment on his part. When he reminded her it was forbidden among the Cherokee to marry within their own tribe, she'd said it did not matter she would gladly leave the Ama and sail with him on the Falcon. There had been no more he could say to convince Raven there was nothing between them.

A woman's cry came from the front of the line. He pushed his way through the Ama to see what it was. He stopped short when he saw Star Dancer laying on the ground, pale, her skin a light shade of blue, and scarcely breathing. Her black hair and dress were wet. He looked for Tsura, afraid of what he might find, but she was not there.

He went to Soaring Eagle, who knelt on the ground beside his wife. Beautiful Meadow gently laid her head to Star Dancer's chest. He saw the tears fall from her eyes, and his heart broke for the woman whose child was very sick.

"She does not go into the water. We have told her the river is too strong," Soaring Eagle said solemnly.

He laid his hand on the bare shoulder of his cousin.

"There is blood here, and footprints," White Owl said. He crouched beside the mess of footprints.

To the left of where the girl lie Red Wolf could see Tsura's bare foot imprinted into the sand. Beside the print was blood, a lot of blood. The dirt was disturbed, a sign she'd struggled with someone. He walked the perimeter seeing more blood. The grass was flattened as if someone were dragged along the ground. Tsura. She was in danger, and he knew by the way the blood smeared the grass it had been her who was shot. His stomach turned. He knelt by a pine tree to pick up a small piece of hair from a rope. A horse had been tethered here. He stood and spotted the note stuck to the tree. *Bring the ruby, or she dies.*

Romulus wanted the pendant. The one Tsura wore upon her neck. Red Wolf was aware of the powers the gem held. He had been told of the lineage to the Chuvani and what would happen if it was placed into evil hands. Did Tsura not wear it upon her now? He'd never seen her without it. She must've hid it or placed it back in his lodge knowing she was going to the river. He clenched his jaw, every muscle in his body tightened. He'd not release the pendant to the Corsair…but he would kill the bastard for what he'd done to Tsura.

He went back to Soaring Eagle.

The chief lifted his daughter from the ground to cradle her in his arms.

"How is she?" he asked.

"She is not well. Beautiful Meadow can hear the water gurgle inside of her."

"Romulus has done this." He crumpled the note in his fist, not wanting to show it to his cousin.

"He drowned my daughter?" Soaring Eagle's face grew dark.

"I do not know, but he shot Tsura and has taken her."

"We will kill this Corsair."

Red Wolf shook his head.

"No, you will take Star Dancer back to the village to be cared for. I will find Romulus."

Soaring Eagle placed his daughter into Beautiful Meadow's arms and walked Red Wolf away from them.

"Cousin, do you remember when we spoke of your woman…and her gifts?" he asked.

Red Wolf stiffened. He knew what Soaring Eagle wanted, but he did not know if Tsura would comply with his wishes.

"Star Dancer will live. The shaman can give her some medicine to clear her of the water," he said.

"No, she is dying."

"Surely, the—"

Soaring Eagle held up his hand.

"I have seen this before. There will be nothing the shaman can do for her. Too much water has been inhaled."

"You cannot give up."

"Bring your woman back. If what you say is true, she can help my daughter."

"Cousin, I—"

"Do this one thing, and I will never ask anything of you again."

The sheer depth of Soaring Eagle's pain showed in the two tears he let fall from his eyes. Red Wolf heard the plea, the desperation in his words, and he could not refuse.

# CHAPTER TWENTY-THREE

The pain in Tsura's ankle pulsed and vibrated into the bone. The slug had slashed her skin, leaving a gash an inch wide. The blood had slowed and was no longer flowing from the wound as it did before. The injury needed to be wrapped and stitched, but it was the least of her worries. She had to break free of the bonds holding her hands behind her back. Her head pounded, the ache resonating from her neck to the temples. The twine pulled tight when she moved, straining her shoulders as they were yanked further behind her.

Romulus had taken her to a wide valley in the belly of the hills. They were out in the open except for the two oak trees she sat near. Darkness shadowed the land, but she could smell the lilacs that grew close by. The scent calmed her nerves, and she was able to purge her mind of the fogginess. She watched the Corsair snap a branch into small pieces and throw them onto the fire. The wood crackled and hissed as the flames grew larger, lighting the area for a moment.

Tsura scanned the meager camp looking for some way to escape. She knew the magick could aid her in this exploit, but set her jaw against it. What if the memories came back? How was she to handle the images when they surfaced? She'd surly die from the pain of it all.

She thought of the child, Star Dancer—a whole life to live awaited her. She was young, free, and full of love, but what if she perished? What if no one had found her? Tsura's chest ached at the thought. Did she suffer alone at this very moment? She swallowed the worry as it crept up her throat and blinked back the tears that hovered within her lashes.

The petticoat she wore offered no warmth from the cool evening air, and she scooted closer to the fire.

Romulus' head shot up, and his black eyes scowled.

"Tell me, Baroness, where did you get the pendant?" he asked as he chewed on a piece of dried meat. He sat close to the fire without his bottom touching the ground.

"The necklace does not exist," she said.

"Ah, but it does." He bent closer the firelight cast his face in long shadows. "I have seen it."

"How do you know it was the pendant providing me the power and that it was not from my own will?"

He picked at his teeth with his fingernail.

"Simple. You would've saved your brother."

She bent forward, curving her back to ease the pain in her ribs from his words. How she wished there had been another way to rescue James. When she thought of her brother, she was washed in guilt. Her legs trembled as the terrible night came back to haunt her.

"You think me daft, but I've heard the tales of the magickal pendant. Whoever beholds the ruby is granted great powers."

"Who has told you of such things?" She kept him busy while she worked the rope around her wrists.

"It was told to me when I was a lad."

"By whom?"

"My father."

"Your father told you a tall tale, and you were naive enough to believe him."

The Corsair's face skewed, his lips pulled tight against his teeth, and his inexpressive eyes stared right through her.

She refused to be intimidated and glared back at him.

"You do not remember do you?" he asked.

"I do not know what you speak of."

"Tsura the great Chuvani, daughter of Vadoma, the evil enchantress."

She held back the gasp wanting to expel from her lips, and asked, "If you knew who I was why were you not afraid of my powers?"

He shrugged.

"You do not use them."

"How could you know?" she whispered more to herself than him.

"I have followed you until two months ago when you disappeared with Micah."

"But why?"

"For the pendant of course."

She stared at him, examining his features. The beard he wore covered his cheeks and chin, but beneath the hair upon his face lay familiarity. She wondered why she had not seen it before. The resemblance was faint, the dark hair and the round eyes, but she was thrown back to a memory of when she was a child living among the peddlers. It could not be? She pulled at the recesses of her mind and within her vision she saw him, a young boy.

"Radu?"

His beard spread with a wide smile, and he held out his arms. "It is me."

Radu had been one of the Peddlers. She played with him and his sister. He was a kind boy with a giving nature. What had happened?

"Why?" she asked, searching his face for the boy she remembered, but seeing only a man consumed with greed.

"I am a Corsair. I steal, plunder, and take what I want. I did not have this luxury living among the clan, so when I was old enough I set out to make my own destiny."

The Peddlers raised their children to be kind, loyal, and above all things humble. They lived off of the land and desired no riches. It was clear Radu did not see it this way.

"You searched for me all this time?"

"I did not. It was pure luck I met the Baron that night in the gaming hall."

Tsura straightened at the mention of her husband.

"He'd won all of his bets, but it was me who came out the victor."

"What do you mean? He lost. Gambled away his money. He did not pay you. It is why you came. Why you burned my home…killed him…killed…" She couldn't finish. Her breath came in quick puffs. Radu's face grew blurry. She pressed her bottom into the ground to steady herself.

He threw his head back and laughed. The sound echoed off of the hills around them.

"He spoke of the ruby his wife wore. Of how he should bring it to the next game to give him more leverage."

"That is why you were there?" she whispered.

"I must admit I was not sure the ruby was the same one I'd been told of until you came to the dock that night."

"Then why did you come?"

"I am a Corsair, I wanted the jewel for its value and nothing else, but I discovered so much more."

"You killed him for the pendant?" Fury boiled inside of her and erupted from her lips as she yelled, "You burned him for the ruby?"

"I stabbed him when he could not find the gem."

"Why could you not have left him? Why did you burn my home?" Her body grew warm, and tiny drops of sweat covered her skin.

"Why not?"

"He was there. He was in his room when you set my home on fire."

He shrugged.

"You bastard." The rope around her wrists burned as her skin heated with rage. Tsura fought the urge to vomit, to lose control and weep. He had known all along she was the Chuvani, and yet he still killed her brother. He watched as she withheld the magick he knew she claimed. He'd duped her. Played her for the fool she was.

"If you knew I did not use my magick why did you not come and take the pendant from me then?"

"Your mother."

Pril had been by her side afterward, and then Micah. Radu had known her mother held gifts of her own, and he could not fight them.

"I waited. Time was all I needed. As the days passed I witnessed your care for life diminish and knew once Pril left your side, I could strike."

"You murdered him for the necklace, the damn talisman," she muttered to herself, unable to comprehend all she'd been told.

"And soon I will have it when Red Wolf comes for you."

He'd taken the one person she'd lived for—stolen a piece of her soul. Ripped from her any chance at happiness. The bastard had trampled her dreams, murdered her existence.

She shook her head from side to side. Her life had been altered once more—driven by greed, lust, and a need for the power the pendant held. She was cursed. The necklace a piece of her life she'd been told to always cherish, to protect above all things, and yet, it had been because of the legacy she had lost him.

The curls along her face were doused in sweat. Tsura's body heated beyond her own control. The bonds broke behind her, and she lunged her hand toward Radu. She could not stop the need as it arose within her. The magick, too strong, overtook her weakness, and she lashed out striking him with such power he flew from where he sat to land ten feet away.

She stood. Fire shot from her eyes as she forced him to take the dagger from his own sheath. Radu tried to fight against the magick, but he was no match for the power she held. She closed her eyes and saw one tiny charred hand placed within her own. Radu had killed him. Her eyelids flew open, the green depths blazed. Her hair blew from her face.

"Cast thy knife of ye own will, unto thy heart to strike and kill!" she shrieked.

"No!" Radu drove the dagger into his heart. His mouth moved and blood-tinged saliva formed at the corners of his lips. He stepped toward her, arms stretched out, before he fell over dead.


Red Wolf dismounted, leaving the reins to hang from Caesar so he could graze upon the grass. The poor animal must be exhausted. When he wasn't checking the ground for tracks, he pushed Caesar to the limit. His worry for Tsura had him thinking of one thing…her safety.

He assessed the situation. She sat before the fire clothed in a chemise, her bare arms and legs exposed. The gash in her ankle where she'd been shot dripped bright red blood. Hair disheveled, she stared at the flames. He went to inspect Romulus. The Corsair lay face down, and Red Wolf used the toe of his moccasin to roll him over. A dagger was plunged in his chest. The evil merchant was dead, but by whose hand? He glanced at Tsura, who rocked back and forth, eyes locked in a daze. No one else was around, was it possible she killed him?

He went and knelt beside her. He ripped the hem of her chemise and tied the cloth around the wound on her ankle to stop the bleeding and protect it from infection.

"What happened?" he asked.

Her body trembled. Red Wolf looked around for something to cover her with. Romulus' horse grazed close by. A blanket hung from the leather satchel tied to the saddle. He tugged it free and gently laid it upon her shoulders.

"Do not help me," she said, her voice no more than a whisper.

He stared at Romulus' dead body again.

"Did you kill him?"

She threw the blanket from her. "I do not need this."

"You are cold."

"No, I am not." She faced him. Torment mixed with anger flickered in her eyes, but as he stared into the green pits, he saw a deep sadness there as well. Sorrow filled him as he thought of all the things she'd witnessed in the past year. He reached out his hand to lay it upon her shoulder, but she shoved him away from her.

She stood, leaving the blanket on the ground. The material of the chemise she wore was thin. He could see her shape as she stood in front of the fire. A need to be near her, to protect her, came over him, and he went to stand beside her. The heat from the fire warmed his bones and chased out the chill in the evening air. He rubbed his hands together nervous of what he'd hear.

"What happened, Tsura?" he asked again.

"He is dead."

"By your hand?"

She swung around. The angles of her face slanted.

"By his own."

"He killed himself?"

She shrugged.

Something was amiss. She was reluctant to tell him anything. Her rigid stature told him she did not want this conversation. Well, he didn't give a damn. She was going to tell him. He turned her toward him. The light from the flames showed the bruises upon her face where the Corsair had struck her, and Red Wolf flexed his hands into tight fists.

"Tell me."

"I have told you."

"Did you do this?"

"I did."

"With your own strength, or with the gift?"

"It is not a gift...it is a curse, a bloody awful curse!"

She'd used the magick. What had pushed her to do such a thing?

"You saved your life. You had no choice."

She stepped into him, her lips pulled down. "Is that what you think? I killed him for my own life? I do not give a damn if I die."

"Then why did you do it after all this time, why did you use the power?"

Her shoulders sunk, and she bowed her head. The hostility drained from her, and once again the sadness he'd seen before filled her eyes.

"I could not control the fury. I wanted him to pay for what he'd done."

"To Morgan," he finished for her.

She did not reply.

"The pendant. It was because of the ruby."

He knew this from the note Romulus had left him.

"He killed for the jewel. The blasted legacy." She paused, her bottom lip quivering. "I could do nothing..."

The vigor he'd seen inside of her earlier had been extinguished. All that remained was emptiness. He'd not seen her like this, even after James had been killed. She appeared defeated, tired, and he reached for her hand. She glanced at him, and he saw the girl he once knew, the girl who when she smiled would have him falling at her feet. He remembered the way his heart had swelled at the sight of her, how with one touch he'd become her slave.

"Let us leave here," he said.

He remembered Star Dancer, and Soaring Eagle's plea for his daughter. He hoped the child was still alive and time had not run out. He peeked at Tsura limping beside him. Now was not the time to ask her to heal the child. He'd wait until they were closer to the village before he brought it up. Unable to watch her struggle any longer, he swept her up into his arms and carried her to Caesar.

# CHAPTER TWENTY-FOUR

Emine hovered over the spell book. The candle she held did little to light the worn pages, but she could still make out the words. She'd spent sixteen years creating the book. Words scribbled onto tattered sheets—curses, potions, and charms. She'd improved and now had most of the spells memorized.

For all the great spells she'd created, the book lacked the one spell she yearned to know—where to find the pendant. She'd tried several times to create a charm, to source the jewel, but they all proved useless. She was desperate to locate the necklace, to hold the ancient gem within her palm and know she had power.

The cauldron bubbled from its perch over the fire, and she went to stir the contents. A new potion steeped. She used the thick wooden spoon to mix the liquid.

As she rubbed her hands together a smile crawled across her lips. The spell was almost ready. Emine could not wait to see her labors put to use. The Witch's berry would be vital in rendering the Branded One useless. Once the brew was poured over top of the leaves and dried, the Chuvani had no chance of defeating the effects. All limbs would cease having movement. The Branded One would be crippled.

Emine cackled. The spell was sure to work on the girl. She'd not be able to use her magick if she could not work her own tongue.

A rap at the door tore her from the pages of the book as she wrote down the new spell she'd created.

"Enter," she said.

Darius walked in with a beautiful Indian maiden. He blew out the candlestick inside the small glass vase, while his other arm held onto the girl's elbow. Emine could not stop the jealousy as it pulled at the corners of her eyes.

"Why have you come?" She walked around the table to stand directly in front of the girl.

"She has news of the pendant," Darius said.

Emine's hand shot out. She grabbed the girl's neck before turning her touch into an eerie caress. "The talisman? You know where it is?"

The girl nodded.

"Speak of it!" She was inches from her face. Desire for the jewel overshadowed any decency she'd had left.

"I want something in exchange first," the maiden said.

Emine released her and stepped back to assess the girl. She had nerve to demand such a thing, but if she spoke the truth, Emine would do whatever she wanted for now.

"What is your name?" she asked.

"Raven."

"And why should I believe you have the pendant?"

"I have seen it upon Tsura."

Emine's eyes grew round at the sound of the familiar name.

"Where is she that you've seen it upon her?"

"She resides with my tribe."

"Which tribe do you speak of?"

"The Ama."

She knew of them. They traded with the Cherokee tribe often. To think the Branded One had been down the mountain from them all this time…

"What do you want?"

Raven tipped her chin, and Emine admired her defiance, but the maiden would soon know the gypsy was stronger.

"If I give you the pendant, I want your promise that you will kill Tsura."

She did not expect this demand. Intrigued, she leaned closer.

"Why do you wish this?"

The girl's eyes watered, but she did not give in to her emotions.

"The man I love yearns for her."

Emine narrowed her eyes as she scrutinized what the girl had told her. The tale made sense. With Tsura dead, Raven could have her man. The Branded One will die, she'd been planning it for years, but she'd not tell Raven of this.

"And you think by killing her, he will love you?"

The girl nodded.

Emine clicked her tongue. Love did not work this way, she knew. The girl's efforts would prove futile if the man's heart belongs to Tsura. The man would love the woman he was destined for, not the one who was forced upon him. She ran her fingernail along Raven's cheek.

"If you bring me the pendant, I will honor this promise."

Raven smiled. She reached around her neck and pulled the pendant out from under her dress.

Emine squealed, and before Raven could give it to her, she snatched the talisman from her hand. The power surged up her arm to pump within her fingers. She clutched the jewel tight.

"I have waited years for this," she said and placed the necklace over her head to rest against her chest. She reached out her hand to touch Darius. Her mind on fire, she wished to scald him. When her palm touched his flesh, he jumped back the skin bright red from her touch.

Emine laughed. She twirled around. Her mousy braid swung against her back, and she threw her hand outward. Without moving her lips or speaking a word, she commanded the table to be lifted and tossed against the wall. The spell book, dishes, and plants spilled onto the floor in a loud crash.

"What are you doing?" Darius asked.

She turned to face him, curled her finger and motioned for him to come to her. He stepped toward her not of his own will, and she sneered at the frightened look upon his face. She brought his head close enough to run her tongue along his lips, igniting a carnal desire inside of him. She felt his need for her, lingered until she had him begging, and pushed him to the side.

She stalked toward Raven.

The Indian maiden ran to the door.

"Come to me!" she shrieked and watched delighted as Raven was thrown against Emine's hand. She gripped the girl's throat, and lifting her from the ground, she squeezed. "Bring me the Branded One."

# Chapter Twenty-Five

Tsura leaned into Red Wolf as they rode Caesar back to the Ama village. She replayed the evening with Radu in her mind. He'd come for the pendant, the bloody blasted jewel. She'd grown to despise the ruby. The talisman had brought nothing but devastation into her life. The desire for the power had influenced evil ever since she was a child, had ruined lives.

Would the hunt ever cease?

She squeezed her eyes closed. The dreadful day perched on the edge of her sanity, waiting to be released from the corners of her mind where she'd kept it hidden. She'd never come back from the desolation if she were to do so, her soul ruined, her heart broken forever. She groaned. The burden was too much, and she willed it away.

Red Wolf had not understood why she'd used her magick to kill Radu. For the last year she'd struggled with the urge, the need, and she rebuked the desire to cast the magick from her hands. When Radu told her the truth of what had happened that day, what he did, she became outraged. She saw no remorse within him, no shame, and she succumbed to the anger and the rage. She exploded and lost all control. She wanted revenge, to strike Radu down—to kill the Corsair.

Her birth mother Vadoma had used the power she held for evil. Had Tsura inherited the dark blood from her? It seemed the only time she could not stop the magick was when she was enraged. The knowledge of what she'd become intensified her need to live away from society. A life alone is what she deserved for allowing him to die that day.

She'd laid her palms upon him, frantic to heal all of his wounds, but she failed. Instead her insides melted, her breath grew shallow, her throat burned…and her body gave up as it began to die. Mr. Willaby, her driver, sat beside her after she'd recovered. His white dress shirt was black with soot, and ashes smudged his wrinkled cheeks. The pendant glowed warm against her chest. She wanted to rip it from her body, expel every part of her lineage to the depths of the earth, but hadn't the strength. Mr. Willaby had pulled her from the fire, while the ruby healed her. She moaned followed by a heart-wrenching scream. Her body shook while she sobbed in his arms.

A single tear slipped from her lashes to nestle within her lips. She licked the salt away. Her soul crushed, she shivered. Why had she lived? She cursed the pendant for what it had brought into her life, for who had been taken from her, and for allowing her to remain alive.

Red Wolf pulled Caesar to a halt, and she slid down the back of the horse. The blanket wrapped around her shoulders fell from her arms.

He turned toward her. As the sun rose in the east, the light cascaded behind him, and she couldn't help but think how he resembled a magnificent warrior.

"Star Dancer is very ill," he said.

She straightened. How could she have forgotten?

"She lives?"

He nodded.

"Soaring Eagle has asked if you could help her."

The chief knew of her power?

"Why have you told him of me?"

"He keeps this secret, but he is desperate. He begs it of you."

She did not know what to say. She could not do it. Seeing the girl would evoke a whirlwind of images, and the dam inside of her would break loose. Tsura did not want to deal with it, did not want to face the reality of what had happened a year before.

"I cannot," she whispered, feeling the shame as it crawled up her spine.

"You cannot?" he echoed, and she didn't miss the scorn in his words.

She shook her head.

The dark eyes she'd once loved to stare into bore down upon her with such intensity she was sure he'd murder her.

"You used the power to kill Romulus, and you will not heal a child?"

"I told you. I cannot do this."

"Why not?" he shouted.

"It will do no good." She tried to make him understand the power would not help the child. Tsura felt horrible for doing so, but she was not willing to face what she'd buried long ago…she was a coward.

"I do not believe you. There is another reason. Speak it."

She set her shoulders against his attack, and placed her features into the grim appearance she'd perfected. It was simpler to be angry, to lash out, to speak horrible words.

"I care not if you believe me."

"Do you care of nothing? Where is the girl I once knew with the yearning to help those in need?"

"She is dead along with whatever has come from the past."

"Morgan is not worth letting a child die."

His words struck her, pierced her heart, and she hardened herself to the pain.

"You know nothing. Leave me." She turned from him, but his steps followed her.

"I am not finished. I refuse to let you do this."

She spun on him. Her finger poked his chest as she advanced.

"You do not decide what I do. I am not your concern."

"No, you're not, but Star Dancer is, and damn it you *will* heal her," he yelled.

She loathed him. He thought to tell her how to live her life, a life she wished to end. If he hadn't left her years before she'd not be here now. She'd not have the constant agony inside of her soul. She'd not feel so alone, helpless, and empty! She'd be whole once more. Her life would have meaning…and he'd still be alive.

"I detest you for what you did to me." Tsura said the words she'd held back all of this time.

"I did nothing that you did not wish."

"Lies."

"You chose Morgan over me. You wanted the fineries the life of a Baron came with. I was your pawn. Cast aside when no longer needed."

"Go to hell," she hissed.

"I am living in hell thanks to you! Every time I look at you I see the life I was supposed to have, the life you stole from me." His handsome face turned ugly, his lip curled as his accusations bit into her.

"It was you who did not return. I waited for you, thought something happened to the *Falcon*." She sucked in a breath to stop her voice from trembling so he did not know how much he'd hurt her. "I was mistaken. You docked that day, but did not come. I am a fool for ever thinking you cared for me."

"I am not surprised to hear of your misconceptions from that day, *Baroness*. It was *you* who wrote the letter after all. *You* who considered me not worthy."

Her words came back to her. The ones she'd said to him the other day to hurt him, to make him think she'd chosen Morgan over him. She refused to tell him the truth. He did not want to hear it, and she would not become victim to his assault from her lies.

"Let me be. I wish to be alone."

"You're a coward."

Yes, she was. God help her, she was horrible she knew, but she did not want to face the pain.

He took her hand in his.

"Please, I beg of you, heal Star Dancer."

"I cannot." The agony her words caused clung to her throat making it difficult to swallow.

"You're pathetic," he growled and threw her hand from him. "And no longer fit to walk among my people."

"Good!" She stepped into him. "Impale me with your dagger. I beg of you to take my pitiful life!"

He stared at her for a long while. Grief carved the shape of his eyes.

"How did I ever love you?" he whispered.

"You never loved me."

He stalked away from her.

"Who is the coward now?" she yelled after him.

He came back toward her, his black eyes lethal, and she planted her feet firmly into the ground. She would not retreat. He grabbed her arms and hauled her to his chest. His nostrils flared, and she met his glare with her own icy stare.

He smashed his mouth to hers, and a spark she hadn't felt in a very long time ignited. The kiss consumed her. His lips and tongue became ferocious as he devoured her. He tasted of the past, of a fresh morning with the dew still upon the grass. The passion tugged at her soul, wanting to heal her heart, and she leaned into him.

He pulled away from her, his breath ragged as he pressed his forehead to hers. It was in that moment she wished for the past to come back, for things to have been different.

"I loved you still," he whispered, "but I cannot love who you've become." He leaned into her, the whites of his eyes red and glossy, and kissed her lips gently. "Goodbye."

Tsura watched him walk away. Afraid to lick her lips and taste him there. He had said everything she needed to hear, but instead of listening, she rebuked him. She stood alone surrounded by the Ama lodges. The faint sound of music drifted toward her, and she walked aimlessly in the direction.

The Ama sat on the ground in a large circle surrounding Soaring Eagle's home. The song they sang tore at her heart. She watched the women cry, the men beat their chests, and she spun unable to face the sadness the girl's sickness brought upon her.


Red Wolf wandered the village, afraid to tell Soaring Eagle Tsura would not heal his daughter. How was he to convey to his cousin, his best friend, that the woman he'd loved was shallow and heartless? His stomach turned at the reality of what Tsura had become. How could she deny Star Dancer the chance to live? He ran his hand through his hair. Frustration settled in his neck, and he clenched his jaw as he fought the overwhelming urge to cry out.

He mourned the loss of the woman he once knew, of the little girl who was so ill that without Tsura's help she would surely die. He couldn't fathom how she'd become so cold. How she was so resistant to heal a child, yet kill Romulus? Her actions made no sense to him, and he'd had no choice but to let her go—to cut off any passion he'd had for her. He always loved her, he could admit that now, but he could not abide by the person she'd become.

He was not surprised at his admission of love for her. He knew the emotion had never left his heart, but the pain of walking away from her could not be measured. His chest burned, the ribs compressing his lungs in his grief. He gasped, swallowing the wretched sob so it did not break from his lips. He continued through the village and found himself at his lodge. The Ama chanting carried over the thatch roofs to cover him. No longer strong enough to battle his emotions, Red Wolf sunk to his knees and wept.

# Chapter Twenty-Six

Tsura stood by the elm tree. She'd fled the scene at Soaring Eagle's lodge and had come here. To the very spot she'd found solace, but today there was no comfort to be found under the large branches and green leaves. This morning the sorrow of what she'd done consumed her, and no matter what she'd told herself there was no comfort to be found. Star Dancer was dying.

"Is it true?"

Tsura did not have to turn to know Beautiful Meadow stood behind her. The woman's voice was as soft as a rose petal, a resemblance to the person she was.

"It is," she whispered. She did not recognize her own voice and coughed to clear her throat of the shame.

"You can save my child with the strength in your hands?"

She faced Beautiful Meadow and was not prepared for the anguish upon her face. The flawless features resonated the sorrow she truly felt, and Tsura had to look away.

"It is not that simple," she said.

"Why is it not?"

"I can only use the magick when angered, and even then I do not want to do it." She held out her hands. "I no longer use the power."

"But you can help Star Dancer if you were to use it?"

"No, I do not believe I can." She tried to make Beautiful Meadow understand without telling her of the past. "The magick is of no use to me any longer."

"When you say you do not believe, are you denying yourself the ability to do so, or are you unwilling to help my child?"

Unable to lie, she moaned and bit off the urge to cry. "It is both," she whispered.

She expected Beautiful Meadow to lash out at her, to slash her nails across Tsura's face for not helping Star Dancer, but instead the woman regarded her with compassion in her brown eyes.

"I have watched you from afar while you have been among us," the other woman said, "I know you suffer deeply, a great pain you hold inside. I know not what this pain is, but I do see how it affects your life. You carry anger upon you like a shield, draping it over your existence to mask the fear of being weak."

Tsura listened to the woman's words, all the while shrinking lower and lower into herself.

"I beg of you, my friend, please try to save my child." Beautiful Meadow's last words came on the edge of a sob.

Tsura fought the tears, the misery, the guilt, and without meeting her eyes, she whispered, "I cannot."

"If you had a child who was ill and dying would you not do anything to help them?"

She inhaled sharply—the breath in her chest did not want to be released, and she wheezed. She could not speak, could not look at her.

"I will fall upon my knees, promise you anything in return, if you'd please try to help her," Beautiful Meadow pleaded.

"I...I...am sorry." Tears fell from her eyes, and she hung her head.

"I forgive you," Beautiful Meadow said through her tears.

She shook her head. "How?" she whispered.

"But will you be able to forgive yourself?"

Tsura watched her walk away. The burden of Beautiful Meadow's words compressed her chest, and she pulled the blanket tighter around her shoulders. The sun rose higher into the sky, and she squinted against the bright rays. She hadn't changed out of her chemise. The thin material offered no warmth, and she shivered. Beautiful Meadow had begged her to heal Star Dancer, and she refused. Tsura's stomach pitched at what would happen to the girl because of her decision.

Star Dancer would die.

She glanced in the direction of Beautiful Meadow and Soaring Eagle's home. She couldn't leave things undone. She needed to see the child, to look upon her and...say goodbye. Her stomach in knots, she twisted her hands within the blanket. She owed Star Dancer a final goodbye.

One shaky leg stepped forward. She feasted on her lip, as she mustered up the courage to continue onward. The Ama sang a low mournful tune as she slipped past them and entered Beautiful Meadow's lodge.

The faint glow of the fire in the hearth cast shadows throughout the dark room. The Ama homes had no windows. The dark area offered reprieve from the hot sun. Star Dancer lay on a bed of furs. Her innocent face was peaceful but barren of the flushed cheeks and smiling mouth Tsura had often seen.

The tribe's medicine man knelt beside the girl, and his thin lips chanted as he held a pipe over Star Dancer. Feathers were tied into his long grey hair. The beads around his neck clinked together when he moved, and his eyes remained closed as he prayed for the girl. He inhaled smoke from the pipe and blew it onto the child. Beautiful Meadow's dark brows knitted together with concern as she sat beside her daughter, rubbing her hand. The hairs on Tsura's arms stood, and she did not miss the contempt displayed on Soaring Eagle's painted face, or his eyes while he glared at her.

She came closer, her palms itched, and fingers grew hot. She observed Star Dancer, and a longing to help the child overcame her. The soft sounds of Beautiful Meadow while she wept resonated around her heart, the sound scraped at her resistance—at her ignorance, and she fell to her knees.

The blanket she'd kept wrapped around her slid from her shoulders to fall onto the ground, but she paid no mind. All her senses were on the little girl who lay before her. Tsura held her palms over Star Dancer without touching her, and the need exploded within her veins. She hesitated, knowing what would happen if she were to do this.

She closed her eyes and silently prepared herself for the ambush of emotions to come afterward. The pounding of her heart intensified, and her mouth went dry. She pulled her hands to her chest as the fear embodied her. She could not do it. She did not want to see the past, hear it, or feel the pain.

She felt the touch of a hand upon her own, and Tsura opened her eyes to see Beautiful Meadow nod as she quietly reassured her. Soaring Eagle spoke to the medicine man in Cherokee, and the old man said a few more words before he got up and left the lodge. She knew what they wanted, what their eyes pleaded with her to do, and she peered down at Star Dancer again.

Tsura's hands shook, the demand so strong, so powerful it caused her vision to blur. She touched the girl's hair, running the soft strands through her fingers. She carefully moved her palms to lie across Star Dancer's chest. The moment she touched the wounded area a shock went up her arms. She straightened her spine. Tsura's lungs began to stiffen and burn. She pushed up onto her knees and pressed harder into the girl's chest.

Tsura took upon herself the child's filled lungs. She wheezed as she tried to inhale. Unable to breathe, she coughed. Spittle dripped from her lower lip, and she struggled to draw in air. She squeezed her eyes shut and focused on making the child well again. Her lungs expanded, allowing the breath to come easier. Star Dancer's ailment gone, Tsura slid her trembling hands from the girl.

She felt her stomach pitch, but held the vomit in while she waited for the girl to open her eyes. The images of the past flashed through her mind, and she inhaled his scent, felt the softness of his cheek resting against hers. She stood on shaky legs and leaned into the pole beside her.

Star Dancer's foot moved, then her small dimpled hands. Beautiful Meadow straightened, and her almond shaped eyes watched intently. A loud yawn came from Star Dancer's lips, and her mother picked her up, smothering the girl in a tight embrace.

Tsura could not hold back the demand to retch any longer, nor could she stop the memories as they flooded her mind. She ran from the lodge past the Ama waiting outside of Soaring Eagle's home and went straight to the elm tree. She made it just as the vomit flew from her mouth. She hunched over, expelling Star Dancer's sickness into the grass. Tsura emptied her stomach three times. The motion left her defenseless against the days she'd tried to bury, and bit-by-bit pieces of the wall she'd placed around her heart began to fall away.

She dropped to her knees, rested her head against the trunk of the tree. The corded wood pressed into her forehead, and she did not care about the pain it caused. She concentrated on ridding her mind of the anguish, but in the moment she'd healed Star Dancer, she'd become fragile. She could feel the grief as it slithered up her spine, twisting the remnants of what she did not want to see. There in the depths of her soul a harrowing scream scratched its way up her throat to expel from her lips. He was so small, so helpless, and she promised to protect him. Her jaw ached from the guilt of allowing him to die. She saw his soft tuft of black hair, the clear brown eyes, heard his laugh and she moaned.

Why him? Why did he have to die? The agony of it all was too much. She was over come with misery—a sorrow so strong she laid on the ground and pulled her knees to her chest.

Red Wolf's arms slid underneath her side, and he drew her toward him to cradle her against his chest. She hadn't the energy to push him from her, to tell him she hated him—despised him for what had happened.

He rocked her within his embrace, protecting her from the outside world. She sunk into him. Unable to stop the torment, she expelled the guilt with each sob that broke from her lips.

"Tsura, release your pain," he whispered into her hair. "Lay Morgan to rest."

"Morgan can rot in hell," she ground out, and she felt Red Wolf's muscles tighten.

"Shush."

She growled low in her throat. How could she have let him die? She wished for him back, wanted a second chance. She gasped, her throat burned, and she wept.

"Allow the pain to come, only then will you be able to heal."

"I will never heal." She saw him then, lying in his cradle, the bed doused in flames. She ran to him, picked him up. His hair singed, she smothered him within her dress to put the fire out on the clothes he'd worn. His once soft white skin was now tarnished with black soot and burned. The memory was too much. Tsura clenched her hands into her hair and screamed.

"I could not save him. I tried, oh, I tried," she wailed.

"Who, Tsura? Who did you try to save?"

"He did not have a chance. He was so small. I was supposed to protect him. I should've been there to protect him!"

The images slammed into her, and she could do nothing to stop them. He was dead, gone from this world and there wasn't a damn thing she could do about it. She tried to give her life for him, heal him, but she had failed.

"He was innocent." Sobs wracked her body. She did not want to let go…did not want to acknowledge she'd not see him, kiss him, smell his skin, or feel his small hand cling to her finger ever again. She let the terror come, the pain so intense, she gasped. "My baby…my sweet, sweet son. Why him?"


Red Wolf held Tsura to him. The raw pain dripped from her lashes and onto his chest. She moaned, the sound so forlorn and desperate he could not stop the tears as they fell from his eyes. She had been burdened with far more than he'd ever thought. A child, her child had died. Shame settled over his conscience, and he hugged her to him. All this time he'd thought she loved Morgan when in fact it had been a baby she'd loved…and lost.

Tsura wept into him, and the sound tore at his soul. He wanted to help her, to take the pain from her, but he did not know how. Red Wolf sensed she'd not dealt with her child's death until now, and he was beginning to see her differently. All this time Tsura had distanced herself from the grief, her only defense the anger she put forward onto those around her.

"Tell me of your child," he asked, his lips pressed into her hair.

She sat up and scooted away from him. Her hair was messed, eyes bright red, and cheeks soaked from her tears. He reached out and rubbed his thumb across her trembling lips. He noticed the change in her immediately, the rigid features upon her face appeared once more, her back straightened, and her eyes cast disgust toward him.

"It is because of you!" she lunged at him. Red Wolf had no time to shield himself from her nails as they slashed into his face. "I despise you."

He grabbed her wrists and held them away from him.

"Damn it, woman! What the hell is wrong with you?"

"My life has no meaning." Tsura's lip quivered, and she broke down once more. "He died because of you." She placed her head into her hands and cried.

"What are you speaking of? I knew not of your child. He was Morgan's."

She jumped at him again, and he had to restrain her arms once more.

"You did not return. You left me alone with no choice...no choice but to marry him." She swung her fists into him.

He turned her so that her back was against his chest and held her tight.

"You wrote the letter. You told Morgan you loved him," he said into her ear.

She kicked her legs out, and the bandage around her ankle let loose and blood ran from the wound.

"The letter was for Morgan. I wrote it to him!" she shrieked. "You did not come for me. You left me." She thrashed against him again, and her hair filled his mouth. "Our son died because of you!"

Red Wolf's heart seized. He let his arms fall to the side. Tsura scrambled away from him to stand. He looked up at her and did not need to ask if what she'd said were true. Her green eyes belied to the torture she'd endured, the burden she carried, all because he had not returned.

"I will never forgive you," she whispered.

He did not know what to say, and so he let her go. The child was his. He'd had a son? The thought sent his mind racing. He remembered the day she made love to him under the rowan tree. She'd become his, the other half of his soul then, and he never stopped loving her.

He heard the quiet steps of Soaring Eagle as he came closer. The longer he remained with the Ama the more he became as they were. He could hear the silence just like when he was a child.

His cousin sat beside him, clad in buckskin pants and no shirt. Red Wolf's heart ached from what he'd learned, and he did not know how to express this to Soaring Eagle. He stared out at the lodges. The Ama mingled, but his eyes strayed to the small boy standing with his mother. Red Wolf's mouth worked, his vision blurred, and he blinked back the sadness of a life he'd never known.

"Your woman healed my Star Dancer," Soaring Eagle said.

Red Wolf did not correct him on his statement regarding Tsura. She'd always be his even if they were not together. "I am glad she has done this."

"I did not believe such a thing existed, but I am grateful just the same."

"The gift she has is difficult to comprehend."

"You have known of this gift all this time?"

He nodded. Tsura had shown it to him the fist day he'd met her, after his arrow had killed Silas Monroe.

"How does she live with such a gift?"

"What do you mean?"

Soaring Eagle shrugged.

"The power she holds must come at a great cost."

Red Wolf thought of what Tsura had lost because of the gift she'd been given, and he finally understood why she'd called it a curse. Why she despised anything to do with the magick.

"Yes, it does."

Soaring Eagle nodded.

"She lost a child." Red Wolf blurted the words, desperate to release what he'd learned to his cousin.

"I have seen this hurt within her."

"You knew it was a child?" How had his cousin known of such a thing without Tsura ever telling him?

"I did."

"But how? Did she speak it to you?"

He shook his head.

"She did not have to."

"I do not understand. How did you see this in the short time you have known her, and I did not in the last three weeks I have been in her company."

"You viewed her with contempt, with resentment, and so you could not see who she was. You saw only what she wanted you to see."

Soaring Eagle was correct. He had not seen Tsura as the woman he'd left behind three years before. Instead, she now portrayed a woman scorned and filled with anger. His pride crushed, his heart broken, he despised her for choosing Morgan over him. The Baron had cleverly duped Red Wolf, and revulsion dusted his teeth. Why had he believed him? He should've gone to Tsura. Regret filled his eyes, and he placed his head into his hands.

"She waited for me, and I was a fool."

Soaring Eagle remained silent, and Red Wolf continued, needing to expel the truth he'd learned. "Morgan had given me the letter Tsura had written to him." He swallowed the misery. "She was with child...my child, and I left her."

His cousin placed a hand upon his shoulder—the gesture did little to ease his guilt. "You did not know," Soaring Eagle said.

"She blames me for the death of our son...and damn it, she is right."

"You cannot change the past."

"I know this, but I will forever live with what I did." He looked at Soaring Eagle, and he could not hide his remorse any longer. "Had I stayed, went to her, we'd be together still—my son would be alive." One tear slid down his cheek.

"Cousin, I cannot tell you not to grieve for you must, but do not wish for the past to be different."

"How can I not? My life would not be as it is now had I stayed, had I fought for her."

"Yes, but you did not know she was with child." Soaring Eagle leaned close to him. "Nor did you know she loved you still."

"It does not matter. None of what you say holds stock. My son is dead because of me. He is dead," he wept, "and I never saw him, never held him. He did not know me, nor I him."

"Do you wish for your parents back?"

He wiped the tears from his face and glared at Soaring Eagle.

"Of course I do. I miss them terribly." What the hell was his cousin rambling about? He did not know what his parents had to do with the loss of his child and Tsura from his life.

"If you had stayed with us, you would be married to a Cherokee bride, living among her tribe."

"Yes."

"You would not have met your woman and fallen in love with her."

"And my son would not have died."

"He would not have lived!" Soaring Eagle's voice softened. "Cousin, your child would not have been had you not fallen in love with his mother."

"I'd have saved Tsura from the pain she's experienced had I not been captured that day."

"Yes, but you were not to be with us—you were meant to be with her."

Red Wolf sighed. "Knowing does not make this any easier."

"Look at the elm tree we sit under."

He glanced up at the magnificent splendor with its long branches full of green leaves to shade them from the sun.

"If it was yours would you care for it?"

"Of course."

"You'd water your tree, making sure it had sun so the leaves can flourish. You are its nourishment, taking care of its every need. But a storm comes and you cannot protect the tree from the winds. Branches are broken and fall to the ground, now dead. Are you to blame for the death of those branches when you have done all you could to keep them alive?"

"No."

"Will you give up on the tree, after it has been damaged?"

"Of course not, it is still alive."

Soaring Eagle smiled. "And so is she."

Red Wolf thought of Tsura. She'd endured a hellish year, but Soaring Eagle was right, she was still alive and so was he. Could they heal together? Was it possible for her to trust him once more? He had to try.

# CHAPTER TWENTY-SEVEN

Tsura sat in the metal basin, her knees bent. She rested her chin upon them. The sunlight filtered through the cracks in Red Wolf's lodge, and she watched as the tiny motes of dust danced around her. The water taken from the river was cold, and she squeezed her knees closer to her chest. Beautiful Meadow held a fur blanket while she waited for Tsura to step from the basin. The woman had come to thank her for healing Star Dancer.

She wanted to crawl into the bed of furs and lay there for all eternity. Every part of her ached for her son, as she'd finally accepted the truth. He was gone from her forever. Tsura felt the moisture drip from her lashes. Before, she'd been able to bring forth her anger, to despise those who lived, now she was void of any emotion. She held no malice toward Soaring Eagle's wife and therefore hadn't the strength to be cruel to her.

"Come from the water. You are shivering," Beautiful Meadow said.

She stood on weak legs, her shoulders turned inward, and her soul downtrodden. The fur from a wolf was draped around her, and she hugged the soft blanket to wet flesh. She sat on the ground, no urge to dress or brush her hair. A moment of truth slipped past her barrier, and she gasped. The depth of what was now shattered the lies she'd told herself the past year. She'd refused to acknowledge the death of her son, denied the truth of it ever entering her heart, and now…she had no choice.

The certainties of that day suffocated the anger, the hate, and the withdrawal she'd so carefully placed around her. She was left with the emotions she did not want to face. The pain, sorrow and misery compounded with the grief and she could not breathe. She did not want it to be real—did not want the horror to be relived over and over again. Tsura could not control the rush of angst as it swelled in her throat, choking her. She allowed more tears to slip from her lashes. How was she to go on now?

She felt the porcupine comb slide through her hair as Beautiful Meadow brushed the wet curls.

"What was your child's name?" the other woman asked.

Tsura's chest ached and her stomach turned, but she could not speak his name.

Beautiful Meadow's hand rubbed her shoulder. "You will say the name without the heartache when you are ready."

"It is not possible. I wish to die."

"You could not heal him as you did Star Dancer?"

"No," she said, and her voice dipped with agony, bringing forth a sob.

"Your loss is great, and it will live within you for the rest of your life, but you must go on."

"I cannot. He was my life."

"You are unwilling to forge ahead."

Tsura turned, ripping the comb from Beautiful Meadow's hand.

"Do not speak to me of how to grieve the death of my son," she said through clenched teeth. "You do not know the pain of losing a child. I saved you from feeling this."

The maiden's brown eyes lightened, and her full lips smiled sadly. "I know of this pain you feel." She placed her hand over her heart. "It is so great you are sure death is the only peace from the agony you face each day."

Tsura stared at the ground. Beautiful Meadow's words touched on the truth she'd faced each day.

"It is during the nighttime as you lie awake, the quiet surrounding you, when the memories invade your mind." The woman continued, "Your existence is not centered, you are no longer whole, and you do not know what to do."

"How?"

"My first child, Moonbeam, died minutes after she was born." Beautiful Meadow released a tear, and Tsura felt a bond take hold between them.

"How did you go on? How did you have more children? You...you do not show this loss."

"Soaring Eagle refused to let me die too. He waited for me to grieve, and when he thought I was done, he pushed me to get out of the lodge."

"He loves you very much."

"He does, but I could've stayed with the grief had I wanted to. He would not have stopped me."

"Then what made you not?"

"Love."

Tsura did not understand, and so she waited for Beautiful Meadow to finish.

"I wanted to love." She reached out and took Tsura's hand. "I wanted to laugh, to feel joy, and I could not do those things if I held hatred inside my heart."

"But were you not afraid to lose another child?"

"Of course, but I cannot influence what is to be no more than I can change the seasons. The sorrow from losing Moonbeam will live with me forever. I will not forget her as you will not forget your child, but a life full of resentment is not what I wanted."

"We are different."

"Once you let go of the anger and bring forth all you've kept inside, then you will see what I have spoken."

"I do not feel the way you do. I am without love. I cannot bring myself to convey such an emotion ever again."

"Even toward Red Wolf?"

The woman was perplexing. She had a keen sense of Tsura's emotions even without her showing them.

"I hold no love for him."

"You withhold your love for him," Beautiful Meadow corrected.

Tsura shook her head. "He chose another life above the one we had planned together."

"And so you hold the past wrongdoings against him?"

"He did not return. He believed a letter I'd written to Morgan was for him. He denied me the chance to explain."

"You must see he was not at fault."

"I care not. I will never forgive him."

"I am sorry you live with this bitterness inside of your heart."

Tsura did not know what to say, and for the first time in a long while, she felt horrible for how she'd treated Red Wolf. Instead of allowing the sentiment to push its way into her heart, she removed it from her thoughts and placed her resentment toward him first.

"This Morgan, did he loved you?"

"He did not. He loved the impression of having me as his wife. He wanted nothing from me other than my presence upon his arm."

"You became his wife."

"I...I was with child."

Beautiful Meadow's eyes lit with understanding.

"Do not deny yourself the happiness you deserve."

"I deserve no such thing..." The agony came again, and she could not stop the pain as it fell from her eyes. "I could not save my own son." Her hands trembled, the guilt too much, and she gnashed her teeth together.

"My friend, you must cleanse your soul of the shame you feel."

She brought her eyes to meet Beautiful Meadow's. "It is not possible."

"But, it is."

"No, I cannot. I deserve this." The edge she'd carefully stayed away from came closer and closer as she fought with her sanity. "I am the reason." Tsura's whole body shook, the sorrow so intense, her ribs ached.

"It was not your fault."

There were no words Beautiful Meadow could say to stop Tsura from slipping over the cliff of emotions she did not want to acknowledge. Without warning they slapped, cut, and punctured her soul. She bit back the scream, the anger at herself, until she could no longer stop it—no longer deny the reality of what had happened and how she'd been a part of the tragedy.

"You do not understand," she sobbed. "You cannot possibly understand. My son died because of my gift. He died because of the bloody pendant, the damn Chuvani lineage." She inhaled and the breath set fire to her lungs. "I could not heal him, and—" she clenched her jaw, rage surged through her blood, "and the damn talisman let me live, instead of saving him!" She leaned forward, her chest constricted, her heart aching, and she growled. "He should have lived, and I should have died. I should have died!" The pain beat down upon her, and she slammed her fists into the bed of furs. "Why?" Tsura could not control the misery as it swept through her like a vicious storm, pulling at all reason, all sanity, all things that made sense, and cast her into a black hole. The shame she'd felt for the past year squeezed her throat, cutting off all air into her lungs. She pulled at her hair, tore the blanket from her while broken sobs burst from her lips. "It was all because of me," she wept.

Beautiful Meadow's arms encircled her. "My friend, my friend, you are loved."

Tsura shook her head. How could anyone love her, a cursed woman, and a mother who let her own child die? Another wave swept over her, and she let it come, taking the shame and expelling it from her body with each tear she shed. Her throat raw, she continued to cry out until there was nothing left, and her body slumped into Beautiful Meadow.

"It is good you have said all of this."

She did not answer.

"In time you will see."

Tsura felt nothing except lost, and no matter how hard she searched she'd not find the love she once had. She pushed herself up to sit across from Beautiful Meadow.

They sat in silence for a long time until Tsura could no longer hold herself up. She eased down onto the bed of furs, and closed her eyes. She heard Beautiful Meadow leave, and the loneliness of the lodge engulfed her. She missed the woman's presence already.

The enormity of today's events had left her exhausted and spent of any more tears. She needed the solace of her own company to reflect on the past—and present. The room quiet, she brought forth every bit of reason she'd given herself to remain distant, angered, and cruel. She knew the moment Star Dancer lived she could no longer dwell on those emotions and had to face the depth of what had happened.

Beautiful Meadow had let Tsura confess the blame she'd cast upon herself for the death of her son, the tragedy so harrowing she was sure she'd die once the words came from her lips. She ran her hand along her curls, twisting the hair around her finger. She ached in every part of her body, yearned for the son she'd lost and knew she'd never hold again.

The wicker door creaked. She opened her eyes and watched as Red Wolf entered the lodge. His presence commanded her attention, but she looked away. She did not want to see his handsome face and know, because of the past she'd missed out on a wonderful life.

Tsura pulled the fur closer using the blanket as a shield she could hide behind.

He came toward her and sat down.

She noticed the small bowl he held, and when his hand reached for her ankle she scooted away. He inched closer. His fingers caressed the skin, and she was shocked at the way her soul longed for his touch.

He turned her ankle so the wound faced him. With careful fingers, he gently rubbed the salve into the cut there. The gash should be stitched, but too much time had passed and the skin had begun to scab. She recognized the mixture of herbs he used upon her now and inhaled the memories of her mother, Pril. How she missed her.

She glanced at him through her lashes. She was not prepared to see the sorrow upon his face, and a piece of her wanted to fall into his arms. She stiffened, afraid to let herself be vulnerable to his touch, to his scent, to his presence. To love him meant loss, heartache, and misery.

"Tell me of him," he asked, his voice raw.

She wanted to deny him this knowledge, but when she thought of her son, of how precious he was, a desire to speak of him overcame her. She slowly pushed herself up, keeping the fur close to her skin.

"His hair was black and grew only on the crown." She motioned with her hand to the top of her head.

"What color were his eyes?"

"The color of a chestnut, and when he smiled they became bright with wonder." She closed her eyes, remembering everything about him. "In the evening after Morgan would leave for the gaming halls, I'd sit with him cradled in my arms and inhale his scent. It was a fresh, milk and honey mixture that stayed upon my clothes. He brought sunlight to the dreary days within my marriage."

She yawned. She hadn't slept after being captured by Radu, and her body was desperate for reprieve. Instead she'd bled herself of the burden she'd kept hidden. The release had not been welcome, and she wished for the day a year ago back more now than ever.

"He resembled you." Her heart lightened and as she let the words come from her lips the grief she'd carried began to lift. "Morgan did not care for him because of this."

Red Wolf's jaw flexed.

"He was my reason to wake each morning."

"He was loved," he said.

"With every part of my heart." She blinked, and two tears fell from her lashes. "He was all I had."

Red Wolf wiped the tears from her cheeks.

"Had I known, I would've fought for you."

She did not know what to make of his words, and too tired, she dismissed them from her mind. The need to be comforted, to feel safe took hold of her, and she leaned into him, placing her head upon his shoulder. Tsura knew she'd not open herself to Red Wolf again, but for this moment she seized all thoughts of tomorrow and let him place his arms around her. She yawned, her eyelids heavy. The world around her began to fade.

"What was his name?" Red Wolf whispered into her ear.

"Rowan," she murmured, before she fell asleep.

# CHAPTER TWENTY-EIGHT

Tsura woke to the merriment of children's laughter, the easy chatter between women as they cooked, and the grate of a blade while it chopped through wood. She must've slept for hours. The scent of corn bread floated into the lodge, and she knew it was morning. The Ama used the first part of the day to bake their breads.

She did a quick survey of the lodge and relaxed her shoulders when there was no sign of Red Wolf. He had comforted her yesterday when she'd been exhausted from the grief. Her emotions in turmoil, she'd given in to his presence, taking from him the shelter she needed. Tsura knew she could never love him the way she once had. Her heart was incapable of such a thing, and she'd not allow him to hurt her again.

The newfound ache resonated around her ribs to encase her chest, and she knew the pain would forever be with her now that she'd acknowledged the death of her son.

She stretched her arms, and the blanket fell from her back. She was still naked and scanned the lodge for the deerskin dress she'd worn days before. She had no desire to wear the heavy skirt and high-buttoned blouse. Beautiful Meadow's dress was much more comfortable and was soft upon her skin.

She found the dress folded neatly beside her, along with the moccasins she'd worn since coming to be with the Ama. The leather shoes were a far cry from the laced boots and confined slippers she'd been accustomed to wearing in Bristol.

The beads stitched into small flowers on the front offered a feminine touch to the moccasins. She went to slip them on her feet when she remembered placing the pendant inside of one at the river. Her hand hovered over the top. The necklace had been the very reason her son had perished. A part of her wanted to throw the talisman into the fire and end the sacred legacy forever, but Tsura was reminded of her promise to keep it safe. She decided to remove it from the shoe and place it somewhere no one would find it until she left the Ama.

She reached inside until her hand met the end of the moccasin. There was nothing there. She searched the other and found it empty also. Where could it have gone? Red Wolf might have come across it when he found her things and tucked it away.

Tsura tossed the blanket from her and pulled the deerskin dress over her head. She slipped her feet into the soft leather shoes and left the lodge in search of Red Wolf.

The bright morning sun greeted her with a welcoming embrace as she stepped outside. The warm air was a sign summer approached. She passed Running Bear and his wife, Wild Rose, as they worked in their yard. Wild Rose stared at her with curiosity while Running Bear waved. She wasn't sure if what she'd done for Star Dancer had been known among the Ama, or if Soaring Eagle had kept the healing to himself and Beautiful Meadow. She didn't feel inclined to explain the magick she held, and she did not want to be accosted for it either.

Tsura kept her head down. She had no desire to make eye contact with the passing Ama as she searched for Red Wolf. She walked toward Beautiful Meadow's lodge. She was sure Soaring Eagle would know where his cousin was. The urgency to find the pendant shocked her, especially after all the evil it had brought into her life. She figured the reason she was in such a hurry to locate the jewel was from her mother instilling the need to keep it safe no matter the cost.

She thought of the Chuvani lineage, of the power within the pendant alone, and of the wicked that coveted it. She had decided long ago not to use her magick because of what had happened to Rowan. Was it possible for her to do the same with the pendant? Could she hide it away, teaching each new Chuvani the perils it would bring if found or if known to exist by those with impure hearts?

Tsura was pushed forward, her knees bent, as small arms encircled them. She glanced down to see Star Dancer hugging her.

"Tsisquaya, how are you?" the small girl asked. Her long black hair was braided on either side of her face and left long and untouched in the back.

Tsura could not keep the small smile from her lips as the girl stared up at her with innocence.

"I am well, thank you," she said and knelt so she could stare into Star Dancer's beautiful eyes.

"I have made you a gift." The girl opened her pudgy hand to reveal a small leather medicine sack.

"You did not have to—"

"I know." Star Dancer smiled and placed the homemade pouch into Tsura's hand.

She stared at the beaded bird on the front. "What is this?"

"It is you, Tsisquaya."

She nodded, and slipped the medicine pouch around her neck. "Thank you."

The girl nodded.

"Have you seen your uncle?"

"Edutsi has gone with Edoda into the mountains to hunt."

Tsura stared at the large rocks beyond the Ama village and sighed. She would need to wait until he returned to ask him of the pendant.

"I lost my hair," the girl said, and she touched one of Tsura's curls.

"When did you lose it?"

"In the river."

It must've been the reason the child almost drowned while they were in the water. Tsura felt horrible. "I will give you another."

Star Dancer clapped her hands and smiled.

The girl's purity melted away another piece of the iron she'd barricaded around her heart.

"Come, Tsisquaya let us go and pick the corn for Etsi."

Tsura had nothing else to do with her time, and had enjoyed toiling in the garden with the other women days before.

She nodded, and Star Dancer took her hand.

They walked together into the field where the Ama garden stood. The rows of corn were the furthest from the village and three times the size of the regular plot. She was handed a basket from one of the women passing by, and Tsura accepted it with a gentle smile.

The longer she spent with the Cherokee tribe the more she began to feel at ease. They accepted her not for what she could do, but for who she was even though she hadn't been very kind to them. Star Dancer ran ahead of her, stopping to pull the corn from the tall stalks and drop them into the basket sitting on the ground.

She gazed out over the valley, and for the first time since the death of her son, she felt a longing to be welcomed, loved, and cared for. She thought of Red Wolf, of the love she'd had for him, and the loss she'd endured draped over her. She could not ignore he had not returned, nor could she see a future for herself filled with love. It was not to be.

She was not strong enough to sustain another heartbreak. Yes, she was weak, she was afraid, and therefore she'd not step into those emotions again.

"It is good you are well."

Tsura turned to see Raven standing between the rows of corn. She did not know the maiden well, only of her assistance when she escaped with Miles, but she was aware of her feelings for Red Wolf.

"Do you wish to remain among us?" the girl asked, and Tsura did not misplace the tone of Raven's voice for compassion. The maiden was annoyed with her.

"I will be on my way soon enough," she said and plucked a husk of corn from the thick leafy stalk.

"He will not travel with you." Raven's thin lips disappeared to form an evil grin.

"*He* can do whatever he chooses."

"He will choose to remain here with me."

Tsura refused to be pulled into Raven's game. Red Wolf was free to do as he pleased. He owed her nothing, nor did she wish anything from him. She ignored the slight sensation to have Red Wolf remain by her side.

"I will be all he needs."

"And what if you are not?" She could not stop the question from being asked. After all, she'd thought the very thing years before. Red Wolf had not fought for her, he had not questioned the letter, and instead he set sail and never returned. Why did his betrayal still hurt? She'd accepted he did not want her years ago, but today while she stood across from Raven, a part of her heart longed for the past to be different.

Raven stepped toward her, but Tsura was not threatened by the maiden and remained where she stood.

"I do not question such things. I will make him happy."

Tsura felt sorry for the girl. She clearly did not know how love worked. Even though it had been evident Raven did not care for her, Tsura could not let the girl believe Red Wolf would want her.

"You cannot make a heart desire you if there is no hunger to begin with."

"He will choose me."

The girl's obsession with Red Wolf was unsettling, but she was not about to argue with her.

"Very well." Tsura dismissed her, pulling another husk of corn from the stalk. She could feel Raven's anger as it radiated toward her. The fury poked and pricked at her skin.

"You seek the necklace," the girl said and it sounded more like a snake's hiss.

Tsura could not keep the shocked expression from crossing her face, and she blurted, "Do you know where it is?"

Raven smiled. "I do."

Star Dancer began speaking to her aunt in Cherokee and Tsura could not understand what it was she said, but by the way the small girl's eyes slanted, Tsura knew she was cross. Raven dismissed the child with a wave of her hand and stepped closer to Tsura.

"I found it within your moccasin by the river. Come with me, and I will take you to it."

Star Dancer pulled on Tsura's hand. "No, Tsisquaya, it is not right."

She looked down at the child and knew there was a reason she did not want Tsura to go with Raven, but she could not ignore the necessity to have the pendant back and put somewhere safe.

"It will be fine," she reassured Star Dancer and followed Raven out of the garden toward the hills.


Red Wolf pulled the whitetail deer from the ground to lie across Caesar's rump. A gash to the middle where he'd gutted the animal gaped open, and flies buzzed around the carcass. He mounted his horse and waited for his cousin to return from the bushes where he'd left on foot to search for more prey.

Soaring Eagle had insisted Red Wolf join him on his morning hunt. He did not want to leave Tsura's side for too long, but knew she needed time to heal. She had let the emotions come forward and was now left to deal with the repercussions. He ran his hand through the long hair that draped down his back. She'd confided in him last night, told him of their son. He wasn't sure she'd open up to him, given that she did not trust him and blamed him for the past, but he'd been wrong.

The moment she laid in his arms, empty of any blame, malice, or resentment, he could feel the woman she once was. Tsura was still there amidst all of the wreckage, a torn, tattered soul longing to be loved. Red Wolf understood her now. The pain, the loss, and the rejection gave way to the anger, hate and shame she placed upon those around her. She was lost and searched for somewhere to belong, a moment without the hurt, without the memories, without the anger.

The thought of Tsura's pain turned his stomach, and he clenched his jaw. He'd not leave her. He owed her that much—damn it he owed her so much more. He growled. He loved her still and knew he'd love her until the day he died. Somehow he needed her to see that. He needed her to know how sorry he'd been for not returning, for not being there when she had their son.

Red Wolf could not deny the shock, or his own shame when she'd told him of their child. He did not know what to say, but did not question her accusation either. He'd known it was true. The realization brought forth his guilt at what he'd done, and he felt terrible. He'd not known his own child, his own son, and his soul cried out for another chance. When he'd gone to Tsura, he was prepared to beg her to tell him of their child and was humbled when he did not have to.

She'd named him Rowan, the very tree where he was conceived. It was a testament to how much she'd loved Red Wolf and how she'd held onto the memories. To name their son after a place only they would know tugged at his heart and caused his eyes to water. She had waited for him even after she'd married Morgan, and like the selfish ass he was, he'd not returned.

Red Wolf gripped the reins, his knuckles turning white. He could not take back the past, even though he wished with every part of him that he could. He'd sacrifice his life for Tsura to be happy, and their son to be alive.

He was determined to help Tsura find her way. To stand still as she berated, beat, and cast hatred toward him. He'd let her fists pummel his chest, her nails slice his flesh, but he would not stop loving her. He'd never leave her again. He knew she'd resist him—deny him any chance at having her within his life once more. Red Wolf would not cease in his affection for her, even if it meant he'd have to love her from afar

# CHAPTER TWENTY-NINE

Tsura walked deeper into the forest behind Raven. The tall pine and elm trees concealed them from the Ama village below. They'd been climbing upward for sometime, and her legs began to ache. She plucked a blackberry from the short shrub as she walked by. A twinge at the base of her neck signaled something was not right. The urgency to find the pendant had pushed aside any distrust she'd had for the girl, and she'd followed her into the forest

"How much further?" she asked.

Raven did not reply, and instead increased her pace.

Tsura stopped. "I will not take another step until you tell me how much longer."

The maiden turned, and as the sun reflected off of her black tresses they glowed a dark blue. "It is just past this hill."

"Why have you taken the pendant there?" It was clear Raven did not hold the pendant. She may have seen the necklace if it had been Red Wolf who had lifted it from her boot, but the girl did not have it now. Tsura turned to leave.

"Where are you going?"

"I was a fool to follow you this far. You do not have my necklace."

"No, dear, she does not...it is I who hold the pendant."

Tsura swung around the voice unfamiliar to her. Dread shrouded her previous concern with Raven the instant her eyes fell upon the woman at the top of the hill. She was a Renoldi. The long tanned skirt, loose top, and green sash tied around her waist were familiar. Her mother wore similar clothing for years after they moved to Bristol.

"You do not remember me?" the woman asked as she came closer. Her long straw colored hair hung past her knees in thin wisps. This woman was not her aunt Magda. Tsura remembered her aunt's coal black hair and dark eyes.

She retreated a step. Every part of her hummed, the magick wanted to protect her—to strike down the evil woman. Tiny pebbles of sweat glistened off of her forehead as she utilized her strength to control the need. She'd not be able to defeat the woman if she held the pendant. Tsura had been born a Chuvani, inherited gifts and powers no person could understand. While under her mother's instruction Pril had repeated countless times what would happen if someone other than a Chuvani took hold of the talisman. Tsura swore to keep the heirloom safe. However, if practiced, the Chuvani was the only one who could defeat the evil.

But Tsura was not proficient in her abilities as a Chuvani. She hadn't used her magick consistently in years. When she was married to Morgan she hid who she was, afraid of what he might do if he found out about her gift. She only used the magick when it was needed.

"You are a Renoldi," Tsura said.

The gypsy smiled, and Tsura did not miss the wicked edges of her lips.

"You remember." She waved her hand to call someone from behind her, and two other women stepped forward out of the trees.

She recognized her aunt immediately and could not stop her hands from shaking. Long black hair streaked with silver and parted down the middle hung past a gaunt, jagged face. The woman's murky eyes held no kindness—long lines pulled her mouth down into a grim frown. She glanced at the other woman, Sorina, her mother's friend. The gypsy woman had cared for Tsura when she was a child and living with the Peddlers. Her mother had grieved Sorina's betrayal with the same sadness as her brother Galius'.

"Do you hold the pendant?" she asked. The ends of her fingers pulsed, and she pulled her hands into tight fists.

"Are you afraid?" the woman asked.

Tsura did not know who this woman was, but she seemed to be superior to the other two.

"Who are you?"

"Why, I am your cousin, Emine. Pril killed my sister and father."

All the stories she'd heard rushed back, and vivid narratives replayed in her mind. Pias had been Emine's father, and she held certain powers all on her own. If her cousin did have the pendant, Tsura knew she'd not defeat her.

"Where is my necklace?" she asked again, her voice a little stronger this time.

"It is here." Emine held up her hand and opened the palm to reveal the red ruby.

Tsura sucked in a breath. She watched horrified as the gypsy placed the pendant over her head to rest against her chest.

"Give it to me," Tsura demanded.

Emine laughed. It was a shrill sound that scattered the birds from the trees. "Now you shall see what I can do." She thrust her arm out toward her.

A searing pain sliced through Tsura's stomach. She heaved forward, wrapped her arms around the middle, and squeezed. The muscles twisted and burned. She held her breath to ease the discomfort, but the agony intensified. The blood filled her head and pressed against the skin. Black dots danced within her vision, and she blinked rapidly desperate to remain conscious. She fell to her knees, the broken branches and roots digging into her bare legs above her moccasins.

With the same force the pain came it disappeared, and she remained on the ground, too weak to stand. Her long curly hair fell onto her face, and she remembered her promise to Star Dancer. She'd not be able to give the child a lock of her hair. The gypsies would kill her.

"Stand," Emine shouted.

Tsura could hear the crunch and rustle of the leaves while the woman came toward her. With the strength only the pendant could offer, Emine hauled Tsura up. Her legs trembled, and she grabbed hold of the tree beside her.

"You hold no power as great as mine," Emine hissed.

"Without the pendant you are no more powerful than a rock."

"You shall pay for all you've done."

Tsura met Emine's dark glare with one as intimidating. "I do not fear you."

"We shall see."

She knew these were her final hours, but she refused to make her death simple for the Renoldi. She owed it to her mother to fight for the pendant—to destroy it before her life was taken. She cared not for her own life, but to leave the pendant within the hands of the Renoldi meant disaster for all who came within the gypsies' fold. Yes, she would destroy the ruby somehow before she drew her last breath.

"Walk. We have a special place waiting for you." Emine gave her a shove.

The magick coursed through her veins, to travel throughout her body. Her skin heated, and she did not stop her body as the skin began to burn. Sweat trickled down her temples, and her temperature rose.

Emine shrieked and released Tsura to stare at her singed hand.

She did not wait for the gypsy to gather herself before she placed both hands upon Emine's face. The skin sizzled. The air filled with the acrid smell of burned flesh. Tsura gagged, desperate to control the urge to retch. The pendant glowed and she reached for it.

Emine bared her teeth and hissed. She struck Tsura in the chest with such force the wind flew from her lungs. She crumpled to the ground. The dirt rubbed into the sweat on her cheeks, and she slowly inhaled the earth. Each breath was paired with an agonizing pain, and she was sure Emine had broken some of her ribs.

"I am stronger," the gypsy growled from above her.

Tsura curled into her knees and remained there. The incessant ache in her side throbbed, and she took shallow breaths.

"What are we to do with her?" Sorina asked.

Tsura knew they spoke of Raven. She pressed her head into the leaves and twigs, to glance at the girl standing off to the side. Raven's eyes were wide and exuded fear. The girl had betrayed her, taken her to the enemy knowing they wished to kill her. She tried to bring forth the anger, but it did not come. Instead she was filled with pity for the young maiden.

"We shall bring her along," Emine said.

"I do not need to go. I brought you the girl," Raven said as she stepped backward.

"Quiet!" Emine shouted.

"But, you did not say I needed to stay—"

"Enough." Emine's eyes flashed with wickedness.

Tsura's senses heightened, her ears rang. She had to help the girl. She slowly rolled onto her hands and knees. The pain in her ribs increased, and she gasped. She couldn't see for the hair falling around her, and she prayed Emine did not hear her. With great care she pulled herself up to stand. The forest spun into a blur of green and brown. Her stomach turned, bile pushed its way up her throat, and she swallowed, unwilling to yield to the pain. She brushed the hair from her face and waited.

Emine's cheeks were a gnarled mess. The raised flesh was red and swollen, an opposite to her pale complexion.

"Please, I wish to leave," Raven's voice trembled.

Emine curled her lip. "Halt all words to pass thy lips, and severe thy tongue rip, rip, rip!"

Raven let out a sickening scream. A single stream of crimson escaped from her lips to roll down her chin. She opened her lips, blood spilled from her mouth, and a piece of her tongue fell to the ground. The girl slumped to her knees, picked up the cut off muscle, and clutched it to her chest. Big tears fell from her lashes as she whimpered.

The sound haunted the woods, and Tsura shivered. The urge pulsed through her. The palms heated, and she wiggled her fingers. Her concern for Raven overshadowed any sense to stay put. She shoved Emine to the ground, ignored the pain as it radiated across her back and into her sides, and raced toward the girl. She took the bloodied muscle from Raven's hand, thrust it in her mouth, and squeezed. The girl didn't fight her, too shocked at what had happened to her tongue. Tsura knew the instant the muscle began to meld with the cut off flesh when her own tongue ached, and she tasted the metal upon her lips. The maiden's eyes changed from frightened to serene, and Tsura knew the tongue had been healed.

A deafening pain erupted in her scalp as she was yanked backward. Emine clutched her hair and dragged Tsura away from Raven. There'd been no time to move, to step aside, and so she vomited all over Emine's dress.

"You ingrate!" The gypsy threw her to the ground.

Raven turned to run.

Emine pointed her fist at the girl. Raven flew through the air with such potency the leaves rustled, and a surge of wind moved Tsura's hair from her face. The girl's body slammed into the trunk of a pine tree before she fell to the ground. Emine could throw a beam? The power of the pendant aided the Renoldi in way's Tsura was not prepared for, another reminder she could not defeat her.

"I've grown tired of these games." Emine stalked toward her. "Cease all movement from head to toe, rob thy senses steal thy foe."

Tsura could not move, frozen still by the spell.

Despair did not touch on the hopelessness she felt. She'd been told not to let the pendant out of her sight, to keep it safe always, and never ever let it fall into malicious hands. She did not fully understand the depth of power the pendant held. The necklace had saved her life while she tried to heal her son, but other than the one incident she'd not witnessed the magick within the heirloom.

Sorina knelt beside Tsura, opened her lips and shoved berries into her mouth. The fruit tasted oddly familiar as the juicy berries slid down her throat. Emine's booted feet paced and the sound of twigs snapping intensified in her ears. She blinked. The motion seemed to take forever, and the trees distorted.

Fear spread across her chest to press on her heart, and lungs. She'd tasted the berry before, when she was small and Pias had given it to her. Witch's berry made her weak, lightheaded, and unable to focus, but there was more to these berries. The small dose would've made her weak but not immobile. Emine must've placed a spell on the fruit to strengthen the poison.

She was powerless to stop the gypsy from killing her, or anyone else. Tsura's eyes closed again this time she could not make them open. She'd fight for the pendant. Her mind slowed, and she could feel herself slipping into a deep sleep. Tsura would destroy the ruby, and in doing so she'd die.

Red Wolf rode alongside Soaring Eagle. The valley was shrouded in grey silhouettes as the sun descended and evening approached. They'd been gone all day hunting, and he was anxious to see Tsura. He was unsure what would greet him when he rode into the village, but he hoped she'd not cut him out of her life like she'd done before. He wanted to know more about his son, and ached to show her how much he still cared.

The Ama village was edged in orange hues reflected off of the rooftops from their fires. The smell of corn bread fanned across the valley, and Red Wolf's nostrils flared. His stomach grumbled, and he kicked Caesars side to quicken the horses pace.

"You rush, Cousin," Soaring Eagle said from beside him. The white chief's braid dangled to the middle of his back, an eagle feather tied at the end.

"I am hungry."

They had been successful in their hunt today. Soaring Eagle had slayed three rabbits and each of them had killed a deer. He glanced back at the carcass hanging over Caesar's rump. Red Wolf sat taller in his saddle. Pride pulled his cheeks up into a smile. He'd remembered how to hunt. The days spent with his tribe had been a reawakening for his soul, and he longed to remain among them.

"I think it is more than your stomach rushing you home."

"You think too much."

Soaring Eagle snickered.

Red Wolf ignored his cousin. The teasing did not bother him as it had before. He knew where his heart lied, and to whom it belonged.

As they approached the village he scanned the faces of the Ama for Tsura. The men and women went about their chores, while the children ran in between the lodges. They neared Soaring Eagle's home when Star Dancer and Beautiful Meadow came running toward them, their eyes big and wide, worry etched into the dark circles.

Something was wrong.

He jumped from Caesar, but Soaring Eagle beat him to his wife and child, concern evident on his face.

"Where is Tsura?" Red Wolf asked.

"She has not returned since this morning," Beautiful Meadow said.

"Star Dancer took her to the garden to pick corn, but…" She averted her eyes.

"Speak what it is you know," Soaring Eagle said and placed his arm onto his wife's shoulder.

"Raven took her into the forest," she finished.

Did Beautiful Meadow know of Raven's affection for Red Wolf and how he'd turned her down?

"What for?" he asked. None of what she said made sense. Why would Tsura follow Raven into the forest when it was clear neither girl cared for each other? Red Wolf felt a tug on his pant leg. He glanced down at Star Dancer. Her big brown eyes misted, and her bottom lip trembled.

He knelt in front of her.

"Tsisquaya is in trouble," the girl said.

"How do you know?"

"Raven spoke of a necklace. The one I saw at the river the day I got sick. It is special."

Red Wolf knew of the pendant, and just how special it was.

"What of the necklace?" he asked.

"Tsisquaya lost it. She asked me if I knew where it was, but I did not."

"Did Raven know?" he was going on a hunch.

Star Dancer nodded.

"She told Tsisquaya she had the necklace and to go with her if she wanted it."

Red Wolf knew Tsura could not let the pendant into the hands of anyone other than a Chuvani, and now he understood why she'd gone with Raven.

Soaring Eagle called two young braves over. He instructed them to remove the deer and rabbits, leaving them at his lodge.

"Can you show us which way they went?" Red Wolf asked.

Star Dancer walked in the direction of the garden. They stayed close behind her so they didn't lose sight of her as nightfall neared. They came to a row of corn, and Star Dancer pointed above it to a wall of pine trees.

"They went into the forest there," she said.

Red Wolf looked at Soaring Eagle. They did not need to speak knowing neither would abandon the other in their time of need.

"Take Star Dancer back to the lodge. Send Running Bear and White Owl to follow our tracks."

Beautiful Meadow nodded. She cupped Soaring Eagle's cheeks within her palms and gently placed her lips against his in an affectionate kiss.

"Heyatahesdi, be careful," she whispered while she pressed her forehead to his.

A pang of jealousy entered Red Wolf's heart at the love between Soaring Eagle and his wife. He'd been blessed with such a love once, but because he was a fool it had been taken from him. He rubbed his molars together, and brushed the self-pity aside. He needed to find Tsura, and right all wrongs between them. Caesar whinnied, and nudged his snout into Red Wolf's side. It was time to go.

He walked into the forest. The tall trees shrouded any light from the moon, and the woods were swallowed in darkness. He waited for his eyes to adjust before he searched the ground for footprints. Soaring Eagle stood off to the side, watching the perimeter for any signs of danger.

"Their tracks lead this way." Red Wolf pointed up the hill.

"Why has Raven taken your woman there?" Soaring Eagle asked.

He hadn't told his cousin of the girls behavior toward him, or her annoyance at Tsura because of their past.

"I do not know."

"If she has this necklace wouldn't she keep it within her lodge and not up the mountain?"

Red Wolf sighed. Soaring Eagle's attentive behavior was one of the many reasons he made a great chief. He knew something was not right. The girl would not take a necklace into the woods unless she was trying to lead Tsura away from the Ama. They continued to walk on foot, their horses trailed behind them.

"Cousin, I must confide in you," Red Wolf said.

Soaring Eagle nodded.

"Raven has lured Tsura from the tribe to hurt her."

"You speak out of worry for your woman."

"No, I speak the truth."

"How do you know of this?"

He stopped, and knelt. His hand felt the flat print in the ground, to the left there was another. He stood and wiped his hands on the breeches before taking Caesar's reins.

"Raven has expressed her affection for me."

"She cannot. The Cherokee law states she must marry a brave from another tribe."

"I told her this, but she did not care."

Soaring Eagle exhaled.

"You have a woman, why would she care for you?"

"I do not know, but I feel that is why she's taken Tsura."

"To harm her?"

"Yes."

They walked in silence for a long while. He knew his cousin absorbed all he'd been told. If Raven had hurt Tsura, the Ama would need to punish her, and Raven was Beautiful Meadow's sister. The act would be extremely difficult for Soaring Eagle.

The trees were no longer clumped together, and the moon lit a clear path for them. Red Wolf stared at the twinkling stars set against an almost black sky and said a silent prayer that Tsura was safe.

Red Wolf was thankful for the bright moon while they continued to search. A wolf howled in the distance, and the horses startled.

He pulled Caesar's snout close and rubbed the hair to calm him. "Shush, friend."

Once his horse had settled Red Wolf searched the ground for Raven and Tsura's trail. He followed the small steps further into the woods, where the trees did not grow.

"There are more prints," Soaring Eagle said further up the hill at the edge of the small clearing. His cousin squatted, and trained eyes roamed the small opening in the forest. "Others were here."

He went to where Soaring Eagle sat, and there on the ground pressed into the dirt were four prints. The footprints were small, and Red Wolf knew it had been women who met with Raven and Tsura. He was scanning the area when he saw something far off to the right of them. It could be a rock, but instinct told him otherwise. He sprinted toward the ominous shadow.

As he drew closer his heartbeat quickened. It was a woman. He fell to his knees and turned her over.

Raven's beautiful face reflected off the moonlight, and Red Wolf released a sigh. His relief was soon overshadowed by his concern for the young girl's injuries.

"Does she live?" Soaring Eagle asked as worry creased his eyes.

Blood stained her cheeks and chin, and he felt her face for any wounds. She was not cut anywhere. He could not see how she'd been hurt. Where had the blood on her face been from?

He placed his head to her chest and heard the faint pounding of her heart. The beats, too far apart, were a sign that Raven was worse off than she looked. He shook her, but she did not wake.

"She lives, but I fear her injuries are within."

Soaring Eagle assessed his sister in-law. His face creased with concern, and Red Wolf knew he'd come to the same conclusion. The girl would likely die.

"Your woman is not here."

He knew this. Tsura had been taken, and he knew by whom.

"Are there gypsies near by?" he asked.

"Tsiquisi? Yes, we trade with them."

"Do you know the clan name?"

"Renoldi."

His breath seized within his lungs. All this time he'd tried to keep Tsura safe, he'd led her right to the gypsies. The very damned ones who wished to kill her.

"Damn it." He stood and went to Caesar. "Which way is their village?"

"Cousin, you cannot go alone."

"I cannot wait. Tsura is in grave danger."

"From the tsiguisi?"

"Tsura is a gypsy. She hails from the Renoldi clan, and they wish to kill her."

He didn't have time to explain. He needed to get to her. He pulled his quiver from the saddle and looked inside. There were only two arrows left.

"I cannot leave Raven."

Red Wolf nodded.

"I cannot leave Tsura again. I must go now."

Soaring Eagle went to his horse. He returned with four more arrows.

"I am a better shot than you," he said with a smirk and handed the arrows to him.

"Thank you, Cousin."

"Wudeligvi, west. The village is at the crest of the mountain."

"How far?"

"No more than three hours."

Red Wolf nodded. He placed the arrows Soaring Eagle had given him into his quiver, checked his sheath for the knife he always wore, and mounted Caesar.

"Donadagohv, till we meet again," Soaring Eagle said.

"Donadogahv."

Red Wolf turned Caesar west, kicked his moccasins into the animal's sides, and took off. He clenched his jaw, flexed his muscles, and set off to rescue Tsura.

# CHAPTER THIRTY

Tsura woke groggy and listless. She blinked to try and regain her composure, but the effects of the Witch's berry were still inside of her. She licked her lips, her mouth dry, her tongue coated as if she'd chewed on a dozen moths. She sat with her back against a wooden pole. She slumped to the side, and if she hadn't been tied, she'd have fallen over. The spell on her body had worn off, and she could now move her legs and arms, but the Witch's berry had taken away her wits, and she was sluggish.

Night had fallen, torches lit the area, and a large fire burned to her left in the center of the village. Emine had brought Tsura home, to the very people who had cast out her family and tried to hand her over to the Monroes. She watched the Renoldi through droopy lids. None of them looked familiar to her, and she wondered if Sorina and Magda were the only Peddlers living here.

The village had been tucked away hidden among the tall pine and oak trees on the mountain. It was the very hill she'd watched while sitting under the elm tree days before. She thought of the Ama. The village had become the one place she'd felt safe—welcome. Before she'd been reluctant to see how much others cared for her, and now since she'd released the anger, she'd been able to witness it. Beautiful Meadow had become a good friend—one Tsura could count on whenever she was in need. The Ama had nestled themselves into her cold heart and warmed it with the compassion they showed her. She'd not let any harm to come to them because of her.

Tsura stared past the small homes, built much like the Ama lodges. There were a few vardos scattered among the other buildings, and she remembered the small wagons from her time with the Peddlers. Two boys tossed a rock near the home directly in front of her. Their knitted brows told her they concentrated on their task to hit something on the ground. A pang resonated in her chest, and she thought of her son. She closed her eyes and saw him, a chubby baby with midnight colored hair. The ache within her soul still remained, but she did not feel the desolation like she had before. Was it because tonight she'd perish, or had it been from the comfort she'd found with the Ama and possibly Red Wolf?

She rested her head against the post. In the recent weeks Red Wolf had been a constant thorn in her side. He'd insisted on protecting her from Romulus, and in turn she'd been nothing but cruel to him. She'd treated him with unjust anger, despised him for the life he'd led without her. Not once had she allowed him to explain, given him the opportunity to express what he knew. She was too hell bent on ruining him, and herself to even consider such a notion.

Tsura hadn't been aware of how Morgan cheated Red Wolf, and how his heart must've broken from her denial of him. She refused to acknowledge his feelings. The bastard Baron chased Red Wolf away, and because of him, Rowan had died.

She accepted what Red Wolf told her as truth. He'd never have left her, or their baby. He loved her. A tear slipped from her lashes to slither down her cheek. She mourned the loss of the life she should've lived, but too much time had passed between them for their love to ever be rekindled. She hung her head, more out of defeat than from the Witch's berry she'd consumed.

Red Wolf deserved much better than she could ever give him. His duty confined him to her, and soon he'd be released of the obligation. This night she'd destroy the legacy, end the relentless hunt for the pendant and all who coveted it. She'd set Red Wolf free of his promises, and she'd be free of the loneliness.

"I see you have woken," Emine said. Her cheeks looked awful, the flesh where Tsura had burned was pitted and red. The skin peeled away, and oozed making the wound appear wet. The pendant glowed upon the gypsy's chest, and Tsura wanted nothing more than to snatch it from around the vile woman's neck.

She tried to form a spell, to place the words in the right order, but they were jumbled in her mind.

Emine snapped her fingers, and a handsome man she had not noticed before stepped around the woman. His blonde hair and muscular arms were only a few of his striking qualities. She watched as he stepped closer to Emine, his shoulder brushed against her frail one.

It wasn't until he stared at the gypsy, did Tsura see the lust reflect within his gaze. The man pined for the older woman, devoured every part of her with his eyes. He was much younger than Emine, and Tsura figured him closer to her own age. What could he possibly see in her? There were plenty of young maidens among the clan he could have chosen, but instead he desired this one.

"Darius, move her to the scaffold." Emine's voice cut into her thoughts, and Tsura turned to where she pointed.

Raised crossbeams were erected behind her, but the ropes around her wrists detained her from seeing the full structure. She struggled with the twine, pulling it tight. The braided hair bit into her flesh and cut the skin. Tsura leaned away from the pole, and swiveled her hips toward the platform. She gasped. A noose hung from the center of the wood. She counted thirteen loops before the knot had been tied.

She swallowed.

The Renoldi's were going to hang her, and by the thickness of the rope they wanted success. She squeezed her eyes closed until black dots formed behind her lids. She had to get the pendant before they hung her. Still dazed, but with time running out, she called upon the power to flow through her veins. Her body grew warm, but before she could throw a beam, or count a spell, her skin cooled, and she slumped to the side. The Witch's berry, and whatever else Emine had placed over the fruit, had knocked the sense from her body.

Tsura inhaled through her nose, and exhaled slowly out of her mouth, desperate to clear her mind of the haze.

"You will not rid yourself of the brew," Emine snarled. "I have perfected the potion so, when placed with the berry, it increases in strength."

"What do you want? You have the pendant. Why do you wait to kill me?" She tried to stall the gypsy.

"I want you to pay for all that you've done!" Emine stepped closer. Her long fingernail jutted out and sliced Tsura's cheek.

Pressed against the pole and tied with her arms behind her, she could not avoid the attack. The skin broke, when the air hit the open flesh, the scrape burned.

"Move her!"

Darius pulled a knife from the sheath around his waist, and cut the ropes holding Tsura to the pole. Her wrists relaxed, and she flexed the joint. With one swift swing of his arm, he hoisted her up over his shoulder and carried her toward the gallows.

"Do you love her?" Tsura whispered into his ear.

Darius' step faltered.

"She is my Empress," he said.

His tone belied to what Tsura now knew, Emine had charmed him.

"She does not care for you. She uses you to do her bidding."

He tightened his hold on her legs, and climbed the three steps to the gallows. She tried to pull away from his shoulder, but the muscle pressed into her midsection. The berries, combined with her fears, increased the unease and nausea swirled in her stomach. The sensation crept up Tsura's throat, and she swallowed the urge to retch all over him.

She waited, until the sickness passed, before she whispered, "Emine has placed a spell over you. Do you not feel it?"

He let his arms fall to the side, he no longer held her, and she fell to the ground. Her bottom ached, and she tried to right the dress, before he yanked her up to stand. Tsura's legs collapsed, and Darius caught her before she crumpled to the scaffold floor. He hauled her back up again, this time keeping one arm around her back. He waited until she found her footing, before he slowly removed his hold on her.

"You must believe me. I can help you."

Darius' blue eyes darkened, and his plump lips laid flat. He pulled her arms back and tied her hands behind her. He fitted the noose around her neck, not bothering to pull her hair free of the rope. His wide hands, and thick fingers tightened the heavy cord and, when she swallowed, the threads from the horsehair rope pressed into her throat.

"Please, you must listen to me," she begged one last time, but Emine's sentry wrenched on the ropes around her wrists, and neck. Once he was satisfied she could not escape, he stepped to the left away from her. It was clear Darius was to guard her until the rope squeezed the life from her.

She stared out at the gathering Renoldi's and wondered when they'd drop the wooden floor from beneath her. She thought of James, of the rope, the tree he was left to dangle from, and how she'd tried to save him. The remorse she felt over the loss of her brother knocked the wind from her chest. How could she have been so cruel? She should've rescued him. Tsura fought the tears clinging to her lashes, even more determined to destroy the pendant. The act would end her life, and the legacy, but she could not allow Emine to keep the ruby.

Emine picked up a torch walked to the fire and lit it. She swung around to face the crowd. "It is time! Come, come and watch the Branded One die."

The Renoldi's came from their homes and vardos, men, women, and children. They circled the scaffold where Tsura stood. Hatred exuded from their faces. They desired her persecution just as their leader. Tsura's stomach turned, the Renoldi's would enjoy her suffering. The clan was sick, demented, bred to believe the Chuvani should perish.

Magda and Sorina came through the crowd to stand beside Emine. The women had their own reasons for revenge, Tsura knew, but she had to stall them until the Witch's berry wore off, and she could use her power to abolish the pendant.

"You have brought me here to hang," she shouted, mustering all the courage she had left. "You seek my death and nothing else?"

Magda walked toward her. Tsura spotted the small dagger she clutched within her boney hand. The metal reflected the torches, and she held her breath.

"You killed my daughter. You are the reason my husband hung from a tree," she hissed. "You will know the agony I have endured before your heart stops forever." Magda plunged the knife into the side of her leg.

The shock expelled the air from Tsura's lungs, followed by an intense pain.

"I did not kill your daughter…Galius did," she wheezed.

"Lies!" She slid the blade from her flesh, and without waiting pierced Tsura again closer to the hip. Magda repeated the vicious attack, Tsura helpless, bound by ropes. Her mind dizzy, she felt another slash on her arm.

She couldn't hold herself up any longer, and her knees buckled. The weight of her body pulled the noose snug around her neck, cutting off all breath. The pressure in her head intensified. She could not defeat them. Blood flowed down her leg and into the moccasins she wore. She closed her eyes as the darkness approached…she'd failed.

Darius' strong arm wrapped around her waist and pulled her up to stand. Too weak, she drooped into him. The rope had not loosened, and she felt his fingers tug it away from her neck.

Tsura gulped. She tried to speak, to thank him, but the words were no more than a whimper.

"The Branded One is here in the flesh, and we shall destroy her," Emine shrieked.

Tsura heard the light step of a woman coming toward her. Too frail to open her eyes and see who it was, she lay against Darius. His arm tightened around her waist. She shuffled her feet. The hem of her deerskin dress lifted, a cool breeze caressed her bare thigh, and the calm sensation lasted mere seconds before a scorching hot pain erupted in her leg. She screamed. Terror scratched the back of her throat as she continued to cry out. The skin bubbled and hissed, and the pungent smell of her flesh filled the air.

Sorina stood before her, a metal poker pressed into Tsura's thigh.

Bile rushed up her throat and spewed from her lips. The intensity too much, the agony beyond anything she'd ever experienced. Please, let them end her life. She leaned forward. Darius' arm, still around her waist, supported her so she did not fall over. She continued to vomit, the shock of the burn too much for her body to consume.

Sorina removed the metal prong and pressed it into Tsura's leg again.

She tossed her head back, the rope taut on the long strands of hair, and let out a guttural sound. Vomit clung to her chin, neck, and the front of her dress. The pain lingered with the smell, and she heaved. The stomach, empty, convulsed instead.

"Enough," Darius growled. "She has had enough." He brought her body into his, shielding her from anymore torture the gypsies might have.

"Quiet," Emine growled, and without further warning, Darius' arm left Tsura's side and she fell to the ground choked by the rope once more. Loud groans came from beside her, and she knew Emine had struck him with a beam. The magick constricted his heart in a vise like grip. There was nothing she could do to help him, the power buried in the crevices of her mind. She didn't try to stand, instead letting the noose strangle her. Soon the pain would leave, the heartache she'd endured would disappear, and she'd feel no more.

"Lift her!" Emine shouted.

Darius' arm was around her once more, but the same strength he'd had before was not there. He struggled with her weight, and she did little to help him. The rope around her neck loosened, and she could not help but wish he'd not done so. She had been close to losing consciousness and knew death would soon follow, but he'd saved her again.

"I will say when she dies." Emine's voice came closer. "Until I speak the words, she will remain alive."

"What more do you want from her? She has nothing left," Darius argued.

Tsura admired his perseverance to stand against Emine and the pendant, but she also knew what the gypsy was capable of doing now that she held the power.

A loud smack saturated the darkness, and Tsura peeked through her lashes to see Darius holding his cheek with his right hand.

"If you do not obey as I've instructed, you too shall die this night!" Emine screamed.

Darius stood, lifted his square chin, and nodded. He shifted Tsura, holding her away from him. She shook uncontrollably, and her teeth chattered. She did not feel the pain when she bit her lip, only aware she'd done so when she tasted the blood upon her tongue. She could not endure much more. Death would soon come.

Sorrow at what she'd left undone washed over her, and she closed her eyes. "I'm sorry, mama."

# CHAPTER THIRTY-ONE

Red Wolf crept through the trees, his moccasins silent against the forest floor. The gypsies had two guards placed at the top of the hill. He slid an arrow from the quiver on his back and aimed the weapon at the larger of the two men. Forty feet stood between Red Wolf and the watchman's. He gripped the bow, his sight trained on the guard to the left. He inhaled, released the twine and the arrow flew through the air. Before the stick lodged into the man, Red Wolf took off toward them. Branches accosted his face, slapping his skin, but he did not stop.

He knew the moment the arrow struck the gypsy, when the other man quickly pulled a knife from his sheath and aimed the blade toward the dark forest. Red Wolf lunged from the trees, his dagger drawn. He tackled the man to the ground. The gypsy fought underneath him, but Red Wolf pinned his arms. With no time to dally, he plunged the knife into the man's side until the gypsy stilled beneath him.

He wiped the blade on his pants, slipped the knife back into the sheath on his leg, and went to check the other guard. Red Wolf's arrow had been accurate, striking the man in the heart. He didn't bother to feel for a pulse, but instead emptied their quivers of their arrows. A bloodcurdling scream echoed off of the treetops and shrouded Red Wolf in a luster of cold sweat. Tsura.

Arrows still in hand, he ran the rest of the way up the hill to where the Renoldi village lay. The leather pants clung to his legs making it difficult to move, and he wished he'd worn the breechcloth instead. He stopped himself just before bursting through the trees and into plain sight of the gypsies. Red Wolf's chest expanded, his heart in his throat, and he scanned the village for Tsura. A sudden coldness stirred in his gut, and he growled low in his throat.

She stood with a noose around her neck, lacerations on her face and body. She slumped into the sentry beside her. The man seemed to be protecting her from another attack, and Red Wolf was grateful, but before he could breathe a sigh of relief the sentry fell forward. Tsura dropped from his arms, and the noose tightened. Red Wolf had just begun to step from the wall of trees concealing him when a hand upon his shoulder stopped him. Soaring Eagle, White Owl, and Running Bear stood in the woods, their faces painted for war. He stared at his cousin, sending him a silent question of Raven.

Soaring Eagle shook his head, and Red Wolf knew the girl had succumbed to her injuries. Another tormented cry filled the air, and Red Wolf watched horrified as a gypsy with long black hair held a branding iron to Tsura's flesh.

He jerked the dagger from the sheath on his leg and curled his lip. The gypsies would pay for their attack on Tsura tonight.

"You must wait," Soaring Eagle said. "There are too many of them."

He shoved his cousin's hand from his shoulder. "She will die."

Soaring Eagle stared at Tsura. His wide brown eyes turned to narrow slits as fury secreted from their dark depths. He knew Red Wolf was right. She would not hold on much longer. The torture the gypsies had inflicted upon her was too much for one person to endure.

"We will circle the village." Soaring Eagle paused and a lethal smile spread across his lips. "On White Owl's call we attack."

The warriors and their chief disbanded without further conversation, and Red Wolf was left to wait for the hoot of an owl. He watched the display of unearthly torture upon Tsura and vowed to kill every single damned Renoldi for what they'd done to her.

He bounced from foot to foot as anger stoked the rage smoldering inside of him. He tightened his grip on the handle of the blade. An owl hooted and Red Wolf burst through the trees, his moccasin feet trampling the ground, his eyes trained on Tsura.

The sentry had been struck with an arrow, and Tsura hung from the noose once more. He had to get to her. The panicked screams of the Renoldi surrounded him as arrows rained down upon them. Thankful for Soaring Eagle and his warriors, Red Wolf knew he could not have rescued Tsura on his own.

She'd dangled from the rope far too long. She'd die if he did not get there quickly. He had stopped to grab his bow when an arrow flew from the trees and hit the rope but did not slice through. Before he could ready his arrow, another one whizzed from a different direction breaking the rope, and Tsura fell to the ground. White Owl and Running Bear had saved his woman.

A weathered gypsy climbed the steps and pulled Tsura's head back. Red Wolf saw the knife, reached for his dagger, and threw it before she stabbed Tsura's porcelain flesh. His blade struck the gypsy in the arm, and she went down. He jumped onto the scaffold and fell to his knees. He pulled the noose from Tsura's neck and sighed when her chest rose. He drank in the sight of her. The cuts and bruises did little to taint the beauty that was all her. He brushed the hair from her face. He pressed his hands into her arms, stomach, and legs evaluating the wounds. He came to the spot on her thigh where she'd been branded. Nausea turned his stomach, and he had to keep from spitting the remnants of disgust from his mouth.

Red Wolf was thrown backward when the gypsy he'd stabbed flew at him. Her nails slashed into his face as she barred her teeth and hissed from above him. He pulled his arm back and punched her in the jaw. She rolled from him and the scaffold to land in a pile of skirts on the hard ground. He did a quick assessment for any more gypsies. Soaring Eagle, White Owl, and Running Bear's arrows protruded from the gypsy to his left and the sentry behind him. Both were dead.

Red Wolf focused on Tsura who began to move. She opened her eyes, and he smiled.

"You...you came for me?" she asked.

He nodded afraid to speak for the emotions she stirred within him.

"After all I've done?" Tears shimmered in her green eyes to resemble the most magnificent emeralds he'd ever seen.

He helped her to stand.

"I told you, I'd never leave," he whispered.

"She must die!"

Red Wolf pushed Tsura behind him and faced the horrid woman. Hollow cheeks gave way to muted skin and a crooked jaw. Long, uncolored hair blew from her face, and her brown eyes glowed with a red rim. She held out her arms and the wind gusted to lift leaves, dirt, and the thatched roofs covering the Renoldi lodges. He shielded his eyes from the dust but did not miss the pendant upon the gypsy's chest.

He straightened, tightened his muscles, and prepared himself for what she'd do.

She walked toward him, arrows lodged into her arms and back. The power of the pendant kept her from death.

Tsura stepped from around him.

"Get behind me. I will protect you," he shouted.

She ignored him. He saw the moment the Renoldi's eyes moved from him to Tsura. Without thinking he lunged in front of her. A force struck his chest, crushed his heart, seized his breath, and he blacked out.


Tsura stared in disbelief at Red Wolf. He'd sacrificed himself, stepped in front of the beam Tsura was to take from Emine...the very one that would've killed her. Admiration settled around her heart and chipped away at her resistance toward him. Gratitude caused her bottom lip to tremble at what he'd done…for her. He loved her. Tears bled from her eyes. He had always loved her. She'd pushed him away, resisted everything about him, and she'd been wrong to do so.

Tsura forgot about Emine and knelt beside Red Wolf. Her senses tuned into him. She absorbed the depth of what he'd just done. She lifted a shaky hand to trail her fingertips along the line of his lips. She loved him.

Emine stepped closer, and Tsura hadn't much time. Once the magick invaded her blood, she'd destroy the gypsy, the pendant, and herself…but Red Wolf would live.

Tsura ignored the pain in her leg from the burns, moved to sit on her knees, and planted her palms onto his chest. Her spine straightened as heat radiated up her arms and into her own heart. The heaviness caused her to gasp. Sweat beaded on her forehead, and her stomach turned. She pressed harder. Her heart kicked against the ribs almost knocking her backward, but she held on as the power vibrated through her.

The pain lessened, and she knew he'd been healed. The urge to vomit came quickly. She leaned across Red Wolf and purged on the other side of him. Weak, she could barely lift her arm to wipe the remnants of vomit from her mouth.

"You love him," Emine said, and Tsura knew she'd kill Red Wolf because of this knowledge.

Determined to save him, she closed her eyes, recalling all she'd been taught, all she'd ever known. The power coursed through her blood, pumped into her heart, and flooded every part of her body. It had been years since she'd felt the magick. She wiggled her fingers. Tsura relished in the reunion, and a smile creased her lips. She'd come home.

She stared down at Red Wolf. Her heart swelled with affection and trust, and her throat ached for the undying love she felt for him. He had protected her all of his life, and now she'd return the service. She leaned into him and inhaled his scent. Aware she'd never touch his lips again. She came closer and brushed her cheek against his and gently, ever so softly she kissed him. Tears fell from her lashes to pool between their lips, and she tasted the salt.

"I love you still," she whispered before she pulled herself from him, wiped her eyes, and stood on shaky legs.

"You are nothing without the ruby!" Emine shrieked.

Tsura raised her arms and spread them wide. She motioned to the fire burning in the middle of the village. The Renoldi reign would end this night.

"Spin, spin, spin," she shouted, and the fire grew taller, vicious. Flames licked at the sky, while the molten blaze turned. "Go." Tsura commanded the cylinder flame to twist about the village and burn it to the ground. The gypsies fled into the forest.

Emine thrust her hand toward Red Wolf, but Tsura stepped in front to block the magick from killing him. She braced herself for the pain, the seizure, the agony...but nothing came. Her power was too strong. The moment had come for her to end the sacred legacy. She walked down the steps of the scaffold toward Emine.

The gypsy's eyes filled with malice, rage and death, and she ran at Tsura.

They crashed into one another. Emine's fists pummeled her body, and she did not protect herself from the attack. She wanted only one thing from the gypsy.

The pendant glowed upon Emine's chest, and Tsura grabbed hold of the ruby.

"Stop thy heart and cease thy breath, blast ye from thy soil and bring forth thy death!" she yelled.


Red Wolf squinted against the bright light illuminating from Tsura and the Renoldi. A gust of wind shook the scaffold knocking the wooden structure to the ground, and missing him by mere inches. When he looked back at Tsura, both women lay on the ground...neither moved.

He scrambled to his feet, kicking up dust, and the debris lying around him. He reached her in seconds. Black curls covered her face, and she clutched the pendant still around the gypsy's neck. Red Wolf fell to his knees and placed his head to Tsura's chest. Silence...a cold hollow silence.

He shook his head.

"Tsura...Tsura." He swept the hair from her face. "Please wake...wake damn it." He shook her.

Soaring Eagle knelt beside him. Red Wolf placed pleading eyes upon his cousin.

"She...she..." He couldn't say the words. He could not voice the reality of what he'd soon have to face. His eyes misted, and he searched the faces of the Ama tribe around him. He did not know when they had arrived, but they stood with spears, bows, and knives clutched in their hands. They'd fought for Tsura. He heard the quiet weeping of the men and women who had come to love her as much as he did.

"Cousin, I am sorry," Soaring Eagle said, utter sadness reflected on the White chief's face.

He let his eyes fall upon Tsura's body once more. He'd heard her whisper of love, felt her lips upon his, and knew she'd sacrificed herself for him. He couldn't comprehend the loss of the only woman he'd ever loved from his life, and he shook the remorse from his bones. He owed Tsura more than to lie across her body and weep. No. He'd bring her home, back to the Ama village.

Red Wolf went to lift her into his arms, when he noticed the pendant she still clasped. The legacy needed to be returned to Pril. He yanked the necklace from the Renoldi's neck, breaking the chain.

He straightened. The lineage, he remembered Pril telling them, the pendant held its own power, but together with the Chuvani it was boundless. He had no idea if what he was about to do would work, but he had to try. Red Wolf pried the pendant from Tsura's grasp and placed the ruby to lie over her heart. He waited, but nothing happened. The pendant did not glow. He hung his head. One tear dripped from his chin to fall onto the ruby. The gem flickered.

"It has life," Soaring Eagle said. "The necklace lit."

Red Wolf stared at the pendant dull and muted. "You see what is not there."

"No, Cousin, I see what you do not." Soaring Eagle grabbed Red Wolf's hand and laid it over the pendant.

Red Wolf felt the blood within his veins swell, and his palms throbbed with a need he did not recognize. His heart slammed into his ribs with one strong beat, and he thought only of saving Tsura. He pressed his palm into the pendant that lay over her chest. Warmth radiated up his arms and into his body. An immense pain blasted through his entire body. He straightened. His legs ached, arms burned, and head spun. Red Wolf's brow glistened, his vision blurred. He blinked. The agony increased until he thought he could bear no more, and then it disappeared, gone from his body as if it were never there.

He turned to the side and threw up. Drained of all energy, he leaned on his elbow while sweat perspired on his cheeks and chin. He heaved once more, and his body listless, he laid his head onto the dirt. The pendant had used his body to save Tsura. He'd felt all of her wounds as if they were his own, but was it enough?

Too weak to move, he continued to lie there. The stars twinkled above him, and he closed his eyes.

"Red Wolf?"

He bolted upright and regretted the movement when his stomach dipped. He steadied himself against White Owl who sat beside him.

"Cousin, your woman has woken," Soaring Eagle said elated.

Red Wolf cupped Tsura's cheeks within the palm of his hands. When her emerald eyes focused on his face, she smiled, and his heart soared.

"My woman," he whispered.

"Yes, my love, I am." Tsura smiled.

# EPILOGUE

*Willow Creek, Colorado 1890*

Nora cuddled into Hawk on the small settee in their living room. After dinner had been eaten and the dishes cleaned, they'd retired into the small room with a cup of tea. She wanted to tell him of the diary, of what she'd learned.

Morning Star played on the floor with Joe, and Nora smiled at the bond the two had formed. She had been blessed, and her heart was truly full.

"What has my wife so happy?" Hawk asked as his chin nuzzled into her neck.

"Remember the trunk you brought in?"

He nodded, and his lips trailed up to her ear. He had a way with her, and she could not wait until the house was quiet and they were nestled under the blanket in their room.

"I found this in a secret compartment on the bottom." She held up the weathered book.

"What is it?"

"My great-grandmother's diary."

"On Jack's side?"

Nora shook her head. "My mother's."

He sat taller.

Nora knew nothing of her mother, or how she'd acquired the gift to heal people. He knew she'd struggled with unanswered questions, and often told her the past did not matter, and together they'd build a future. But to Nora it did.

Hawk pulled her onto his lap. "What does it say?"

"We are gypsies."

He burst out laughing, and Nora slapped her hand onto his chest playfully.

"Darlin', I knew you were a thief when you stole my heart."

"Oh, stop it." She laughed. "I am a Chuvani, a queen among the gypsies, and all first born daughters born to a Chuvani receive the same gifts."

"Gifts?"

She nodded and couldn't keep the excitement from her face. Within the diary several spells had been written, and Nora had tried a few. Remarkably they'd worked.

"I can count a spell."

Hawk raised an eyebrow.

He was so handsome, especially when he smiled.

"You can count, yes," he said.

"No, silly. I can start a fire in the hearth by commanding the logs to do so."

He snorted.

Nora kissed his whiskered cheek. She'd show him.

"Simmer to hot, burn thy wood and boil thy pot."

The two logs within the stone fireplace lit. The orange flames licked the timber, and the wood crackled.

Hawk sat up, hugging her closer to him.

"I'll be."

"There is more." She left his lap to grab the carved box on the shelf above the fireplace. Earlier in the day she'd examined the detail of the engraved lilacs and sparrow, but it was the unique flower carved on the side with a dozen petals she'd not recognized that drew her interest. She traced the outline of the petals. Her finger pressed into the wood to feel the detail when a small compartment flipped open.

Nora sat beside Hawk, the box in her hand, and she winked at him before she pushed her finger into the flower. The side opened. She pulled out a leather pouch with a beaded bird on the front.

Hawk leaned into her, and she couldn't help but scoot closer to him.

With careful fingers, she removed the necklace tucked inside. Nora held a silver framed ruby, and when the pendant touched her skin, the gem glowed bright.

"What is it?"

"My legacy."

A power unknown passed unto ye,
spared of light, of love, of destiny.
Keep buried of evils desire to covet,
thus shall remain your sacred legacy.
~ Tsisquaya

*Keep reading for a note from Kat and a sneak peek from*
Chasing Clovers.

# Message from the Author

Dear Reader,

When I started this journey I knew the end had to go out with a bang. I struggled after I'd lost my brother, and to be honest I didn't foresee any writing within my future for a long while. However, God had other plans for me, and so did my brother. The need to write this story with the emotion I did was necessary for me to heal, and for my readers to experience these characters the way I intended.

The loss of a loved one cuts deep, and sometimes the wounds never heal. If you've ever experienced such a loss know that I truly understand what you're going through. I chose to write Tsura's loss and her emotions the way I reacted when I lost my brother, and the way I feel anyone would react when they lose a child. These are real, raw, and sometimes difficult emotions to endure; it is how I write all of my characters.

However, always remember that even in your darkest hour there is light, and with light, comes love…followed by hope.

Love,
Kat

*Excerpt from*

# CHASING CLOVERS

*Calgary, 1884*

The stagecoach pitched to a stop, jostling Livy Green from fitful nightmares of a past she longed to bury and the stranger she was about to marry. Her neck stiff and her back aching, she massaged her shoulders. She straightened and tried to stretch her arms, but the tiny space wouldn't allow it.

A loud sigh blew from her lips when she realized how rumpled her clothes were. Frowning, she ran her hands along her skirt. Nothing but a hot iron would get the wrinkles out. With only two other dresses in her wardrobe, and no time to change anyway, she had no choice but to meet her fiancé looking as she did.

Her stomach dropped. *What if I'm not what he's expecting?*

She peered out the window and wasn't surprised to see a few North West Mounted Police mingling with the other townspeople. Their bright red uniforms stood out like apples on a tree. She reached for her satchel and held it tightly before she stepped out the small door. *You can do this.* She squeezed the handle on her luggage. *You have to.*

Fort Calgary was a bustling town with two hotels on either side of the street, a small dress shop with ladies hats and fabric displayed in the window, and a red-bricked bank on the northwest corner. She watched people walking along the wooden planks and filtering in and out of the shops.

A loud squeal sounded behind her.

Livy jumped. She was almost trampled by a young boy running from his mother. Her heart lurched at the sight of the child. The familiar ache inside her soul willed her to look away. But she continued to watch mother and child until they disappeared inside the mercantile.

She took a deep breath, forced all thoughts of the past out of her mind and scanned the streets again. Her face flushed when she thought of what she was about to do.

Bag in hand, she spotted the blacksmith across the street next to the barbershop. Her stomach twisted at the sight of the saloon two buildings down. The all too familiar swinging doors waved back and forth, taunting her. Two drunken cowboys left the saloon, weaving their way down the boardwalk.

Livy clenched the satchel and tensed.

She turned away, closed her eyes, and took another deep breath. Here she would be the wife to John Taylor—a man she'd never met—and stepmother to his two children.

She took another breath. She would start over. *Again.*

She surveyed the busy boardwalk in search of a tall man with dark hair. Almost every man she saw fit the description he had given her, so she decided to move over to the bench in front of the mercantile and wait for Mr. Taylor to find her. Hands folded together on her lap. She tapped her toe restlessly. Where could he be?

A rough looking cowboy sauntered toward her. His brown greasy hair, and ripped denims were paired with an evil smile.

Livy tucked her chin into her chest. *Oh, please don't let that be him.* She'd seen his type before and knew what they were capable of. The man lingered beside her for a few moments before continuing on down the boardwalk.

She sighed with relief. *How am I going to do this?*

No longer Angel Green, she was now Olivia Green. The past was far behind her, except on those long dark nights that would not allow her to escape it.

She chewed on her bottom lip and stared at the busy street.

Her new life would begin here. She would survive.

She blew out a shaky breath. It was all she knew how to do.

"Olivia?" a male voice asked.

A tall man stood beside her, his hat pulled low so she couldn't see his eyes. He hesitated, then extended his hand. "Olivia?" He had a polite, resonating voice.

She shaded her eyes with a hand. "Livy will do fine." She was uncomfortably aware of his presence as he towered over her.

He smiled and took off his hat. Wavy black hair curled above the collar of his coat and his skin was tanned from the sun. He looked nothing like the dirty cowboy. *Thank goodness.* Instead, he wore a clean flannel shirt tucked into faded denim pants.

"John Taylor. Good to finally meet you. My buckboard is over there." He pointed the way, then peered around. "Where are your trunks?"

"I only have this one."

Her cheeks reddened as she lifted her tattered brown satchel. She held it slightly behind, not wanting him to see the holes and stains on it.

Nodding, he offered his arm. She ignored it. Friendly eyes stared back at her. After what had happened to her in Great Falls, she hated being touched by men.

"Do not be insulted, Mr. Taylor," she said, staring at his boots, "but I'd rather you show me the way instead."

She headed in the direction he'd pointed out earlier. When she heard a low chuckle from behind, she pursed her lips and walked faster. *I need no one, least of all a man.*

In truth, she needed John Taylor more than she could admit.

As soon as she reached the buckboard, she tossed the satchel up onto the seat, gathered her skirts and climbed up. She had sat down when she noticed he was still standing on the walk.

"Uh, Miss Green?" He tipped his hat back, crossed well muscled arms and smiled at her. "That's not my buckboard."

Her face flooded with heat.

If this wasn't his wagon, why hadn't he said something earlier, instead of watching her make a fool of herself?

Her eyes misted. How had she gotten here, in this place, with a man she didn't even know? She swallowed. How could she have thought he was the answer to her problems?

Standing, she clutched the satchel and moved to the edge.

*How am I going to get down from this blasted wagon?*

Out of the corner of her eye, she saw John Taylor step toward her. She didn't want his help, nor did she want a stranger's hands on her. Determined, she held her breath and climbed down before he reached her.

He shrugged broad shoulders and strode toward another wagon. She watched his massive frame climb up with ease. Reins in hand, he waited for her.

The buckboard looked brand new, the wood oiled so it glistened in the warm afternoon sun. Lumber and a crate filled with supplies were piled in the back.

She set her satchel in back and climbed up beside him. "This is your wagon?"

He laughed, showing perfectly aligned teeth. "Sure is, ma'am."

Instead of waiting for her to sit, he whistled and the team jerked forward. Livy grabbed the side of the wagon and muttered a curse beneath her breath. If he wasn't her intended, she'd give him a tongue lashing he'd never forget.

Once seated, she ran her shaking hands along the front of her skirt and took a deep breath. *Be more civil, Livy.* It wasn't in her best interest to lose her temper and go flying at Mr. Taylor.

She closed her eyes. *Be kind. Smile.*

Her lips lifted at the corners, but then faltered. How could she smile? How was she supposed to be happy when all she felt was empty, incomplete and—worst of all—alone?

The buckboard rolled past shops, hotels, and even though she didn't want to see it, the saloon. Relieved to be putting the town and its harsh reminders behind her, she stared at the fields.

The stage master was true to his word when he had said, "You'll never see a sight like the prairies. It looks like a patchwork quilt, green and yellow with a touch of orange when the sun hits it."

Lost in the array of colors, she stared at the stalks swaying in the breeze. The hot sun beat down on her and she remembered the bonnet hanging around her neck. She placed it atop her head, not bothering to tie it but letting the strings dangle in the breeze.

"Sun gets real hot during the summer months," he told her. "Best to always wear a hat."

Unsure of what to say, she stayed silent.

They had traveled for almost two hours. Livy was grateful when he pulled the wagon to a stop below a large oak tree. Her bottom was beginning to go numb and she needed to stretch.

"I'm hungry. How about you?" John lifted a red blanket and a basket from behind the seat. He jumped down from the wagon and strolled toward the tree. "Coming?"

As soon as her feet touched the ground, she stretched and tried to work some of the kinks out of her sore muscles. Feeling a little better, she moved toward him, who fanned out the blanket and plopped down. Motioning for her to do the same, he opened the basket and handed her a piece of cheese and a slice of buttered bread.

Her stomach grumbled as she bit into the moist bread.

"Mmmm," she hummed.

"Yeah, Alice can sure make good bread," he said before taking a bite of his own.

"Alice? Is that your housekeeper?"

He shook his head. "No, I don't have one."

She was mesmerized at how his work-worn hands transformed into a light, almost feathery touch while he blotted his lips.

"Alice and Hank own the ranch that borders mine. She bakes my bread and watches the children from time to time."

"Oh."

He took a deep breath. "Look, Livy...I know we've only written each other a few times," his dark eyes studied her, "but I hope I made it clear that you'll be cooking and cleaning as well as looking after the children." He took another bite of cheese.

He *had* made it perfectly clear in all four letters she'd received. But she had lied when she told him she knew how to cook. She purchased two cookbooks and read a few pages on her journey, but she had not put any of this knowledge to use.

"Um, that will be fine." She hesitated. "But I must tell you, I have little experience cooking."

He stopped chewing. "How little?"

With nowhere to go and little money left, she lied. "I know enough that you won't starve."

He must have believed her because he didn't question her any more. Instead, he finished his lunch.

"You remember the children's names?" he asked after a while.

Of course she did.

"Ben and..." She didn't want to say the little girl's name. "Em—" She cleared her voice. "Emily."

Emotions that she had kept locked up began to escape. The panic that always came when she thought of her daughter started to crawl up her chest. A sharp pain slashed across her heart. Her throat felt thick and sticky.

She grabbed the flask of water and took a long drink. Her eyes grew moist. She swallowed hard.

"Are you okay?" He touched her shoulder.

Heat from his hand radiated down her chilled body, but she couldn't move away. She was forced to endure his touch.

"I had a piece of bread caught in my throat."

She coughed, lying for the second time in five minutes. This time she didn't feel guilty.

He eyed her for a few seconds. "Are you all right now?"

"Yes." She blinked back tears. "I'm fine, Mr. Taylor."

Only she wasn't fine and wasn't sure she ever would be.

He stood and offered his hand. "Call me John."

She hesitated. Part of her wanted to take his hand, to feel wanted, accepted. But she knew all too well what her touch could lead to.

Her fingers dug into the blanket beneath her. With an impatient huff, he grasped her hand. She felt the calluses on his warm palm and slowly closed her fingers around his, so he could bring her to her feet.

"Em's my little angel." A sad smile lay across his face. "Sweet as the woman who gave birth to her."

He let go of her and she felt the instant cold on her palm.

"I'm sure she is," she said.

The mention of children put her on edge. Most times she'd walk away, but today there was nowhere to go and her mouth had taken liberties yet again.

"Livy, does it bother you that I have children?" The blanket dangled from his hands. "Because if it does, say so now. I won't have a wife who doesn't approve of my kids." His lips formed a straight line, grim and full of displeasure.

"No. I...I like children."

This wasn't a lie. She *did* like children—what she knew of them anyway. She hadn't grown up with any other kids. Living inside a saloon didn't exactly make you front-runner in the friendship corral. Most of the kids she came across either teased her or were afraid of her. And what she knew of having her own children, she'd rather forget.

He would take her back to town and put her on the next stagecoach if she didn't make this right. If truth be told, that's what she deserved. To be alone, a castaway thrown to the slums without another thought.

She tried to smile, but her efforts proved futile. "I'm sorry." She wasn't the least bit sincere. "I'm a little irritable from the long ride. Please accept my apology...John."

"Apology accepted."

Relief washed over her.

"When will we get to your ranch?" she asked.

"You're already on my land. Have been for the last half hour."

When he grinned, she had never seen a more handsome face in all her life. His dark eyes brightened and he seemed to relax before her eyes.

He had said they'd be traveling for another couple of hours.

*How big is his spread?*

She scanned the fields.

"The T-Bar Ranch is one of the biggest cattle ranches this side of the mountains." The pride in his voice was unmistakable.

It had been so long since she'd felt proud, since she'd been happy. Would she ever feel those emotions again?

"Y-you own all of this?"

He pushed his hat back, grabbed the flask and took a long drink. "Yup, I sure do. Worked my fingers to the bone gettin' it that way too."

"You must be proud."

"Damn right I am," he replied. "I live and breathe this land. It's a part of me. Like my son and daughter, they all sit right here." He patted his chest.

"Your wife must've loved it here."

His expression changed from one of delight to regret. She instantly felt horrible. She knew his wife had died. He'd said so in his letters. She also knew what it was like to lose a loved one, and the emptiness that came with the loss.

"Yes, she did," he whispered.

She couldn't look into his eyes. She didn't want to see the pain that lay in their dark depths.

"I'm sorry."

"For what?" he demanded, disgust on his face. "She's gone and there ain't a damn thing you or me or anybody else can do about it."

One minute he was beside her, the next he was at the wagon.

The rest of the ride was spent in silence.

When the ranch house came into view some fifty yards after the wagon crested a hill, Livy inhaled at the vast picture before her. The large whitewashed house stood two stories tall and a porch wrapped around the entire dwelling. The house and the brightly colored flowers planted along the walk were a welcoming sight.

Two barns were situated to the left of the house. She could hear the clucks from the chicken coop. Fenced corrals with cows penned inside were scattered all around. Cattle sprawled over the land, grazing in the fields. Beyond the house she could see the Rocky Mountains. The mammoth jagged rocks were intimidating yet stunning.

"It's so beautiful," she said, awestruck.

John smiled for the first time since they left their resting point. "Yes, it is. I never tire of seeing it when I come home."

"How could you not? It's perfect."

He stopped the wagon in front of the house, jumped down and came around to help her. Although she attempted to wave him away, his strong hands wrapped around her waist and brought her to the ground.

"Go on ahead and wait for me inside," he said.

Nervous, she glanced up at him and only relaxed when he gave her a kind smile. His hands were still on her waist. As he stared down at her, she couldn't quite make out the play of emotions that flickered in his sable-colored eyes. Uncomfortable with having him so close, she tried to step out of his grasp, but his hands tightened on her waist.

"Mr. Taylor, please." She pressed her palms against his chest. "Let me go."

He didn't move.

"I said let me go."

She shoved him hard and he released her so quickly, she lost her balance and scrambled to correct her footing.

"Go into the house," he commanded, "I'll be in after I put the horses away."

Picking up her satchel, she ran toward the house.

CHASING CLOVERS is available in a new 2018 edition!

# ABOUT THE AUTHOR

Kat Flannery's love of history shows in her novels. She is an avid reader of historical, suspense, paranormal, and romance. She has her Certificate in Freelance and Business Writing.

A member of many writing groups, Kat enjoys promoting other authors on her blog. Kat enjoys teaching writing classes and giving back to other aspiring authors. She volunteers her time at the local library facilitating their writing group. She's been published in numerous periodicals throughout her career.

Her debut novel *CHASING CLOVERS* has been an Amazon Top 100 Paid bestseller. *LAKOTA HONOR* and *BLOOD CURSE* (Branded Trilogy) are Kat's two award-winning novels and *HAZARDOUS UNIONS* is Kat's first novella. Kat is currently hard at work on her next series, *THE MONTGOMERY SISTERS*.

VISIT KAT AT: www.katflannerybooks.com
FIND HER ON FACEBOOK: Kat Flannery, author
FOLLOW HER ON TWITTER: @KatFlannery1
GOODREADS: www.goodreads.com/author/show/5284914.Kat_Flannery
GET KAT'S NEWSLETTER: http://eepurl.com/druxu9

www.ingramcontent.com/pod-product-compliance
Lightning Source LLC
Chambersburg PA
CBHW071908220626
47052CB00002B/259